Vivian Conroy is a multi-publish... CW00349443
25+ contracted titles. Away fr...
hiking, crafting and spending to
where readers can connect with her under @VivWrites.

Murder Will Follow Mysteries

An Exhibition of Murder

Under the Guise of Death

Honeymoon With Death

A Testament to Murder

A FATAL ENCOUNTER IN TUSCANY

Miss Ashford Investigates

VIVIAN CONROY

One More Chapter
a division of HarperCollins*Publishers*
1 London Bridge Street
London SE1 9GF
www.harpercollins.co.uk
HarperCollins*Publishers*
Macken House, 39/40 Mayor Street Upper,
Dublin 1, D01 C9W8

This paperback edition 2023

1

First published in Great Britain in ebook format
by HarperCollins*Publishers* 2023
Copyright © Vivian Conroy 2023
Vivian Conroy asserts the moral right to be identified
as the author of this work
A catalogue record of this book is available from the British Library

ISBN: 978-0-00-854932-9

Printed and bound in the UK using 100% Renewable Electricity
by CPI Group (UK) Ltd

Chapter One

Miss Atalanta Ashford sat at a table in the tearoom of the Grand Metropolitan Hotel in Paris, watching with a smile as the immaculately clad waiter transferred silver trays with sweet treats from his cart onto her table. Macarons in pink, yellow and green, bonbons with elegant gold decorations, paper-thin rolled butter biscuits and madeleines.

She really deserved this feast, having just concluded the rather delicate case of the Marquis of Merion's letters. When his secretary had appeared on her doorstep to engage her, she had believed it would be about some indiscreet love letters the marquis had sent to someone he had been enamoured with in his younger years, physical proof of a youthful folly that now threatened his upcoming marriage to a German princess. But it had turned out to be something completely different. The marquis, a fervent horse lover and breeder of excellent jumpers, had written a letter to a friend expressing doubts about a horse he was training that he considered too headstrong to ever make a successful showjumper. The letter had fallen into the hands of an unscrupulous young woman who was after the friend's fortune but had seen a chance to get into the marquis's pocket instead. She had threatened him that she would make his letter public, by handing it to the press for instance, and would ruin his reputation as a breeder for ever, unless he paid her a ludicrous sum for her silence. Aware that blackmail never ends, the marquis had been quite desperate, and his devoted secretary had hired Atalanta to negotiate a deal for the return of the letter with assurances this payment would be a final one and no contact would be made later for more money. Atalanta had hesitated to take the case because she really had seen no way to persuade a woman of dubious morals to be honest in returning the letter, but Renard, who had overheard part of the conversation while pouring coffee, gave her a signal to accept. He had later, after the secretary's departure, told her that he had contacts that could help to convince the young lady it was in her best interest to come to a deal. "We must simply make her an offer she cannot refuse," he had said with a smile.

"*Merci,*" Atalanta thanked the waiter, who stepped back with a slight bow and wheeled his cart back to the double doors leading out of the room. It was quiet on this Wednesday afternoon and with a sigh of satisfaction she picked up her teacup and savoured the delicate aroma of the jasmine in her green tea. She was just about to pick a first macaron off the silver tray when the doors through which the waiter had vanished were flung open dramatically and the hotel's manager rushed in.

He had seen her arrive fifteen minutes earlier and escorted her to her table personally, enquiring how she liked it in Paris and if she had recently travelled anywhere interesting. She had told him she had visited Santorini, conveniently omitting that she had been there posing as an old lady's companion to investigate an accidental death that might have been murder. Not only had it turned out to have been murder but there had been another death and Atalanta had worked hard, and risked life and limb, to bring the killer to justice. The hotel manager's enthusiastic response to her mention of the Greek island had probably been provoked by images of her exploring the whitewashed village dotted with pink blossoming bougainvillea, olive and fig trees, trying delicious seafood, and admiring the views across the azure water from atop the famous red rocks. But she knew she had come back from the trip hardly rested and new cases had immediately engaged her attention. She was incredibly grateful to her grandfather, Clarence Ashford, who had left her his entire fortune, along with his vocation to sleuth discreetly for the higher circles, but at times that very vocation left her little room to enjoy the freedom that had come with the wealth.

The manager halted at her table, clasped his hands together in front of his chest with typical French dramatic flair, and whispered in a low voice, "Oh, Mademoiselle Ashford, I must be the luckiest man alive because you are here on this very afternoon when I could become the unluckiest man alive."

Atalanta raised an eyebrow at this rather cryptic statement. "Has something happened?"

"Yes …" He looked around him, lowering his voice even further. "A crime."

"Here in the hotel?"

"*Oui. C'est un drame.*" He pulled his hands apart and gestured wildly. "*Une catastrophe.* Madame Versaint is one of my best clients. She stays here for months on end. She—"

"Calm down, monsieur, and tell me in an orderly fashion what happened and how I may help."

"You will help? Oh, I knew I could count on you. Come with me." He reached out as if to pull her off her chair. Atalanta cast a regretful look at the table full of delicacies.

The manager said, "I'll of course ensure you can enjoy your tea later. And at the expense of the hotel. But right now I need your assistance. That fool Doriot is making a mess of it."

"Inspector Doriot?" Atalanta asked with a rush of apprehension inside. She had come across him before, and he had made it very clear that he had never liked her grandfather interfering with what he considered official police business, and that he didn't want her to follow in his footsteps. "I'm certain he is very capable and will do anything in his power …"

"Oh, he is doing anything, yes; anything to upset Madame Versaint, her maid, the sculptor and the staff." The manager gesticulated again as he walked beside her, leading her up the elegant stairs to the first floor. "He has had the audacity to have a female member of his police force search the persons of everyone who was in the room at the time of the theft. One maid already told me she is taking her leave after this affront."

"What theft?" Atalanta asked, to cut her way through his indignation over the police's way of handling the case to what had happened to the honoured guest.

"Madame Versaint has a ring she always wears. A gold ring with a large diamond in it. It was a gift from her husband. Years ago he acquired an African mine and the best stone found there he had made into a ring for her when they married. He is currently on a business trip in Spain and she is staying here at the hotel, where she can have the best meals and entertainment at night."

"Yes, and something happened to this ring?" Atalanta tried to focus on the essentials while the manager led her through a corridor with a dark blue carpet decorated with the golden entwined Gs and Ms of the hotel logo. Potted palms stood along the walls and oil paintings depicted elaborate scenes from the court of Louis the Sun King.

"It vanished," the hotel manager said with a dramatic sweep of his hand in the air. "Madame has lost some weight recently and the ring is a little loose on her finger. She stood up from the sofa and the ring fell and bounced away across the floor. Everyone helped to look for it, but it was not found. Madame rang for me and I contained all present in the suite until the police arrived."

He stopped in front of a door of white-painted wood embellished with gold detailing of fruits and leaves. He knocked. After a few moments the door was opened by a uniformed policeman. Past him Atalanta saw a sofa carrying an elegant woman in her forties with blond hair and a peach dress that hugged her slender figure. She had been crying and was still dabbing her blotched face. A maid in dark blue stood half behind the sofa, handing her a new lace handkerchief. By the marble fireplace in which no fire was burning, two hotel maids stood with their heads bowed. They both had their hair down and, in their hands, held the white head adornment that was part of their uniform. A few feet away from them stood the policewoman who had apparently been called in to search the persons present for the missing ring.

A voice with the sharpness of a foghorn rang out from the adjacent room. "How can the wretched thing be gone? Are there cracks in the floorboards? Did it slip into a dusty corner?"

The manager flushed and cried, "We have no cracks in our floorboards here and there is no dust in our corners."

A tall man marched out of the other room, pulling back his shoulders and gearing up to retort. But then he saw Atalanta and his expression fell. "What is she doing here?" he barked.

The manager said, "I asked her to come and help us. She will know what happened to the ring without tearing the entire room apart."

Doriot huffed in disbelief. "How? By some trick? For it isn't humanly possible to find this missing ring without actually looking in places. And we have looked everywhere. My people have felt the curtains and checked the vases and—"

"Monsieur Doriot here," the manager said to Atalanta with a grim expression, "thinks that one of the people who helped to look for the ring after it had fallen slipped it into some hiding place to retrieve later. But so far he has been unable to point out what hiding place that was."

Doriot was scarlet now and seemed ready to yell at the manager.

Atalanta raised a hand to stop both men from saying any more. "That's a very good thought," she said quietly.

"If it worked," the hotel manager scoffed. "But he has searched my staff, even forcing the maids to undo their hair as if they could have hidden the ring in there."

"I'm just being thorough," Doriot snarled. "We know for certain that no one left the room. The ring *must* be in here."

Atalanta let her gaze wander the room. There were two tall windows, but they were closed. No one could have tossed the ring out, and indeed that made little sense as it would have fallen on the pavement below and be picked up by any passer-by with an interest in the glittering stone. The windowsills were full of potted plants. She walked over to see if the ring had been hidden in the earth.

"I already looked there," Doriot said. "Not in the earth, or under the plants in the pots."

Atalanta ignored him and continued her survey of the room. Because it was full of ornaments there were many potential hiding places, but Doriot constantly reminded her that they had already been checked. She felt his hostility as a live presence in the room, threatening to dim her reasoning. But she forced herself to pretend she was all alone here and merely exercising her mind. What was logical?

Would the maid of the guest have tried to steal the ring? But why on this occasion? Surely there would be other, better ones?

The maids in service at the hotel? They both looked like frightened young girls who would not have the wit to use such a chance the second it occurred.

Her gaze came to rest on the man in the room, an artistic type of about thirty with a goatee, and metal-rimmed spectacles resting on the tip of his nose. He blinked at her as if he wasn't quite sure who she was and what she was doing here. Beside him stood a high wooden stool with a bust resting upon it. Made of clay, it was modelled in the likeness of Madame Versaint. Atalanta's gaze descended to the man's hands, which were dirtied with clay. He had been working on the model when the ring had fallen and the frantic search had commenced.

She eyed him and smiled. "That is a very good likeness."

"It is just a model for a marble bust," Madame Versaint declared. She still dabbed at her eyes. "My husband insisted on me having my very own bust to put on the piano in our winter residence. I had to sit for this clay model so the artist has an example to work from when he starts work on the marble. I have no patience to sit for that. It would take me days." She shuddered.

Atalanta looked at the bust again. "Inspector Doriot, have you checked the bust?"

"Pardon me?" The inspector glared at her without understanding.

"You say you have checked everything in the room. Does that include the bust?"

Doriot blinked in confusion. "What is there to check about it?"

Atalanta walked over. The artist said sharply, "Don't touch it or you will ruin the likeness."

"I'm interested in the bottom of it." Atalanta stopped in front of the stool and looked at the artist with a friendly smile. "I'll touch it very gently to turn it over."

"It is easily ruined. The clay is still soft."

"Yes." Atalanta's smile deepened. "That is the point,

isn't it?" She held the artist's gaze. "When the ring fell and bounced away, you helped to look for it. You picked it up and pushed it into the soft clay. In an instant it was swallowed and couldn't be seen any more. All you had to do was wait until the police gave up their search for it and you could carry off your bust to your studio. Your now very valuable bust."

"Is that true, Antoine?" Madame Versaint asked. "I thought you were such a wonderful artist, so talented. Why ruin a good career with a reckless theft?"

Antoine sighed. "Spur of the moment. Just too good to let pass by." He reached out and overturned the bust gently. With an expert movement of his index finger and thumb he pushed something out of the clay.

The policewoman gasped as the ring surfaced.

Doriot swore under his breath. He stared at Atalanta. "How did you know that?"

"You should read more books, Inspector." Atalanta smiled. "All the great crimes have been done before. By making a catalogue in your mind you will have a very valuable encyclopaedia to draw upon."

The hotel manager beamed. "I knew I could count on you, Mademoiselle Ashford. Merci."

Atalanta waved it off. "I was here at the right time."

"For you, that is," Doriot muttered with a sour expression.

Madame Versaint said, "I think my husband will have to acquire the bust elsewhere. I don't want to do business with a criminal."

The policeman and woman led the artist away. Doriot moved as if to say goodbye to Madame Versaint but she turned her head away from him and ordered her maid to make her tea as she had a terrible headache.

Doriot glowered at Atalanta before disappearing after his people and the caught criminal.

Atalanta smiled at the two hotel maids, who looked as if they couldn't believe what had happened. "You can now resume your duties. All is well."

"But first make yourselves presentable again," the hotel manager said. "*Vite, vite.*" He ushered them out of the room with a hand gesture.

Madame Versaint said, "Really, I never believed it was one of them. I've never had any trouble staying at this hotel. I could have known it was the sculptor. He did have shifty eyes."

Atalanta suppressed a smile at Madame Versaint's sudden insight into human nature. "I'm glad that the ring has been recovered. It must be very precious to you given that it was a gift from your husband."

"I rarely see him." Madame Versaint waved her hand languidly. "Our marriage works best when we are far apart from each other. I live here and enjoy myself and he goes on business, wherever he believes he can find another fortune. I must admit, he has a nose for opportunities." She studied Atalanta through her eyelashes. "Do we know each other? Have we met? You look vaguely familiar. Why don't you take tea with me and we can chat?"

Atalanta didn't much feel like being questioned and evaluated by this woman she barely knew, and politely declined, checking her watch with feigned shock. "Is that the time? I really must dash."

Outside the room, as she made her way past the potted palms and opulent banqueting scenes again, the manager spluttered, "But your afternoon tea is still waiting for you. I can have it brought up to Madame Versaint's room with new tea and—"

"Please pack my treats for me so I can take them along. I do have another appointment," Atalanta felt obliged to claim. It would be awkward for the manager to learn she didn't want to socialize with his prize hotel guest. "I wish I had more time but—"

"I'm so sorry your tea was disturbed and … But you were brilliant. Simply brilliant."

"A simple matter of recalling a story I once read." Atalanta smiled at him. "Thank you for your belief in me."

She waited in the lobby while the manager had a

waiter pack her treats into a large box with the hotel emblem emblazoned on the side. Carrying it carefully in her hands, she walked outside and down the steps in front of the hotel's spectacular columned facade.

A car horn honked. She looked to her left and spied a fiery red sports car, an open two-seater, with someone behind the wheel furiously waving at her. She narrowed her eyes against the bright sunshine to see who it was. The figure unfolded and jumped out of the car without even opening the door, then came towards her with long athletic strides.

"Raoul!" Atalanta clutched the cardboard box. "I had no idea you were in Paris." She surveyed the man who had helped her in two cases and who, during those difficult times, had become a close confidant and friend. At least, she thought they were friends, but with Raoul it was near impossible to judge what he truly felt. "You could have called."

"I did call at your house. Renard told me you had left for tea. It gave me time to conspire with him."

"Conspire with him?" Atalanta repeated, not quite understanding. Although her faithful butler knew Raoul had assisted her before and treated him with all due respect, she couldn't shed the feeling that Renard didn't really like Raoul or was perhaps wary of the rumours that Raoul was looking for a wealthy wife to support his extravagant lifestyle. Having been her grandfather's manservant for many decades, Renard felt protective of her and would defend her against any danger, real or imagined.

"Yes." Raoul's handsome suntanned face split in a dazzling smile. His brown eyes twinkled as he leaned towards her and whispered, "I am abducting you."

Chapter Two
<hr/>

"Abduct me?" Atalanta echoed perplexed.

"Yes. I heard from Renard you've been working far too hard."

Ah. Renard was still protecting her, but in another way. He had to be truly worried if he'd set aside his suspicions of Raoul for this greater good. "Renard shouldn't gossip about me when I'm not there."

"He merely shared his concern with me. He told me that since you came back from Santorini, you have taken two cases and only turned down a third because he advised you strongly against the client in question. He thinks you're overdoing it with the detection."

"Renard hasn't said anything to me." Well, not in so many words. Or had she conveniently ignored his remarks because she didn't want to hear them? She hurriedly added, by way of an excuse, "I need to sharpen my skills and I'm not going to do that if I don't take cases."

"Still, you promised me when we left Santorini that you would pick up your vacation where you had left off. Remember? Murano? Your plans to continue to Florence …?"

"I intended to, but when I came home, there were letters waiting for me and later the secretary of a … an influential man called on me and asked for my help."

"Yes, well, you can try and convince me whatever way but I'm saying you need a little holiday away from crime. So I made some plans with Renard …"

"With Renard?"

"I could hardly have gone up to your bedroom to pack your cases myself. You must agree it wouldn't have been proper." His eyes glinted with amusement. "Your faithful butler did all the packing for me and even put the luggage in the back of my car." He gestured to the gleaming two-seater.

"My luggage is in the back of your car?" Atalanta asked.

"Yes. It is a lot to a man's mind but then ladies need a lot of dresses and other articles if they are travelling in style. And we're going to enjoy some extra special luxury."

"I don't follow."

"Atalanta, Atalanta, why do you always want to know everything ahead of time? Why can't you simply accept a surprise? Let me take you along and you'll find out what we're going to do as we're doing it. How about that?"

Atalanta felt excitement wriggle in her stomach that Raoul was back in her life once more. That he wanted to spend time with her, that he cared that she was working too hard, that he had worked out a surprise for her ...

At the same time her rational mind told her that she shouldn't allow herself to enjoy this so much, as Raoul always had a way of endearing himself to her and then again irritating her with his ideas, his life choices ... As a race car driver, he risked his life every time he got into the car for training or for a race, and he simply laughed at the fear others had for his safety. He was always surrounded by adoring women and never missed an opportunity to flirt, even if he himself called it mere politeness. He easily formed opinions about people, without checking if they were grounded in facts, and let himself be led by sympathy or antipathy, placing loyalty where it didn't belong, at least to Atalanta's rational mind.

Had anyone told her when she still worked at the boarding school in Switzerland, before she had come into her grandfather's fortune and his sleuthing work for the elite, that she would meet such a man as Raoul, she would have thought she'd dislike and avoid him. Never would she have believed that she would enjoy his company and long to know him better. This seeming contradiction confused her and made her cautious in his presence; wary that, under his influence, her common sense might go out of the window.

She was glad he couldn't read her thoughts. Feeling an inconvenient flush creep up, she looked for an excuse to reject his invitation. "I don't know if I should go with you. On the other two occasions we spent time together it wasn't exactly relaxing."

"Because it was work. You were undercover then. First in Provence, then on Santorini. We were trying to catch a coldblooded killer. There wasn't exactly time to unwind. But today I'm inviting you on a purely private trip. No crime, no work. No cases, no clients. Just you and me and a beautiful journey to places you've always wanted to see. Now what do you say?"

Atalanta had a feeling this couldn't be real. It had to be some dream from which she would wake up. Raoul here, inviting her to spend time with him? Not for a case, but ... *just you and me.* Had he really said that?

"I'll take this." Raoul pulled the cardboard box from her hands.

"Careful. The contents are fragile."

"What can it be?" He looked at the box from all sides. "A hotel logo. Not from a shop. No gloves or scarf. Too bad as you do need a scarf to hold your hair in place as we travel in this thing." He patted the two-seater on the hood in passing and placed the cardboard box in the back. In the same movement he extracted a parcel in thin, pink wrapping paper and threw it at her. She caught it in both hands, feeling the soft contents shift under her touch.

"Open it." He encouraged with a carefree laugh.

The somewhat heavy feeling that had accompanied her from the hotel where she had concluded the unexpected case of the missing ring vanished completely and she laughed as well as she tore the paper open. In her hands was a gorgeous thin silk scarf in an elegant black-and-white-striped pattern.

"Bought it in Rome," Raoul said as he came over to her and gently pulled it from her hands. "Here, let me …" He folded it into a triangle, placed it over her hair and knotted it under her chin. The back of his hand brushed her cheek and her heart somersaulted. She was going on an adventure with Raoul. Destination unknown. This was so exciting. And special. How could she say no? She'd forever regret it. Life was meant to be lived, fully, not merely fantasized about from the safety of her armchair at home.

Besides, she had faced murderers and come out victorious, so what did she really have to fear from spending time with Raoul?

"Mademoiselle …" Raoul opened the door of the car for her and she clambered in. The padded seat moulded itself to her back. They could drive this thing to … Yes, where to? He hadn't told her a thing.

She glanced back to look at the luggage stashed behind her and indeed recognized the blue and gold of her own cases.

"Ready?" Raoul asked as he started the engine. He smiled at her and winked.

Atalanta felt like holding up her arms and shouting with joy. This was simply wonderful.

"Off we go." Raoul smoothly inserted the car into the stream of traffic. "I bet there are sights in Paris you've never seen."

"Logically, as I've only lived here since June." Atalanta sighed as she studied the passers-by on the pavement, hurrying past shop windows and restaurants. "It's been three months now, but it feels like much longer. Last week I looked at a calendar and got a shock thinking I should have been back at the boarding school. That I was actually late for the start of the new year. Then I realized I don't work there any more and no one is waiting for me."

"Do you miss it?"

His question took her by surprise. She studied his profile. "Why would you think I'd miss it? I have so much money now, opportunities to travel, see places, meet people. How would I have time to miss it?"

Raoul shrugged. "You get used to things. Before I was a professional driver, I had several jobs in order to make enough money to get on a team. You know, to go to parties where you can forge connections, make sure you meet the right people. I liked working hard. These days I get up around ten and then I stand in the living room of my apartment and wonder what to do with my day ..."

"You make yourself sound like a rich dandy without a proper job. But I wager you work very hard. You have to train a lot to do the racing and ..." Her stomach contracted as it always did when she thought of what he did for a living. Every time he got into his race car, he risked injury. He could die.

I could lose him.

But he isn't mine to keep.

Raoul said, "Oh, of course. But still people think it's a life of parties and cocktails and ... Like it isn't real work at all." He glanced at her. "And because I know what it is like to have a normal job, I even understand them. A little." He scoffed. "Here I'm talking about all this serious stuff, while you want to have a good time away from everyday life."

"No, I'm glad we can talk about anything."

"Like what you have in that cardboard box."

"You would never guess ..." Atalanta told him all about her afternoon tea at the hotel and the unexpected case she had been called into. "Doriot really hates me now."

"Well, he did search the entire room and then you waltz in and find the ring within – what? Ten minutes?"

"I guess if I were him, I'd be a bit sour too. But anyway, my tea was cold and I asked the manager to pack the treats to take along. My grateful client, or perhaps she wasn't really a client, but you get my meaning, had wanted to socialize so I practically ran. I would have to explain everything about ... well, you know. How I live and why I'm not married and ... It's just tedious going over that again and again."

"Well, those treats will come in handy now. We can stop and eat them at a very special place I know that has a wonderful view. Just wait and see."

Atalanta stood at the railing and looked down on the houses and churches and parks of Paris. Her head was light with the height and the champagne Raoul had whisked out of the back of the car before he had escorted her up here. She had never seen the city quite like this. Her grandfather had collected old maps of Paris and she had pored over them a few times to see what he had liked so much about them. She wanted to know him better, learn more about him, as she lived in his houses and followed in his footsteps. Now standing here, she recognized all the landmarks: the grand Notre-Dame, Montmartre with the beautiful white Sacré-Coeur, and the Arc de Triomphe dwarfing the traffic moving round it. She tried to memorize the layout of the city that she now called home.

Raoul came to stand by her side. "Deep in thought?" he asked.

She looked up at him. It felt so familiar to have him with her. As if it had always been like this.

She remembered how she had suspected him during her first case in Provence and smiled. "I was just thinking how little I know of Paris and how much I want to know about it. Because my grandfather loved it so much. His library is full of books about the city and he collected maps. I wish I ... could have talked to him. Known how he felt about living here, far away from England, from his homeland."

"Well, you have a homeland because of your place of birth. And a homeland of your own choosing. You know, I was born and raised partially in Spain, partially in France. But ever since I started racing, I'm often in Italy, especially in Tuscany, and that feels like home to me. The landscapes, the food, the friendly people. So perhaps your grandfather had that sensation coming here, to Paris."

Atalanta nodded. "I guess so." She smiled up at him. "Thank you for the champagne and this view. It was amazing."

"You make it sound like it's already over."

"Well, I don't know what your surprise is."

"You're a detective. You can deduce. You need luggage for this trip, or else I wouldn't have asked Renard to pack for you. So we're going away overnight. But where to?"

Atalanta tilted her head. "Do you actually want me to guess?"

"No, not really." He checked his watch. "We'd better go. We don't want to be late."

"Late for what?" Her mind raced. A play? The opera? Fireworks somewhere in the open air? Or dinner at an exclusive restaurant? The treats had been delicious but at seven-thirty in the evening her stomach could also use something more substantial.

Raoul put his arm around her lightly. "Come on. Find out."

They got into the car again. He navigated the still busy traffic with ease, even finding time to point out sights to her. She tried to guess where they were going but it seemed impossible as they kept taking turn after turn.

At last they arrived at a train station. Raoul snapped his fingers to call a porter, who loaded all their cases onto his cart and wheeled it ahead of them to the platform Raoul had mentioned. Atalanta's sense of excitement increased. Where would he be taking her? Deeper into France? Or to the north, to Belgium with excellent cities like Antwerp and Brussels?

Then her gaze fell upon the gleaming metal carriages, the steam engine way up ahead, the fashionable passengers ascending amidst a flutter of silk and satin, cases being handed up into the luggage cart.

And a staccato voice overhead named the destinations: Lausanne, Milan, Venice, Belgrade, Sofia, Istanbul.

Atalanta grabbed Raoul's arm. "We're travelling on the Orient Express?"

"Yes. The one taking the Simplon Pass. It leaves at

twenty past eight and we should be in Milan a little after ten tomorrow morning. There I have another car waiting and we're going to explore my second home, Tuscany."

Atalanta resisted the urge to wrap her arms around his neck to hug him. It wasn't like her to be so emotional. But this trip, so suddenly, so thoughtfully prepared and …

"Let's get on board and find our compartments," Raoul said. "I got two side by side, full service included. I want you to feel totally glamorous on this trip."

"I already do. Oh, but you really shouldn't have spent so much money …"

"Atalanta …" Raoul grasped her shoulder. "Don't talk to me about money. I have it, you have it. It's no issue. I don't want to spoil this experience."

"You're so right. I'm sorry. I won't say another word about it. Now lead on."

Chapter Three

Atalanta couldn't believe that she was actually walking past the doors of sleeping compartments on that famous train. The Orient Express had often featured in her dreams about world travel, and she, a simple boarding-school teacher, had often imagined herself in evening dress, leaving her compartment to go to dinner, where she'd sit with other well-dressed passengers sampling the exquisite dishes on offer. She had seen travel posters depicting the train's interior but they had done no justice to the sophistication and luxury of everything around her now. She followed Raoul with a sense of awe and the urge to pinch her arm to ensure she was indeed awake and not dreaming.

"Here we are," he said, halting before the door of compartment 14. "This is yours and mine is just next door." He smiled. "Normally you'd have to share it with another passenger but I made certain we each had our compartment completely to ourselves. There's a connecting door that can of course be locked and bolted. But I'll knock on it to let you know I'm ready for dinner."

"I'll hurry to get dressed," she assured him.

He waited while she opened the door and looked inside. The compartment had gleaming wood panelling with gilded accents and luxurious dark blue padded seats by the window. Her cases had already been placed in the rack.

Raoul reached over her shoulder to point at another door. "There is a washing basin behind it if you need to freshen up. The lavatories are at the end of the carriage."

"Thank you. I'll be ready soon."

Atalanta waited until Raoul had closed her door then she quickly locked it. She didn't want the conductor or someone else on the train to bolt into her compartment while she was dressing. She reached up and pulled her largest case from the rack. Renard had excellent taste and would no doubt have packed appropriate garments. She leaned the case on a seat and clicked it open. On top of her clothes was an envelope with her grandfather's strong handwriting on it.

Atalanta had received a bundle of letters after his death, each marked with a few words referring to the contents, to use during her cases. She found his advice helpful and comforting as it connected her with the man she had longed to know. As an orphan, and without siblings, any form of family connection, even if it was only in writing, meant the world to her. This envelope, however, was not from her bundle. She had never seen it before. It was of very good quality and the words on it read, "When you're on the Orient Express."

Atalanta's brow furrowed. How had her grandfather known in advance she'd travel on the Orient Express? Had he once met Raoul and ...? No, he couldn't have instructed him to take her on this trip as he hadn't known whether she would even accept his inheritance after his passing.

How then?

She used her little finger to open the envelope – something that would have made Miss Collins at the boarding school frown – and slipped out a note. She folded it open and read:

My dearest Atalanta,

Hooray. You've decided to do something for yourself and boarded the Orient Express. It's the train of dreams, connecting the City of Light with all the sights and sounds of the East, the lands of spices and silk. Well, it doesn't quite go all the way to China, but once you're in Belgrade or Istanbul, who knows where you will go next? There's no end to what you can dream of and where those dreams can take you.

It will only be to Milan this time, grandfather, Atalanta whispered. *But that is far enough for me right now.*

She realized with a little shock of surprise that the idea of not travelling further, to those amazing cities her grandfather had mentioned, didn't make her feel regret. No, she was just excited that she was here, that Raoul had taken her on this journey and that she would be able to spend some time with him. As long as he was with her, it didn't really matter where they were going.

She frowned a moment as this conclusion seemed so at odds with her previous aspirations. But it wasn't as if she had given up on travelling. It was just that, for now, this whole trip was perfect as it was and she didn't need faraway places or exotic sights to enhance it.

She smiled to herself and read on.

I hope you have a better time on the train than I had the last time I took it. There was a theft on board and a conductor had been accused. I knew the man and was fairly certain he wasn't capable of doing anything criminal. Then again, a fortune in diamonds can be tempting. Fortunately, the victim knew of my reputation and allowed me to conduct an investigation among the passengers to see if any of them could have had anything to do with it. It was quite a riveting little case, where my suspicions were first directed at a lady's maid who had forged her references, then at a travelling salesman with debts. But in the end, it was all much simpler.

The victim had changed her will before she got on the train. She was a widow without any children of her own and had intended to leave her fortune to a cousin whom she barely knew but who studied in Oxford and was well on his way to becoming a doctor. She believed her legacy would put him up in practice – until she heard that he had lied to her about graduating. He had, in fact, never completed his education but had run off to join the stage. Enraged at his irresponsibility, she had changed her will to leave everything she owned to the local church.

Well, then of course I knew the answer.

I do too, Atalanta said to herself. *The cousin ran off to "join the stage". So he is an actor. She had rarely seen him, so she wouldn't easily recognize him, even without a disguise. But with his acting skills, he could easily alter his appearance and get close enough to rob her and take what he considered as his: her valuable jewellery.*

A knock resounded on the connecting door. No. Raoul was already dressed for dinner? He was so quick. And she had done nothing but read a letter!

She hurriedly put it back in the envelope and hid it amongst her things, then pulled out an emerald-green evening dress with sparkling sequins along the neckline and on the bodice. She slipped it on and brushed back her hair, securing it in a low bun at the nape of her neck and attaching a clip decorated with three emeralds surrounded by bright azure aquamarines. She put on gloves and picked up a small leather purse in exactly the same shade of green as the dress.

There was no time to touch up her makeup, but Atalanta liked a natural look and in the mirror over the washing basin she saw a woman with a dazzlingly happy face. She smiled as she walked to the connecting door and gave a short knock to indicate she was ready too.

She heard the outer door of Raoul's compartment open and within seconds he knocked on hers. She hesitated a moment with her hand on the handle, her breath catching in her throat that this was actually her life now. As she opened the door, Raoul stood in the corridor with a flower in his hand. She had no idea how he had transported the white orchid, for it looked immaculate and fresh, as if he had just picked it. He handed it to her.

"I recall that on Santorini you chose white orchids for your headdress for the festival of saints. I assumed you like orchids so …" He held it out to her. "It has a little pin attached so you can wear it on your dress."

"Thank you." Atalanta took care to attach it without disturbing anything about it. "I love orchids. They were my mother's favourite flowers. I'm growing them in the conservatory of my Paris home now. No matter how busy I am, I take a little time every day to go and see them, care for them."

"Talk to them?" Raoul asked with a grin. "My father had a gardener who talked to all the plants. He was certain they understood what he said and thrived because of his compliments. He also scolded them when they didn't do well. But not too harshly of course, lest he'd hurt their feelings."

Atalanta shook her head. "You're mocking me. But something so beautiful and gentle just evokes a protective feeling in me. I want to be tender with it and treat it … well, almost like a baby. I do know my plants can't hear me but …"

"They connect you with your mother. When you talk to them, you talk to her."

It was a simple statement but pretty much the truth.

"I used to write her letters," Atalanta said, "when I was a little girl. I didn't dare tell anyone about it because I didn't want them to think I was mad, believing my mother was still alive. I knew very well she wasn't, and that she'd never read what I had to say but …." She frowned, looking for the right words to express her feelings. "She was gone from my life for ever, but I needed her to be a part of it somehow. I needed to share my experiences with her, my happiness or my pain. I wanted her to stay a part of who I was, to be there as I grew up, if that makes sense. She died too soon for me to ever really know her, but I did want to know her. And by writing to her, I sort of … created a bond between us. However one-sided."

"I didn't mean to make you sad." Raoul said it softly, his eyes considerate as he surveyed her. "This should be a happy night."

"But it is. You've brought me an orchid and made my mother part of this too. If she was still alive and could know how lucky I am to have the life I lead now … I think she would like you."

"I take that as a compliment." Raoul gestured to his right. "Shall we? Dinner is served until nine on the train so we must move quickly if we want any to be left for us."

"Of course. How did you manage to get me this beautiful flower?"

"I arranged for it to be brought to the train and our personal steward took care of it until we arrived. He brought it to me the instant I was in my compartment. Those personal stewards are very capable and aim to please. We share the same one so you can ask him for anything you may require. Just ring the bell and the light over your door will come on. The steward will come to assist you."

"Thank you. I feel like gentry."

"You should have been gentry." Raoul grinned. "Lady Atalanta Ashford, it does have a certain ring to it."

"I don't see what it might have added to what I already have."

"Titles can open doors. I have titled friends who don't have to lift a finger to get into places where you and I are not welcome."

"I doubt there are places where you're not welcome." Atalanta said it with a disbelieving huff. "You arranged for champagne on the Eiffel Tower. You get private compartments on the Orient Express."

"That's merely a matter of money." Raoul made a throwaway gesture.

"And the fact that you are Raoul Lemont, the celebrated race car driver, has nothing to do with it?" Atalanta laughed softly. "You are gentry in your own right. You have a title you earned by winning so many races."

"Perhaps."

She could tell by the quick jerk of his lips that he was amused by her statement and even flattered.

They reached the restaurant car and entered into a

bustle of animated voices. All tables were taken. At some, four people sat, at others, two. The lamps with their red shades threw a dimmed light across the fine table linen and napkins, the wine glasses and highly polished silverware. Waiters discreetly moved between the tables putting down plates and filling glasses, while enquiring if everything was to the patron's liking.

Raoul had to step aside to avoid contact with a waiter's elbow and his thigh bumped into a table where a young lady was sitting alone. The table shook and her plate touched the stem of her wine glass with a 'ting'.

"*Scusi*," Raoul said.

Atalanta assumed that he instinctively used the Italian he spoke most every day.

The amber eyes of the woman lit and she said eagerly, "*Italiano?*" Those eyes dominated a strong face that had the classic beauty of a Renaissance statue combined with a lively energy that made it impossible to look away.

Raoul smiled. "By choice, not by birth." He reached out his hand. "Raoul Lemont."

"Catharina Lanetti."

"Of the Tuscan Lanettis?" Raoul asked.

Catharina's expression dulled a moment as if she resented being addressed that way. "Yes," she affirmed reluctantly. "But you should hardly say so, as my father despises what I do and often tells me that I disgrace the family."

"What is it that you do?" Atalanta inquired curiously.

Raoul looked at her and said to Catharina, "May I present Miss Atalanta Ashford, my travel companion?"

"Pleased to meet you," Catharina said. Atalanta had the impression the young woman was interested to know what 'travel companion' might entail, but she didn't ask any questions. She said to Atalanta, "I'm an adventuress. I take challenges and I complete them. It was never my family's intention when they sent me to Turin to learn more about winemaking. But life often takes unexpected turns." She pointed at the two seats opposite her and said, "Why don't you sit at my table? I've wrestled my way through the soup and half the main course alone and am simply dying for company." She waited a moment and added, "Unless of course I'd be disturbing a … romantic tête-à-tête?"

"We're not involved," Raoul hurried to say.

For a moment it hurt Atalanta that he denied it so quickly, but then it was the truth. They were merely friends. And sleuthing partners, but Catharina needn't know about the latter.

Raoul let Atalanta take the seat at the window and he sat opposite Catharina, asking her where exactly her family's property lay. "I've heard so much about it. Cosimo Lanetti's palazzo with the vineyards ..."

Catharina smiled. "Cosimo is my father. I grew up in that palazzo and played in the vineyards. We own most of the land surrounding the village of Palino. The villagers work for us as temporary labourers to bring in the harvest. We also have workers who are engaged year round. It's an honour to work for Cosimo Lanetti."

"Tuscany is full of vineyards," Raoul said. "Still, your father's wine has a reputation for being the very best."

"He was lucky that he acquired the best vineyard of the entire territory. It wasn't part of his family property when he was a young man. It belonged to another family who didn't have an heir, only a daughter who needed a husband. My father married her and the vineyard became his. He built his empire from there."

"And you're expected to follow in his footsteps?" Raoul asked, accepting the menu from a waiter who hovered respectfully nearby.

"I'm but a woman." Catharina said it with a mix of regret and resignation. "My father thinks I could run the vineyard if I was married. He has a list of eligible candidates. I despise them all. He sent me to Turin to get some sense into me. I think he believed that if I had worked at someone else's property and felt like a servant there, a hired hand, I'd come back with a new appreciation for my position at home."

"But it didn't turn out that way?" Atalanta asked. She had also accepted a menu.

Raoul suggested that, as they had come in late, they should skip the first course and immediately get to the *tournedos bearnaise* with *pommes noisettes* and peas, followed by the *terrine de canard*.

The waiter removed himself and Catharina leaned back with a sigh. Playing with her fork, she said, "I did feel terrible in Turin. I realized I wasn't cut out to care for a vineyard all the time. I want to do so much more. Make chocolate. Climb mountains. Conquer the sea in a sailboat and see America. Not the cities, but the wilderness. My father hoped that I would miss home and come back with a renewed determination to become his successor. But all I learned was that I want to chase horizons and find challenges and have no day be the same."

"And now you have to tell your father the bad news?" Raoul asked.

"I guess so. But I won't hit him over the head with it. After all, this is the weekend of his birthday celebrations. He's turning sixty and everyone who is anyone in the village, in the family and among his friends is coming to congratulate him. And to drink his first-class wines, of course. It will be a big feast lasting several days."

"Well, if he has all his loved ones around him, he might feel softer towards you and be open to the new direction you want to take," Atalanta suggested.

Catharina laughed ruefully as she threw herself back in the seat. "You don't know my father. He expects the entire world to move according to his wishes. You can't tell him no. Still I'm going to. It's not like he'd be left without a successor if I decline. He has sons from his second marriage."

"So you are the eldest?" Raoul asked.

"Yes. He married my mother when he was twenty-six. She died when I was five, and soon after he married the daughter of a banker friend from Florence. She bore him the desired sons. Three no less." For a moment Catharina's pretty face contorted into a scowl. "Unfortunately, none of them turned out the way my father would have wanted. You see, Lorenzo is interested in the vineyards, he is dutiful and capable, but physically weak. He easily gets out of breath if he has to walk along the vines and when it's summer and hot, he can't be out much or he burns and comes close to fainting. Giovanni on the other hand is like an ox. He can dig and plant and harvest for hours on end. He is never tired and he doesn't complain about anything. But he is careless, forgets about appointments, argues with workers, chases maids. He creates ripples wherever he goes. I guess my father would like to put the good sides of both Lorenzo and Giovanni into one person and then he'd have the ideal son and successor. Now he just has two headaches on his hands."

"How old are these boys? Can't they marry and settle down or something?" Raoul grimaced as he added, "Marriage seems to be the solution to so many problems."

Atalanta had been acquainted with Raoul's ideas on commitment and marriage on her first case in Provence and cringed a little that he was so outspoken with a virtual stranger.

But Catharina tilted her head back and laughed out loud. "Oh, they are certainly old enough for that. Lorenzo is twenty-five and Giovanni twenty-three. In our circles it's common to marry young. Lorenzo is already past his prime in my father's eyes and Giovanni should be forced to choose a bride before the year is through."

Atalanta said, "But you just said your father and his second wife have three sons? You only speak of Lorenzo and Giovanni."

Catharina's expression set. "Their eldest, Thomasso, was abducted when he was fourteen months old. He was never found."

Atalanta cringed under the unintended painful effect of her question. "I'm sorry I asked about it."

"And how about you?" Raoul said quickly, eyeing Catharina. "I would never have guessed your age, but your story gave it away."

Catharina laughed again. "Yes. I can't deny it. I'm thirty-three. That is very old for a woman to still be unmarried. No man would even look at me if it wasn't for the promise of having my father's vineyards attached."

"I'm sure men might meet you without knowing about your father's vineyards," Raoul said. He held her gaze. "You could even lie about your surname."

"Oh, believe me, on my travels I do. I can't wait to get away from it all. I ..." Catharina wet her lips. "I only need to find the right moment to tell my father. I do feel a bit sorry for him because I led him to believe I was interested in taking over. But I guess ... I never thought he would actually want me to. Being a woman and all that."

"Perhaps he doesn't," Atalanta suggested, "and he'll be relieved when you tell him about your plans. He can safely let you go into a different life in which you will be happy, while he can give his property to a man."

"I can't believe I'm hearing you say that," Raoul said

to Atalanta. "You believe in equality. Else you wouldn't be living the life you do."

"Oh, and what life is that?" Catharina asked.

Atalanta threw Raoul a warning glance. She didn't want him to say anything about her work as a detective. She was on holiday. And her grandfather had taught her never to advertise herself but let the client find her.

"I travel a lot," she said hurriedly. "On my own. I don't need a husband to take me places."

"Have you been anywhere riveting lately?" Catharina asked.

"Oh yes, Santorini. Do you know it?"

"Unfortunately, no. I do want to go there. Is it spectacular?"

"Oh, very."

Between mouthfuls of delicious beef in sauce, Atalanta regaled their table companion with stories of her stay on Santorini, painting vivid scenes of the white houses, red rocks, beaches and sea life, the wild gulls overhead and the little sparrows on the terrace at night when the sun sank into the sea. She described the festival of saints and the fishermen who hung the octopuses out to dry like laundry on a line. She conveniently didn't mention the deaths and the case she had investigated and how dark the human heart could be. Her companion clearly wanted light diversion as she was tense about the task ahead, telling her father she wasn't going to do what he planned for her.

Raoul took his turns, filling in details about Santorini, and Catharina observed with a shrewd look, "So you were there at the same time?"

"Yes, Atalanta was staying with friends and I was there to look into the possibility of doing a race there."

"I see." Catharina seemed pleased by the confirmation they hadn't been travelling together.

Atalanta felt slightly disturbed by the idea that the woman might be interested in Raoul and would start flirting with him under her nose.

Would start? Had started already, judging by the way she rested her chin in her hands as she stared across the table at him with a warm smile.

But it was no business of hers whether another woman found Raoul attractive. In fact, she assumed that lots of women of his acquaintance felt that way and he dealt with situations like this every day.

"And what are you up to now?" Catharina asked, still holding Raoul's gaze.

"I have a sports car waiting in Milan and we're going to explore Tuscany. I haven't got a plan yet. Just go where the mood takes us."

"I see. How lovely. Tuscany has this wild spirit. I guess your type of trip is a perfect fit with that. But really, while you are at it, you must stop by and attend my father's birthday party celebrations on Friday night. There will be a big banquet with the sort of stunning dishes they would have served at the Medici court."

"Medici?" Atalanta asked.

"Yes, my father has a bit of a love affair with the Medicis of old. He was called Cosimo after one of them and he also gave all of his children a name that was used by the Medici family. They are the true standard of Italian excellence in his mind. He imagines himself to be one of them almost. He promotes banking, he supports the arts ... following in their footsteps as it were. His birthday party will be as opulent as they come. The food, drinks, dress ... I think everyone will be dressed up like famous people from Tuscan history. You know that lots of great names came from the region."

"Michelangelo, Galileo, Da Vinci," Raoul enumerated.

"Wasn't Dante from Tuscany as well?" Atalanta asked.

The name Dante seemed to surprise Catharina. Her eyes widened a moment and she took her time before replying, "Dante who wrote the *Divina Commedia*? Yes, of course."

Atalanta nodded. "It does seem interesting, such a historical dress-up party."

"Well, if you'd like to go, I agree right away," Raoul

said. He gestured to the waiter. "We'd like our dessert. You do want some, Atalanta?"

Atalanta only half heard him as she debated whether to kick herself for accepting Catharina's invitation. Such a party might be very special, and this opportunity a unique chance to see inside a grand palazzo, but she was practically throwing Raoul in Catharina's path. Something that felt risky.

And that is just why I'm doing it, she said to herself. *I want to know if he's going to flirt with her. If he does, then I will know that his friendship with me is merely that, friendship; an intellectual bond, common interests and all that. Nothing more. Then I will know that I can always rely on him as a friend and helper when things get hard, but I need not expect he could ever see me as … well …*

She shook her head, annoyed at her own thoughts.

"Don't you want any?" Raoul asked with surprise in his voice. "*Glace plombières* is a delicacy."

"Oh yes, of course I do. I was just thinking back to something that happened this afternoon in Paris and I don't want to be occupied by … something that hardly matters now."

Raoul ordered two desserts and the waiter walked away.

Catharina said, "It will be wonderful to have you at the party. Then I have someone to talk to."

"It doesn't seem like you can't talk to strangers," Atalanta observed a little sharply. "After all, you didn't know us either when we came into the carriage."

As she said it, doubt began to niggle at the back of her brain. Had Catharina really not known who they were? Or had she known Raoul from a newspaper clipping and used the moment he had bumped into her table to place herself in his path?

Or was it even worse? Had Raoul's contact with the table been a little act to engage with Catharina and make it natural for her to invite them both to sit down with her and have dinner together?

Atalanta hated herself for this thought, but her brain, always looking for connections, always deducing, didn't want to let go of this sudden lead. Why had Raoul picked her up so suddenly? Why had he taken her on the train when, with his fast car and love of driving, they could have travelled that way? Why take her on the Orient Express where there was a luxury dinner included in a restaurant car where it was easy to meet? Inconspicuous, seemingly coincidental.

Had Catharina asked Raoul to introduce her to Atalanta?

Had she even planned to invite them both to her father's birthday celebrations?

But why?

If Catharina wanted time with Raoul, she could have devised a way to invite him alone. She didn't need Atalanta with him. On the contrary, the presence of another woman could only be distracting.

Did she want her there for ... a case?

No.

No. No. No, that couldn't be true. Raoul would never do that to her. He wouldn't whisk her away on this alleged holiday, woo her with champagne and a white orchid, only to lure her into yet another case.

She was far too suspicious. If she didn't take care, this kind of reasoning would alienate her from him. Would break a special friendship. She had to believe that everything was exactly as it appeared to be. She had agreed to go on holiday with Raoul, they were having a wonderful time, they had met an intriguing woman who had invited them to a Medici-style birthday party. It was just perfect.

There was absolutely nothing suspect about it. It had nothing to do with her work. It wasn't a case. It wasn't going to become a case.

Period.

Chapter Four

When Atalanta was back in her compartment and getting ready for bed, having put on her nightdress and slung a hairnet over her hair, there was a knock at the connecting door. She went over and asked softly, "What is it?"

"Can I talk to you for a moment?" Raoul's voice asked.

Atalanta quickly threw on her dressing gown and removed the hairnet, tucking it under her pillow. Her hair now fell freely over her shoulders. She felt at it with one hand, opening the door with the other.

Raoul had removed his jacket and tie and unbuttoned his top two shirt buttons. He stared at her with a slightly worried frown. "Are you angry at me?"

"Angry?" Atalanta repeated the words with some consternation.

His brown eyes surveyed her. "You can tell me outright."

"Why would I be angry? You take me on a wonderful trip and ..."

"I didn't think at all when that woman, Lanetti, asked us to sit at her table. I enjoyed her stories and yours about Santorini. You made it sound so much more idyllic than it has truly been."

His wink made Atalanta laugh. "I did my best. I can't let the poor woman know I was there to look into dead bodies."

"I know." His expression sobered. "I just didn't realize that perhaps you would have wanted us to have dinner together. Without a third party present."

Atalanta tried to picture it. Raoul opposite her, his focus entirely on her, the looks exchanged over the wine glasses ...

It might have been a little too ... intense for her liking? She was never quite comfortable in his presence, and when he could scrutinize her it became worse. "It was fine this way."

"Are you certain? You were so silent when we walked back to the compartments."

"I was just thinking about what Catharina told us.

How her father expects her to be different than she is. I think it's sad that in families there are often so many expectations, and so much resentment when those expectations aren't met."

Raoul held her gaze. "What did your father expect of you?"

Atalanta thought a moment. "I don't know. He never really said. He had a lot of expectations of himself. He was always fighting a shadow, trying to prove a point. That was tragic really." She looked down. "He felt like he failed me because he could never create the life for me that he'd pictured in his head. But I didn't feel the same way. I loved him and I wanted us to be together. Even when times were rough."

Raoul touched her arm a moment. "I didn't want to make you sad. I feel like I'm doing all the wrong things on this trip."

"That's not like you."

Raoul huffed. "Because ..."

"Because you never doubt yourself. You don't overthink things."

She also said it to herself, again, *Don't overthink it. Don't assume that he feels guilty because it is all a setup, something he agreed on with Catharina, for some reason you can't fathom yet. Take things at face value for once. Enjoy yourself.*

Raoul said, "If you say you're not angry, then everything is fine. I'd better ..." He stepped back. "Unless there's something you want to discuss."

"No, I want to try that bed. I've never slept on a moving train before. It must be very special."

"Well, the noises can keep you from sleeping. Perhaps I should have brought you a sleeping draught instead of an orchid."

"I never take pills or powders. I'd worry I'd be hazy the next day. Don't worry. I'll have a good night's sleep and then once we're in Milan, we can explore." She kept looking at him as she added, "Do you want to take this invitation to the party for Catharina's father's sixtieth birthday?"

"It does seem like a chance to see how those people live."

"I thought you had a friend with a palazzo. You mentioned him once."

"Yes, but he's not that rich. I know the Lanettis by reputation. They throw parties that everyone is still talking about months after the fact."

"So you want to go there?"

"Only if you want to go there."

Atalanta hesitated a moment. If there was some plan to get her to that party, she could test Raoul's possible involvement, and his resolve to make it work, by denying that she wanted to go. She could claim that she loved to see simpler sights or that she wanted to avoid the crowd at such a big party.

Then again, apart from Catharina's flirting with Raoul and the idea that the invitation had a hidden purpose, a dress-up party in grand style was something she'd love to be part of. If she let her suspicions subside for a moment, her choice would be to go.

"We can decide later," Raoul said. "I'm sure Catharina doesn't expect us to tell her now. She'll be asleep already. And we should get some rest too. Good night." He smiled warmly at her, retreated, and closed the door.

She heard him lock it on his side. As if he expected her to barge in in the middle of the night.

The click reminded her sharply that Raoul was always doing that. Locking her out. Out of his innermost thoughts, his feelings. On Santorini she had landed in trouble because she had started to assume things about him – his past with the suspects, his choices – and she could have made a total mess of both the case there and of her friendship with Raoul.

Here she wouldn't make the same mistakes.

She sighed and wriggled out of her dressing gown. Her gaze fell upon the orchid, which she had put in a small glass of water to keep it fresh as long as she could.

A memory of this trip. This trip that was lovely and frustrating at the same time.

There was something about Catharina Lanetti she couldn't quite define. Was it because she had shared so freely that her father disliked her choices and that she was loath to go to the party and speak with him about her future? Wasn't it odd to share such intimate family matters with strangers on a train? Had this incongruity raised Atalanta's doubts about the coincidental nature of the encounter?

Had it felt like Catharina was repeating a story she had already told before – perhaps to Raoul, when she had enlisted his help to meet Atalanta? – but in a manner that didn't seem preconceived?

Her previous clients had hired her. Engaged her, come to her. Why had Catharina not been able to do that? Connect, ask help.

Or was Catharina uncertain that she would need help? Was it more a matter of being insecure about her choices and wanting some support at that party?

From Raoul? From her?

Atalanta rubbed her forehead. She was close to a headache just because her mind was running in circles. She simply didn't have the information to conclude anything with certainty. She'd have to …

What? Find out for herself?

Did that mean she had already decided to take Catharina's offer?

Because she'd never enjoy her trip if she kept wondering what the woman had wanted of her and how that party would turn out ...

Hissing in annoyance at her own curiosity, Atalanta got into bed and settled down for what would be her first night in a bed that moved at high speed through the night.

Atalanta dreamt of being on a ship that was being perilously tossed to and fro by a storm. Water roared from all sides and the mast broke with a snap. She could barely see anything around her but she heard Raoul call for her from somewhere near. She called back and tried to make her way to him across the deck. But the boards were slick with water and her feet slipped out from under her. She tried to grab at the railing but missed, her fingers touching the wood before she fell headlong and crashed down the sloping deck. Raoul kept calling her name, from further and further away. She knew he was in trouble and she had to get to him, but she wasn't able to stop herself from falling. She plunged into a chilly depth and darkness closed around her. She screamed but no sound came out.

Her eyes flew open and she stared into the night around her. Where was she? Why was her bed moving? Was she indeed on a ship? Was there a storm? Where was Raoul?

Slowly the day's events came back to her. How Raoul had whisked her away from the hotel to the Orient Express. The orchid he had brought her; dinner with the mysterious Catharina Lanetti.

Her heart skipped a beat. Had she cried out during her dream? If so, Raoul had to have heard and woken up. Soon he'd be knocking at the connecting door and what could she say? That she had had a nightmare? It would be most awkward.

But no knock disturbed the quiet in her compartment. She did hear someone moving in the corridor. Probably a steward on duty or a passenger making their way to the lavatory. She took a deep breath and relaxed her tight shoulders. There was nothing wrong.

Well, not in the sense that she was on a ship in a storm and ran a risk of drowning. There was of course the slight matter of having met Catharina and knowing, with an instinctive clarity, that something wasn't quite right. About the woman herself, or the encounter.

Atalanta rubbed her forehead. She had worked hard

before this trip. Perhaps too hard? Was she starting to jump at shadows?

Did it even matter? Whether Catharina had conspired to meet them or it had been completely coincidental, Atalanta could make her own choice. Did she want to spend part of her holiday with the Lanettis at their palazzo or not?

She pursed her lips. The truth was that she didn't really know. When she had imagined travelling she had always thought that it would be wonderful to get to know the people of a land and see how they lived. So a party inside a palazzo would be a chance to do exactly that. It was an opportunity to be with people in a more intimate setting than when she visited a village or was sightseeing in a town. She should actually appreciate this invitation that brought her into the heart of the region Raoul wanted to show her.

Raoul, yes. He was the problem, more or less. She wasn't sure that she wanted to share him during this trip. She wanted to keep him to herself and let this trip be personal and something for the two of them.

There was nothing against that, of course, but on the other hand the party was only one night out of their schedule and ... Did it really matter that much?

Atalanta sighed and turned on her side. She shut her eyes firmly. She had to get some sleep or she would be wasted in the morning. She didn't need to decide alone. She would ask Raoul how he felt about it. Later today, once they were off the train and exploring Milan and then driving out into the countryside, towards their destination, there would be plenty of time to discuss it and try to get an idea of what he thought of Catharina, the encounter, and the party. If he had no reservations, then she shouldn't be so worried but just go.

———

The sound of knocking woke her. Light was creeping into the compartment. She yawned and rubbed her eyes. The knocking continued. She forced her still sleepy body out of bed, grabbed her dressing gown and staggered to the connecting door. "Yes?"

"Are you all right?" Raoul sounded a tad worried. "I knocked before and you didn't answer. I thought you had left the compartment to stretch your legs. I always imagined you as an early riser."

"I usually am, but I had a bit of a rough night. What time is it?"

"Nine thirty. We arrive in Milan at twenty past ten, so we don't have much time left for breakfast."

"Breakfast! Do they even serve it at this time?" Atalanta flushed at the idea that she had slept so late.

"I'll go and see. You join me as soon as you can." It sounded like he turned away from the door. Then he added, with a sound as if he had to laugh, "But remember you are on vacation. So you don't need to rush."

"I don't need to rush ..." Atalanta grumbled to herself as she hurriedly opened the door to the space where the wash basin was. "I had so wanted to rise early, have breakfast and a chance to enjoy some of the sights from the train. Now we are almost there."

But there was no point in lamenting. She had to freshen up, dress and find Raoul, who had hopefully managed to secure some breakfast.

When Atalanta, in a bright yellow dress with her hair swept back into a wet look, entered the dining car, Raoul was sitting at a table laid out with a full breakfast of coffee, orange juice, a basket with bread, preserves and cold cuts, cheese. Everything looked most inviting – but for one thing.

Catharina Lanetti stood at the table, in what struck Atalanta as a forced relaxed pose. As if she had just happened to walk past, but in reality had planned it to the last detail. She wore an elegant turquoise trouser suit with a broad leather belt accentuating her slender waist. On her left wrist sat an expensive gold watch.

She looked up when Atalanta approached and smiled, but her cheeks were pale and there were bluish shadows under her eyes.

"Good morning," Raoul said. "I demanded everything they had left for our breakfast." He gestured across the table. "I hope this meets with your approval?"

"It looks delicious." Atalanta smiled at Catharina. "I assume you have already had breakfast? You look ready to tackle the day."

Catharina grimaced. "Looks can be deceiving. I had a very bad night."

"Don't train journeys agree with you?" Atalanta asked while seating herself. She wasn't about to ask Catharina to sit down with them and hoped Raoul wouldn't either.

Catharine shrugged. "Normally I'm fine on trains. On planes, on boats. I'm not affected by the motion or the sensation of speed. However, I find it decidedly unpleasant to get threats under my door."

"Threats?" Raoul echoed. He looked up at her with a frown over his dark eyes. "Someone threatened you?"

"They shoved a note under my door." Catharina reached into the pocket of her trouser suit to produce a white page. She put it on the table. Raoul reached for it but Atalanta said, "Don't touch it. There must be fingerprints on it from the sender."

Catharina looked at her. "Even if there are, how can we see them?"

"The police can—"

Catharina tilted her chin up. "I won't be going to the police with a stupid note."

Raoul leaned over and read it without touching it. "'Don't go to the party or you'll regret it.'" He looked at Catharina. "Why shouldn't you go there?"

"I've been away and some people didn't like my absence."

"If they didn't like your absence, they should be happy you're coming back." Raoul picked up his coffee and took a sip. "I don't see why they should threaten you."

"Let me rephrase that. They blamed me for leaving. They don't want me to come back and get into my father's good graces again. They're afraid he will give control of the vineyard to me."

"'They' being ...?" Atalanta queried. She spread apricot preserve on her bread. Despite this intrusion at their breakfast her logical mind felt quite intrigued by the situation.

"Everyone who stayed behind when I left." Catharina shrugged again. "My half-brothers. My father's steward.

His right-hand man. The secretary. Everyone who could never stand me, a woman, having any say about the family property."

Raoul said, "But if they are at your father's estate, how can they push a note under your door?"

Good question, Atalanta thought. She surveyed Catharina carefully.

The woman pulled an innocent expression. "How should I know?" She grabbed the note from the table and slipped it back in her pocket. "I just wanted to explain why I had a bad night. Enjoy your breakfast." And she walked away.

Raoul watched her go, his hands hovering over his plate where a half cut up boiled egg waited to be distributed on bread. "What do you think?" he asked Atalanta.

"About what?"

"The note." Raoul took another sip of coffee. "Did she make it up?"

"Make it up?" Atalanta echoed, surprised Raoul would think that far. She had imagined he was charmed by the handsome woman, had even known her before this trip, but she had never thought he would make such an accusation.

Accusation? Let's just say 'suggestion'.

"Yes." Raoul looked grim as he focused on the egg on

his plate. "I often have the unfortunate experience of women doing anything to make themselves interesting to me. They sometimes ... invent problems to appeal to my chivalrous side."

"And you think Catharina wrote this note herself to imply she is in danger and have you come to her rescue?"

"Come to her party," Raoul corrected. "I do believe her family won't be thrilled to see her waltzing in again after a long absence and bringing a famous race car driver might help lighten the mood."

"But she could just have told us so last night and asked us to help her out. We might have done it and she needn't have come up with this dramatic threatening note."

"I fear she has a dramatic nature."

"I don't agree." Atalanta sat back and frowned as she went back over the impressions she had formed of Catharina during their brief encounter so far. "I think she's very down to earth and practical. She's also independent and wants to forge her own path in life. Why would she lure you to the party by inventing a danger to her person she needs to be saved from? That doesn't seem to be in line with her character at all."

"I don't know her character," Raoul said, now sipping his orange juice. "And neither do you."

"I know, but when meeting someone for the first time you do form an opinion about them. I can't see her sitting in her compartment writing this note herself and then presenting it to us as if it came under her door. Besides, she did look worn. She slept badly."

"Makeup?" Raoul suggested. "She could be far more cunning than we think."

"To what end? To get you to her father's palazzo? I'm sorry, Raoul, I know you are a wanted guest at parties, but to go to such lengths …"

Raoul said, "She may be the type of woman who always wants to win. She saw me getting on the train. She decided she had to invite me to her father's birthday party. She didn't know I was with you. Last night she sensed that she can't influence me so easily so she decided that more drastic measures were necessary. Hence the note."

"It's possible of course but … Have you met her before? Do you actually know if she is manipulative?"

"She may have been to my races. I have been a professional driver for five years now. I have met hundreds of people. I don't recall all of them."

Atalanta ate in silence. This whole situation reminded her painfully of the Santorini case, where Raoul had kept information from her. In hindsight she did understand why and she wasn't upset about it any more. But … it had somehow damaged her trust in him a little. Perhaps more than she had acknowledged so far. She couldn't help but feel like he might again know more than he revealed and …

"Shall we simply decide not to go to that party?" Raoul said. "I'm sure we'll see her on the platform when we get off at Milan and we can then tell her that unfortunately we can't make the time for it or something along those lines." He reached across the table and covered her hand with his. "I want this trip to be special for you, a relaxing getaway, and I feel like getting involved with those Lanettis won't be relaxing at all."

"I agree." Atalanta felt relieved. "Thank you."

"No need to thank me." Raoul retracted his hand. "This juice is excellent, nice and sweet. Waiter! Could you refill my glass?"

Chapter Five

The arrival in Milan was chaotic. There were passengers coming off the train, others waiting to get on it, porters with luggage, and newspaper sellers. A voice called out announcements in Italian.

Raoul said, "We'd better wait for our luggage here." He drew her to the side, while scanning the platform. "I don't see Catharina. You?"

"Was she getting off here?" Atalanta asked. She was suddenly worried that they had misunderstood and the chance to politely decline the invitation would pass.

"I thought she said so." Raoul sighed. "Come along then, we'd better walk that way to find her."

He ushered her by the arm through the crowd, craning his neck to see better. Atalanta tried to find a flash of turquoise. But perhaps Catharina had donned a coat over her suit? It was a sunny and warm day but still some passengers coming off the train were dressed in expensive coats and gloves, underlining their status.

"There she is." Raoul pointed ahead of them. "We can catch up with her if we try." He lengthened his stride, pushing past a man with two suitcases, one in each hand. The man swore at him in Italian.

Atalanta watched Catharina's dark head bob among the crowd. It seemed that she was also hurrying for they couldn't manage to close in on her. Finally she halted, standing next to a man.

As Raoul and Atalanta reached the pair, they heard Catharina say in a strident voice, "I knew it was you with the note. How can you be so vicious?"

"Papa doesn't want you at his party. He told me so. He said that he hoped you would stay away. That you're dead to him. As dead as your mother."

Catharina paled. She formed her hand into a fist and lashed out, striking the man full on the nose.

He gave an agonized cry and staggered back, reaching up to his face. Blood splattered across his chin. "You broke my nose," he wailed. "Look at all the blood." He crumpled against a stack of crates.

Other passengers came to his aid, asking if he needed help.

Catharina threw him a scorching look. "Coward," she

spat. "You can't even fight a woman. And you think Papa will give you anything?"

Raoul caught her shoulder. "Catharina, this is not the way."

The woman turned to him. "Lorenzo was on the train. He shoved that vile note under my door. Because he is a coward who can't fight for the inheritance. He knows once I come home Papa will take me in his arms and everything will be as it always was." She looked again at her half-brother, who was being helped to his feet by two men. One of them had given him a handkerchief to dab at his bloodied face. "Don't come near me. Or I'll break more than your nose."

Catharina marched away. Raoul took two steps after her, then turned to Atalanta. "What should we do?"

"Nothing. It looks like she can fend for herself." Atalanta nodded at Lorenzo Lanetti, who was still recovering from the blow. "She doesn't need our help."

"Probably not," Raoul agreed with a sour expression. "Where's our luggage? My car should be out front. I asked a friend to bring it here for us."

Lorenzo Lanetti was standing up again, his face contorted with rage. "She'll be sorry," he said. "She won't get away with this." He clutched the bloodied handkerchief in his hand with such force his knuckles cracked.

Atalanta swallowed. "He seems ready to kill someone," she whispered to Raoul.

"He's just upset he got bested by a woman. He won't really harm her."

"But he was on the train. He could have shoved that note under her door." Atalanta followed Raoul, who directed the porter with their luggage through the magnificent station building to the front.

A red two-seater was parked to the left with a young man in a light suit leaning on the hood. He jumped upright when he saw them and raised a hand. *"Buongiorno."*

"Never lean against my car," Raoul said half amused, half serious. "She cost a lot of money."

"She? Are cars female?"

"My cars are." Raoul winked at him. "May I present Signorina Atalanta Ashford, a friend from Paris. She's coming to see Tuscany with me."

"I see." The friend surveyed her from head to toe with a little smile that suggested he thought that the trip would be more than just sightseeing.

Atalanta flushed. "And your name is?"

"Oh, excuse me," Raoul said to her, "that is my good friend and race aficionado Marcelo Bachi. But our ways part here, as we're going to get on the road."

"Not even a cup of coffee to start into the day?"

Marcelo asked with a feigned hurt expression. "I know a little bar here that serves the best coffee in the world. You have to try it."

Raoul looked at Atalanta. "Can the best coffee in the world tempt you?"

"I guess it can."

Raoul asked Marcelo, "Is it far from here?"

"No. If you leave the car, we can walk."

Raoul spoke to the porter, who declared himself happy to watch the car and luggage for them for a small fee. "All taken care of," Raoul said, offering her his arm.

She sighed in satisfaction as they walked away from the station through a street lined with tall, beautiful buildings. In the distance were two spires of an old church with stone saints watching over the entrance. It lay on a square with tables outside little cafés. They sat down to order their coffee. Atalanta cast her gaze past the fountain in the square and the pigeons quietly looking for food. The murmur of Italian around her, the sparkle of golden scales on the river nymphs supporting the fountain, it all contributed to this perfect day.

Perfect? Well, not quite. She kept thinking about Lorenzo Lanetti, who had threatened his half-sister. Who had been on their train. Who could have sent the note. About Catharina's ill-advised blow and the blood she had drawn. A man would not like such humiliation. His hatred had been palpable. How would things go when Catharina came home?

Shouldn't they have accepted the invitation anyway?

They actually had, sort of. After all, because of the altercation between the half siblings they hadn't been able to explain they weren't coming.

The waiter brought their coffee in small cups with a glass of water beside each and a small biscuit to dunk.

"Biscotti," Raoul explained, "amaretto flavoured. There are countless varieties, also with anise and pistachio, but I prefer amaretto."

Atalanta dipped the hard biscuit in the coffee and nibbled. It had a delicious, full, sweet flavour enhanced by the tang of the strong coffee. The sun shone down on them, warming the cobbles of the street and luring bees to the blossoming baskets of flowers at a nearby stall. Everything seemed bright and summery here, the colours shining as in a first-class painting. She had become part of this inviting world and wanted to immerse herself in it.

But her mind kept coming back to the unhappy Catharina, the shadows under her eyes, the hatred in her half-brother's face. But also the violence in Catharina's blow to his nose. She hadn't slapped him in the face, to put him in place. No. She had struck him with the force of a boxer. Intending to cause damage.

Hers was a heady mix of emotions just waiting to explode.

Well, even if it is, it is none of your business, she told herself. *You're on holiday. Raoul said so.*

He didn't want to go to the party. He even thought that Catharina had tried to lure them with a made-up story.

But it wasn't made up. That had been proven now. Lorenzo had been on the train. He'd had the opportunity to slip the note under the door.

How worried was he that his father's legacy would be entrusted to someone other than him? How desperate was he to prevent that? Catharina could be in actual danger. Perhaps they had to attend the party just to see that she was all right.

"Atalanta?" Raoul leaned over and touched her arm. "I asked you something."

"Sorry. I was daydreaming for a moment. This is so beautiful." She gestured around her. "Thank you so much for bringing me here."

Raoul smiled. "I'm glad you enjoy it. But this is nothing compared to what is yet to come."

Marcelo scowled. "Oh, of course our beautiful Milano isn't good enough. He wants to show Tuscany. There's nothing like it to Raoul's mind. I always wonder why he is so fond of it. What special memories he once made there ..."

Raoul rolled his eyes. "You're always riling me, *amico*. But I find something in Tuscany that I don't find elsewhere. Peace perhaps."

"Peace?" Marcelo laughed. "You enjoy crowds and company, parties and races, danger and challenges. Why would you want peace?"

"Probably because it's not very often a part of my everyday life," Raoul said. He smiled as he spoke the words but his eyes were serious. Atalanta wondered what exactly Raoul wanted from this trip. And why he had wanted to take her along.

After they had finished their coffee and returned to the station, they said goodbye to Marcelo and got into the car. They soon left the busy traffic of the city and exchanged the views of shops, restaurants, theatres, and houses for the green lushness of the countryside. The trees were swaying softly on the breeze, birds sang and the landscape rolled away in gentle hills. Soon these became covered with vineyards and Atalanta tried to catch glimpses of the ripe grapes hiding. She knew the harvesting season started in September – early when the summer had been warm and the grapes had been able to soak up much sunshine, later when the weather hadn't been so favourable. She wondered what kind of year it had been this time. Whether the owners who walked between the vines would rejoice, expecting a rich harvest or would worry that it wouldn't be as large as other years.

"We can stop in a village and see if there is a parade with the *novello*," Raoul suggested.

"*Novello*?"

"The new wine. It's actually last year's wine which has had a chance to ripen and mature. It's brought into the village on a cart stacked with bottles. You have to see it to believe it that it doesn't collapse. The cart is hailed by the villagers and in the village square a first bottle is opened and the wine tasted. It's an age-old ritual. If you are in Tuscany in September, you must see it."

"Well, then we must see it." Atalanta relaxed her shoulders and sighed. "This is simply wonderful. I wager that, had I been in Paris, I would have been dragged into some case again. It seems like I can't avoid crime, wherever I go."

As she said it, she thought of Catharina and the bloodied handkerchief in the hand of a man ready to take a swing at someone and break their jaw. Or their neck?

"I know what you're thinking now," Raoul said in a

serious tone. He glanced at her before returning his attention to the winding road. "You wonder when we'll meet crime here."

"Perhaps we've already met it."

"The Lanettis," Raoul scoffed. "They remind me of the Medicis, the family Catharina's father allegedly admires so much. They were also conniving, jealous, greedy, and not afraid to go far when they wanted something."

"How far?" Atalanta wondered out loud.

"They say that some of the Medicis were murderers. And the Borgias were even worse. They were half Spanish. There are tales of a woman among them who poisoned those who stood in her way. But you never know if such tales are true."

Atalanta hemmed.

Raoul said, "And even if they are, it's nothing new. At the court of the Roman emperors poisonings were fairly common. I wonder if those people ever ate anything without wondering if that bite would be their last."

"Seems rather unpleasant having to worry about that all the time."

"They had positions of power. That made them targets." He glanced at her again. "We're just normal people. Luckily."

"Not exactly, I'm afraid. Your competitors must be

jealous. And I bring criminals to justice. I must make enemies. Sooner or later."

"You're not thinking about your own enemies," Raoul said, "but about those of Catharina Lanetti. You like her."

"Well, she's independent, loves travelling. She wants to do things with her life. She is like me in that respect."

"And with her mother deceased when she was little … You feel you have things in common."

"Perhaps yes." Atalanta sighed. "Or it is just that my mind can't stop thinking about puzzles?"

"It takes some time to get into a holiday mood," Raoul agreed. "We just have to forget about the mysteries of our train ride and enjoy the day."

They continued past picturesque villages with grey stone houses under slate roofs, past olive trees and lemon orchards with the fruits shining through the leaves like spatterings of sunshine against the dark green. Children playing in a field looked with admiration at the car and even ran along for a few metres waving their hands in the air. Their cheerful voices resounded in tune with the ringing of a church bell in the distance.

This is the life, Atalanta sighed to herself. *This is what I always dreamt of. Immersing myself in beautiful landscapes that I had only seen in postcards. But it's even better than all those dreams because in those I travelled alone and here I am with a friend.*

She looked at Raoul's expression as he let the wheel run smoothly through his strong suntanned hands. He seemed at ease, relaxed in the driver's seat, which was probably his favourite place to be.

He looked at her as if he had felt her scrutiny. "What is it?" he asked.

"Nothing special. I was just thinking that so many people hate driving and you actually love it. Good for me."

"Oh, you'd love driving too. You just need to take a few lessons. Or on this trip I could show you the basics and you'd be well on your way."

"I'm not going to drive this car while in a foreign country. Suppose I ram into something. Or an animal crosses the road."

Raoul laughed. "You're rather timid for a woman who hunts killers."

"I'm just careful. That makes a lot of sense."

"I guess so. Look, such a friendly little village. Shall we stop and walk through it? Perhaps eat something? It's past lunchtime."

"Would such a small town have a restaurant?" Atalanta asked doubtfully.

"Not a restaurant, but an inn or tavern or other place where the locals come to drink at night. In the daytime they serve meals to those passing as they deliver food or sell products. It won't be fancy, but you can be sure that you have the freshest ingredients. Tomatoes that were harvested at their ripest and sliced onto fresh bruschetta. Herbs straight from the garden. And handmade pasta. Mmmm." He held his index finger and thumb together and kissed them with a look of exaltation.

Atalanta laughed.

Raoul threw her a hurt look and pointed a warning finger at her. "Never laugh at an Italian when discussing food. We take food very seriously here. The local produce is always someone's pride and joy. And offending people ... well, Italians do have a temper."

"Yes, if even the women fight like men ..."

Raoul sighed. "Don't start about Catharina again." He added after a brief silence, "I do feel bad that we didn't tell her we weren't coming. She's probably counting on it."

"And Lorenzo's presence on the train means her note might not have been an invention after all. You feared she had an ulterior reason for acting like a woman in danger but ... perhaps she really is."

"And we should go and save her?" Raoul shook his head. "I don't think so. We made up our minds that we aren't going, so we aren't going. I'm sure everything will be fine without us meddling in what is, after all, a family affair."

They parked the car in the shade of a tall tree in the village square. An old man sat on a weathered bench in front of his house dozing, his chin touching his chest as he snored. A tattered dog lay at his feet, not even bothering to raise its head to look at the visitors.

"Most people will be resting right now," Raoul said. "The siesta after lunch. I hope we can trouble the innkeeper for some food." He led the way to the building opposite. The door was open invitingly but when they went in, there was no one in the dim room, only several rickety tables and chairs. The bar was empty and the smell of stale beer was in the air.

Raoul crinkled his nose. "I don't know if we should eat here." He walked to the bar and tried to peer through an archway into the next room. "I think someone is there. I'll go and have a look." He disappeared behind the bar and out of sight.

Atalanta studied a black and white photograph that hung on the wall. A group of men stood in the square under the tree that was still there. They were cheering and one of them carried something in his hands. A trophy? Did they have a sports team here?

Suddenly a male voice started to shout in Italian. It sounded as if the man was furious. Atalanta froze in fear that Raoul would be smacked in the face as Lorenzo Lanetti had been and he would be unable to drive today.

That they would be stuck here in a village that was hostile to strangers and might even drive them out of town on foot. They'd have to leave the car and …

The male voice continued to rant while another voice shouted back at him at the same volume. It took Atalanta a few moments to realise it was Raoul. Having heard him mostly speak in moderate tones, she was surprised and oddly fascinated that it was him.

She snuck to the bar and tried to see into the room from which the voices emanated. She couldn't make out much, but the discussion was surely not friendly. How had Raoul managed to make an enemy of the man so quickly?

Then Raoul appeared with a wide grin. "His wife made ravioli this morning and there is still some left. I had to bargain to get it as it's actually his own meal for later today, but with a bit of persuasion …"

"I thought he was about to beat you."

"No, no, that is the usual way Italians conduct a conversation. You make a point by raising your voice and gesturing a lot with your hands. It's not violent though."

"Good. You didn't break your nose and we'll get something to eat."

"It would take more than one man to break my nose. I know how to defend myself. Unlike Lorenzo Lanetti, who looked like he hadn't even been in a fight when he was a boy."

"Enough about fighting." Atalanta pointed at the photograph. "Is that from some victory in sports?"

"Probably pigeons."

"Pigeons?"

"Yes, lots of people in these small villages have pigeons and they race them against each other. The pigeons are dropped a hundred miles away and the first to return wins a prize. Villages also compete against each other. I guess that must be some giant win." Raoul cast the photo a dispassionate look. "I don't like their cooing and I have no idea what the sport in it is, but it's a favourite here. So better not say anything negative about it."

"I have to make a list," Atalanta said with a grin. "Don't criticize the food, don't speak slightingly about pigeons ... anything else?"

"Have you got an hour?" Raoul asked.

Atalanta hitched a brow. "That bad?"

Raoul shook his head but his laugh was rueful. "It's easy to get into a discussion here. People have strong opinions about everything. And you're an outsider who shouldn't interfere. We'll have to keep a low profile or we will have constant altercations. I'm used to it and can shout back, but as you were already picturing me with a bloody nose …"

Atalanta huffed and pointed to the door leading outside. "Shall we go and sit in the sunshine while we wait for our lunch to arrive?"

Chapter Six

After a delicious homemade lunch of ravioli with fresh herbs and sparkling water with lemon, followed by a small cup of espresso, they continued their drive. Atalanta was now really in a holiday mood, letting the breeze caress her features and narrowing her eyes so the sunshine turned to rainbows on her lashes. She inhaled the rich scents of the land – earth, sun-soaked grass, and cobbled walls – and when they passed houses, wafts of freshly baked bread or spices worked into pesto. As the heat of the day was over and the afternoon wound down, people were working outside, cleaning vegetables, mending clothes, or taking dry laundry off the line. And time and time again, Atalanta saw the wood and wire cages in which the pigeons lived that the villagers were so proud of.

Close to six they entered a village where the sound of lively music greeted them from afar. In the village square a three-man orchestra – two violins and a flute – was playing lively dance music. Women, in white dresses with red embroidery on the neckline and sleeves, danced, turning left, then right, each with one arm held elegantly over her head while the men, dressed in black shirts and trousers, clapped their hands to the rhythm, going faster and faster.

Raoul parked the car and got out, rounding it quickly to help Atalanta alight. He squeezed her hand as he said, "This is typical of the region – a spontaneous feast in the street. Do you smell that?"

Atalanta inhaled. "It's burning wood."

"Yes, it is. Burning wood from a pizza oven." He pointed towards a large cone-shaped stone structure. "We're going to eat the freshest pizza you ever had. Really thin bottom, delicious tomato spread and toppings straight from the land."

"But we're outsiders. Can we just join in? I thought you said they didn't like people who came from elsewhere."

"*Ciao*, Marco!" Raoul waved his hand high in the air.

A tall man, better dressed than most of the villagers, came over in long strides. "*Benvenuto!*" He continued in such fast Italian that Atalanta understood very little of it, but his wide smile and the way in which he kept pumping Raoul's hand made it very clear he was glad to see him.

"May I present Signorina Atalanta Ashford," Raoul said. "We're sightseeing together."

"Aha!" The man managed to infuse a whole world of emotions in the one word. He took her hand in his and kissed it. "*Benvenuta*. So pleased to make your acquaintance." He spoke English with a charming Italian accent. "I hope you like our beautiful country?"

"Oh, yes, I've only had good experiences so far."

"That's a lie." Raoul wagged a finger at her. "Atalanta witnessed, first-hand, how hot-headed you Italians can be. She was present when someone delivered a pretty good right hook to a man's nose and broke it." He added with a grin, "That someone was a woman too."

Marco laughed. "Our women are the same as we are. They don't like to be treated badly. Did the man betray her? Was he unfaithful and she caught him at it?"

"No, it was her half-brother and it was about an alleged threat." Raoul looked more serious now. "On the train on our way here we happened to meet Catharina Lanetti."

Marco raised his eyes to the sky above and spread his hands in dramatic fashion. "Lanetti. That name is cursed around these parts. We can't stand to hear it."

"And why is that?" Atalanta asked curiously.

"Well, once upon a time we had the best vineyard and the prize wine made there was connected with this village and the surrounding land. We were proud of it. But the master of the house had no sons, only a daughter. He had to accept a husband for his only child as his successor. That was Cosimo Lanetti. They whispered he only wanted to marry her for the vineyard. That he didn't love her."

"Mere speculations?" Atalanta asked.

Marco shrugged. "He treated her well after they were married. He built the villa that is still their seat especially for her. She decorated all its rooms. She was allowed to paint and sculpt, something most husbands don't like. She had staff so she never had to worry about the household. There was never even a rumour that he betrayed her. Everything looked perfect."

"You say that as if there is something wrong with perfect," Raoul said with a laugh.

Marco lifted a shoulder and let it fall again. "Perfect doesn't exist, *amico*. You know that; I know that."

"Ah, so now the fact that they had a scandal-free marriage is the very reason we assume that something was amiss?" Raoul shook his head. "You're just like a paparazzo. You want to find a story no matter what."

"Well, she did die." Marco said, then turned to the

man working the pizza oven and shouted something. The man waved in acknowledgement.

"Die?" Raoul said. "Catharina did mention her mother passed away when she was still young and that her father remarried."

"Yes. He married another woman who could further his business. The daughter of one of the richest bankers in Florence. How convenient."

"Were there suspicions about the death?" Atalanta asked. "That it might not have been natural?"

"Anna Lanetti was killed in a highway robbery. She was travelling along in a carriage her husband had made for her, drawn by a very spirited horse. She was stopped by robbers who took her money and jewellery, even ripping her wedding ring off her finger. They stabbed her to death, probably because she resisted. There had been robberies like it in the area, and shortly after the incident the gang was caught, tried, and hanged for killing her."

"It all seems pretty straightforward," Atalanta said.

"Yes. But the gang leader has maintained that they never killed anyone during the robberies. Just before he was hanged, while standing beside the hangman, he cried out that he was innocent of murder. That they had only taken money and valuables from people during holdups, but they had never shed blood."

Atalanta pursed her lips. "He probably thought that if

it wasn't for the murder, they would never have been condemned to death. He simply tried to save his life and that of his men any way he saw how."

"Perhaps."

The man who manned the oven extracted a large pizza and put it on a platter. He sent a woman over with it. She placed the platter on a table and smiled at Raoul. Marco ordered her to cut the pizza and pass around the slices. She handled the big knife with ease and held Raoul's gaze just a little longer when she handed him his slice on a simple earthenware plate.

Marco said something to her and she returned to the oven, looking over her shoulder as she went.

Marco said, "You seem to have caught the eye of my daughter."

"How old is she now?" Raoul asked.

"Seventeen."

"Too young for me."

"And you are a confirmed bachelor, *nò*?" Marco clapped his hand on Raoul's shoulder. "You should enjoy your freedom a little longer, *amico*. Until the right one comes along." He cast a glance at Atalanta as he said it. She pretended to be completely engrossed by the delicious pizza. It was topped with salami, ham, and a strong cheese. The wood on which it had baked had given it extra flavour. Raoul had not exaggerated. This was the best pizza she had ever tasted.

"But we've diverted," Marco said, his expression serious again. "You mention the Lanetti name. Are you interested in Catharina? She is a beautiful woman who broke many hearts. Some whisper she isn't human at all, but a wood spirit. There was an old belief that there were once spirits who would take the form of a beautiful woman and lure men into the woods, or into swamps, to their death."

"A variation on sirens," Atalanta said to Raoul.

Raoul grinned. "Every culture has a myth where women lead men to destruction. It's a universal problem."

But Marco wasn't laughing. "Catharina Lanetti is a dangerous woman," he said in a low voice. "People around her die."

"What do you mean, people around her die?" Raoul asked sharply.

"People she doesn't like, or those she has argued with tend to die." Marco gestured with a greasy hand. "Years ago she invited a schoolfriend over for the summer. The girl had her own bedroom in the palazzo. One night she climbed out of the window and fell to her death in the courtyard. People whispered that Catharina had put her up to a dare. Catharina never acknowledged this but ...

why couldn't it be true? There's no reason for a girl to climb out of a window in the night."

"That is just one example, and of an unfortunate accident. Who are the other people who died?"

Marco sighed. "Her mother."

"You told us it was a robbery gone wrong. What on earth does Catharina have to do with that?"

"An hour before her mother left on that fatal trip, she and Catharina quarrelled. Catharina was heard exclaiming several times, 'I wish you were dead.'"

"Haven't we all said something like that at one time or another?" Raoul looked sour. "I think it's very cruel to accuse a child of having caused her mother's death. There's no logic behind it either, just superstition or folktales."

"Perhaps you're right. But Catharina is a troubled woman. If she's coming back here, she must want something. She said last time she left she would never return. So why would she do so now?"

"Her father is turning sixty and giving a big party."

"Oh, is it that?" Marco nodded thoughtfully. "She might want to get back into his good graces to get some part of the property. After all, Cosimo isn't exactly fond of his sons. He did draw the short straw with those two. One of them intelligent but physically weak, the other strong and handsome but without any plan in life. He should have taken the whip to them when they were younger. And perhaps he did, but it didn't work out. Neither of them is capable of running his estate the way he wants it to be run."

"So Catharina might actually have a chance to become her father's successor?" Atalanta asked. "Would the workers and the businessmen who buy from the vineyard accept a woman in charge?"

"I don't know. Perhaps if she used her pretty face to her advantage. A little charm can go a long way. Do you want more pizza?"

While Marco handed them both another slice and called for wine to be brought, Atalanta thought of the woman they had met on the train. She had seemed unhappy. Nervous too, perhaps. Or in any case, not at ease, not confident that everything was going to turn out well. The threat shoved under her door. Her half-brother having been on the train.

The robbery in which her mother had died, and the gang caught for the crimes later claiming that, yes, they had stolen, but never killed – did it mean something? Had Catharina's mother died in the robbery? Or had someone only made it look like that? Did Catharina suspect? Not just that it had been murder but also who was responsible?

The father immediately came to mind. He had

remarried soon after, to a banker's daughter. An advantageous match for his business.

Had the villagers been right to assume he had merely married his first wife for her vineyard and had disposed of her so he could marry again and put money into the property? Had all his decisions been based on greed or ambition, whatever you wanted to call it?

Was it a family trait? Would Lorenzo not hesitate to hurt Catharina to keep his father from giving part of the property to her? Was she in danger?

Atalanta suppressed an impatient sigh. She wanted to enjoy this trip, not worry about some woman she barely knew. But why had Catharina wanted them to be present at the party? Because she felt insecure, alone, threatened?

They hadn't told Catharina they weren't coming.

They could still go. Perhaps they even had a moral obligation to find out what was happening there. Her grandfather had left her his fortune on the express condition that she help people. He himself had once, on the Orient Express when confronted with that wrongly accused conductor, sacrificed his holiday time to look into the crime.

Atalanta washed down the last bite of pizza with the rich red wine. It was a delicious authentic meal served in a small village that could come straight from a travel poster. This was the Tuscan experience Raoul had wanted her to have. He had wanted to take her away from murder and cases, from clients and crime. But it felt as if it simply wasn't meant to be. And if she was honest with herself, the whole thing intrigued her. The death of the mother. The death of the schoolfriend. Indeed, why *would* a girl climb out of a window at night?

Marco walked away to talk to his daughter and Atalanta turned to Raoul. "I've been thinking. We don't have a place to stay for the night yet, do we?"

"No, we haven't."

"Then we can go to the Lanetti palazzo and accept Catharina's invitation to stay there."

"I thought you didn't want to." Raoul studied her a moment and then said, "Don't tell me that the story of these deaths happening around Catharina intrigues you."

"Don't you think it is odd?" she asked.

"Odd, perhaps, but she is not a wood spirit. The words she spoke to her mother before she left on that fatal carriage ride didn't cause her death. She was a child at the time. She didn't conspire to have her mother die."

"Of course not. I don't think she caused her mother's death."

"But you think another might have had a hand in it."

"It's possible to use the presence of robbers in an area to kill someone and let them take the blame."

"And do you also have a suspect in mind?"

"Cosimo Lanetti."

"The man whose birthday party we'd be attending. Don't you think it's in rather bad taste to go to someone's party and drink his champagne while suspecting him of murder?"

"The point is" – Atalanta leaned over to Raoul and spoke in a low voice – "that Catharina may have drawn the same conclusion I have. She may blame her father for her mother's death. What is her intention in going to his birthday party?"

"You believe she might want to … harm him, because of some idea that he is guilty? Catharina told us she is over thirty now. Why wait so long? Don't you think she might have drawn that conclusion a little bit sooner?"

"You're probably right." Atalanta hung her head. "I guess my imagination is running wild."

Marco came back with more wine. Raoul declined, saying he still had to drive the car. "I want my passenger to be safe," he said with a nod at Atalanta.

Marco said, "I wish I could invite you to stay at my house, but I have my mother-in-law over and my wife's sister with her two children. We're full to the brim."

"Don't worry about it. We have a place to stay for the night." Raoul gestured to Atalanta. "She just suggested that we attend Cosimo Lanetti's birthday party. Catharina invited us to it."

Marco stared and then huffed. "Well, well, an invitation into the lion's den. To a party the Medicis would have been jealous of. Stuffed peacock, towering cakes, endless streams of alcohol and subtle backstabbing."

"As long as it's subtle and nobody takes it literally."

Marco scoffed. "I wonder what would happen if someone did. I bet the Medicis got away with so many crimes. They were powerful and nobody dared to stand up to them. The police in these parts fear Lanetti. They won't touch him, or his children."

"They'd have to investigate if something happened," Raoul protested.

"Oh, they'd investigate, but the blame would be placed on someone who could be eliminated without any harm coming to the core family."

"Someone like Catharina?" Atalanta asked. Her heart beat quickly as she awaited the answer.

"She has been away," Marco mused. "And no one really liked her in the first place. I guess that if the family would decide who to sacrifice, she'd be top of the list. It would even look better than blaming a servant. That would be too obvious."

"So if a death happened during the party, Catharina

could be accused?" Atalanta said, half to herself, half out loud.

Raoul sighed. "It seems she's dead set on going to see these conniving people for herself. I think it could be quite dangerous to mix with such a crowd."

"I thought you never shied away from risks?" Marco asked. "If you do go there, you must come back here to tell me all about it. I can't wait to hear if I was right about the stuffed peacock."

Chapter Seven

"I still don't understand why we're doing this," Raoul said as he turned the car on to the dirt road leading to the palazzo of the Lanettis. To their left and right and as far as the eye could see, vines grew across the rolling hills. Cypresses lined the winding road. The sun, low in the sky, cast golden light across the land.

"Because I've never seen a stuffed peacock in my life," Atalanta said. "We have the chance to be guests at an extravagant party. Why wouldn't we go? It's a nice way to spend the night and we can leave again in the morning."

"You want to talk to Catharina," Raoul said in a resigned voice.

"I guess I do want to know if she blames her father for murder. I mean, that's such a huge accusation to hang over a relationship. It must hurt both of them. If it's not true …"

"What if it is true?" Raoul clenched the wheel. "I feel like we're putting our heads in a wasps' nest. It's none of our business what Catharina believes."

"Or what her father did? If he's guilty, someone should do something about it."

"Like what? The alleged robbery happened almost thirty years ago. You can't reconstruct what actually happened."

"Probably not." Atalanta played with her gloves. Marco had offered them a room in his house to change and they were now both in evening wear for the party. Her orange dress matched the warm hue spreading over the land. She felt content after the pizza and wine, ready to simply stop the car somewhere and get out to enjoy the view. Be with Raoul without others present.

But she had made the decision to attend the party. And now the palazzo came into full view. It was a tall, flat-roofed building in light stone, with a central entrance consisting of three stone archways. The many windows had dark blue shutters, which were all open allowing light to stream out.

Raoul halted the car and a servant came out to take the keys and park it for them. Raoul told him to be careful as she had a lot of spirit. He led Atalanta to the door where two more servants, dressed in Renaissance garb, waited to show them inside. One of them asked to see an invitation and Raoul said that they had been asked to attend by Catharina Lanetti. The man blinked a moment as if the name was unfamiliar to him. Then he said he'd have to ask inside. He disappeared while the other watched them with a blank look.

It would be ironic if they were turned away, but at the same time it might solve a dilemma. They would not be able to go to the party and they'd have no more responsibility to—

"Good evening." A tall man with dark hair and brown eyes came over, dressed in rich purple embroidered with gold thread. He wore tight white trousers and traditional medieval stockings wrapped around the lower leg. He reached out a fleshy hand. "Cosimo Lanetti. I understand you are a friend of Catharina?"

"Raoul Lemont. I race cars."

"Of course. I attended one of your races a while back. Excellent steering, a deserved win. And this is ..." The man smiled winningly as he kissed Atalanta's hand.

"Signorina Atalanta Ashford. A friend to whom I'm showing the beautiful Tuscan land."

"Then you've made the right decision to come here. Because Tuscany has no better place than this estate.

Allow me ..." Cosimo took Atalanta's right hand, placing it on his left, and then led her, their hands held high between them as if they were a medieval couple, into a great hall. The room had a high ceiling upon which mythological figures had been painted. Atalanta wanted to see which she recognized, but her attention immediately drifted to the beautiful glass chandelier in the centre. The glass elements were formed into bunches of grapes, the cut glass reflecting the light in dazzling rays. A long, gilded table stood along the left side of the room, full of elaborate dishes: fruit in tiers, stuffed pheasants and peacocks, a boar's head with an apple in its open mouth and a mosaic of lobster, shrimp, and oysters.

Cosimo halted and looked at the guests with a satisfied smile. His expression was a bit too smug for Atalanta's liking, but he had a right to be proud of what he presented to them.

"This house was built for your first wife?" she asked. "I heard she decorated all the rooms."

"Oh, yes, she did. She had excellent taste." Cosimo smiled at her. "Every household needs the hand of a woman with style and class."

"Cosimo!" A blonde woman in a deep red low-cut dress strode up to them and eyed them with an angry scowl. "You should be getting ready for the birthday toast."

"I am, *amore*." He gestured from the woman to Atalanta. "May I introduce my wife, Melina. Melina, this is Signorina—"

"Atalanta Ashford," Atalanta rushed to add. "How delightful to meet you. What a fabulous party."

The woman seemed mollified. "It took weeks to prepare. Especially the artist to do the ice sculptures was hard to come by. The sculptures are in the other room." She pointed to an open door. "You must have a look later."

Cosimo snapped his fingers at a servant and ordered a gold goblet to be brought for his birthday toast.

Raoul touched Atalanta's arm and pointed at the peacocks, saying Marco had his wish now. "Too bad I didn't bring a camera – I could have showed it to him later."

Atalanta was only half-listening, focused as she was on the whispered words Cosimo addressed to his wife. "You must always make everything look effortless. If you tell people how difficult it was to organize …" He shook his head with a clucking noise.

Melina's cheeks turned red as she hissed back, "It *was* a lot of work. And you're not even grateful."

"I don't have to be grateful for a party paid from my own pocket. Remember, *amore*, who owns all of this." Cosimo turned back to Atalanta and Raoul and said with a charming smile, "I'll propose the toast and then introduce you to a few people. You'll see that everyone worth knowing is here."

Instead of the servant, Catharina strode up to them. She wore a light blue dress with a gold embroidered corset that closed with a buckle shaped like a flower. She had a gold goblet in her hand. "Papa, don't you think someone else should propose a toast to you?" She held up the beaker.

Her father narrowed his eyes. "Why are you interfering? And what goblet is that? It's not my own."

"Indeed it is not. I bought this for you as a birthday present. Knowing how much you admire the Medici, I found this via an antique dealer."

At the word 'present' Cosimo's eyes had lit up. He now leaned over and studied the expert craftsmanship and the jewels set in the rim. "It looks very beautiful."

"I would advise you, however, not to drink from it."

"Why not? If it is mine, I should drink from it and step into the shoes of the illustrious Medici men who drank from it before me."

"It is a special beaker." Catharina was raising her voice as if she was speaking to the entire room and people were turning their heads and listening to what she was saying. "It has a secret compartment."

"A secret compartment? You mean, for treasure?" Cosimo peered into the goblet. "Does it hold another gift for me?"

"It may hold something, but it isn't a gift you would want."

"Why not? How well do you know me after years spent away?" Cosimo snatched the goblet from her hand. "I'll drink from it. Lucio ..." He gestured at a man nearby with a pitcher of wine. "Fill the goblet for me that I may drink."

"I wouldn't try it." Catharina sounded cold. "The last man who drank from it regretted it."

"I'm not superstitious, don't believe in curses."

"Or poison?" Catharina asked.

Cosimo gripped the goblet. "Poison?" he repeated slowly.

"Yes. This cup has an ingenious mechanism to hold poison that is only released when the drinker holds the cup at a certain angle. Before that it is perfectly safe. But after ..."

"And that is your gift to your father?" Melina's eyes shot sparks at Catharina. "You're a wicked child."

"I know my father. He can't resist owning special things. And this is very special." She looked straight at him, her eyes narrowing a fraction. "Or do you want to give it back to me?"

"No." Cosimo held the goblet to his chest. "It's mine."

"He would be a fool to ever drink from it," Raoul whispered to Atalanta. "He probably thinks he can sell it at a good price and thus benefit from this unusual gift."

Someone started to applaud and everyone present followed suit. Catharina jerked upright as if she hadn't been aware that her conversation with her father had been overheard. She turned red and walked away.

Atalanta looked at Raoul. "What a strange family this is," she whispered, "where they give each other such presents."

"Perhaps it's some joke they both understand?" Raoul shrugged. "We don't know that much about them."

"We know absolutely nothing." Atalanta sighed. "Still, I want to talk to Catharina and now is as good a time as ever. Excuse me. I'll be back soon." She walked after the woman, whose light blue dress was clearly visible among the crowd.

Chapter Eight

Atalanta followed her hostess through a gilded archway into another room where guests in Renaissance costumes were sampling wine and food was being passed around by waiters wearing masks. A long table held the ice sculptures Melina had been so concerned about. The centrepiece was a replica of the Lanetti palazzo and on both sides a swan spread its wings. Crushed ice had been placed under and around the sculptures, but it was warm in the room and, judging by the drops forming, these carefully created works of art were melting. Understandable that Melina felt sorry she had gone to so much trouble for a perishable product.

In the next room, a space had been cordoned off with red and golden cords, and acrobats in medieval garb were building a human pyramid while a musician accompanied their movements, drumming faster as the pyramid got higher and the act more dangerous. Others were doing flips and cartwheels. The guests didn't seem to have much of an eye for the antics as they talked, laughed, and drank.

Catharina's light blue dress kept teasing Atalanta from afar, luring her further into the palazzo's many rooms. In one, a man was fire juggling, in another a magician conjured pigeons from his silk top hat. The many sights and sounds started to make Atalanta dizzy, and gave her the feeling she was caught in a strange maze, looking for a way out but not finding one. Time and time again, she saw a masked waiter watching her from afar but she didn't know if there were simply many of them scattered through the rooms or if it was the same one following her around. She wished she had stayed with Raoul instead of wanting to speak with Catharina.

At last she came into a room where a woman sat playing a piano. There were no guests there, perhaps because there didn't seem to be any food and drink on offer. The quiet was a relief after the bustle she had just left behind.

Catharina had halted in the centre of the room and stood with her head down, listening to the beguiling music. Atalanta walked up and stopped beside her, looking at her expression. It struck her how sad it was, with a tinge of bitterness. Was it hard for her to be back here, in her father's house where she had often felt unwanted? Was she reminded of her deceased mother? Her abducted half-brother? On a night like this, celebrating a family milestone, the past must have felt more alive.

"Are you not feeling well?" Atalanta asked softly.

Catharina looked up with a jerk. "Signorina Ashford …" Her features brightened. "You took my invitation and came. How kind of you. You might have had other plans and I interfered. But you're here now and …" She gestured at the piano. "Isn't that lovely?"

"I love music." Atalanta smiled at her. "And the piano is one of my favourite instruments."

"Really? You must try this one." Catharina went over to the woman playing and complimented her, told her she could go to get herself a glass of champagne. Although her tone was friendly and it made sense to give the artist a well-deserved break, Atalanta couldn't help but notice that Catharina's approach was rather brusque and demanding. She could at least have waited until the piece was finished. Now she practically claimed the piano. Which was logical perhaps as she was the daughter of the master of the house, and the woman nothing but … a hired hand? Like all the other performers?

Still the musician rose with reluctance and threw Catharina an ugly look before retreating.

Catharina gestured for Atalanta to sit at the piano. "Please try it and tell me how you like it."

"It's a beautiful instrument by the look of it." Atalanta caressed the wood before sitting down. "Thank you for letting me play."

"Oh, you must act as if this is your home. Most guests do." Catharina's mouth pinched a moment. "My father allows them too many liberties, in my eyes. Especially when they've drunk a lot, they get rude and ... unpleasant."

"Still you came to the party," Atalanta said, letting her fingers wander over the keys and lure a tender melody from the instrument.

"I had to. My father doesn't tolerate disobedience. Had I not shown up here, I could forget about ever getting anything from him. And I need his support, now more than ever."

"I see." Atalanta continued to play while she asked gently, "Do you need money for your travel plans?"

"Actually I want to expand our business ventures. While I was in Turin, I learned how to make chocolate. It's an art and I've become very good at it. I want the Lanetti name to be famous not just for wine but also for chocolate. I hope I can convince Papa that it's a good idea."

"And in an attempt to pave the way for your request you got him this special gift? Because he is a collector of Medici possessions?"

"Exactly. He sees them as grand examples. You should see his study. It's full of vases and candlesticks that were allegedly once theirs. I think he sometimes gets cheated when his favourite antiques dealer has another unique piece for him. But my gift is truly special. I'm certain it was actually used by a Medici."

"But don't you think that a poison goblet is a ... very unusual birthday present?"

"My father admires the Medici for many things. Their business acumen. Their interest in the arts. How they sponsored artists like Botticelli and perhaps even contributed to the invention of the piano. In fact, many things are said to have originated with them. They played an incredibly important part in the world of their days. My father wants to be just like them." Catharina smiled to herself as she let a finger slide across the piano's edge. "He also admires their ruthlessness. How they did everything to extend their power. Marriages were matches for property. Friendships were begun to further their interests. And they also killed to get what they wanted."

Atalanta looked at Catharina's face as she said, "Do you agree with that?"

"With what?"

"His admiration for murder as a way of getting what you think you need in life."

"I assume you don't agree." Catharina turned away, and with her back turned, it was impossible for Atalanta to gauge her feelings. Then she said, "But you didn't grow up in the family I had. You never had to wonder if ..." She fell silent.

Atalanta stopped playing to focus on the conversation. "What exactly is this gift for your father meant to convey?"

"That I give him what he wants and he should give me what I want in return." Catharina turned to Atalanta, all smiles again. "I want to present him with my chocolate-making plans tomorrow. I need him to be in a good mood. Tonight's party will help, I hope. Do continue playing."

"Thank you, but no. I've had my chance to try this wonderful instrument. And the lady who was playing here first will probably be returning. Was she engaged for tonight like the other artists, the acrobats and magicians?"

Catharina's lips curled up in a derogatory grin. "She'd resent you for saying such a thing. She is a

Lanetti."

"Excuse me, I was under the impression—"

Catharina flicked a hand up. "You've not insulted me. I never liked her. She comes here too often and the way she looks at my father … I think Melina has something to worry about."

"She is family and still you think …"

Catharina laughed softly. "She is not family by blood. She married into the Lanetti family. For a good reason, I assume. She is the wife of my cousin Danielo. They live in a house nearby. He helps Papa with the vineyard. He used to follow Giovanni around like a shadow, always trying to get into his good graces. But I heard that recently he's doing more things on his own and he's actually convinced Papa to give him control of part of the estate." Catharina stared ahead with a frown. "Yes, he is definitely becoming a contender in his own right."

"A contender for what?" Atalanta asked curiously.

"Papa needs a successor. He had a heart attack in the spring. It was nothing major, but the doctor said he shouldn't work so hard. He wants to appoint someone who can take charge of the day-to-day business. Someone he trusts."

"And there are several people interested in that position?"

"Yes. Of course." Catharina stood still, staring with a

frown into the distance. "It would give one so much power in the family. We all want it. Lorenzo, Giovanni, Danielo, even Melina. She knows nothing about wine making, can't tell a grape from an apple, but she has suddenly asked the steward to show her things and … She believes my father would actually allow her to interfere with business."

"But he never would?"

Catharina raised her hands. "The Papa I know wouldn't let her anywhere near his prize vineyards. But the heart attack changed him. He has become softer. At least that's the only way I can explain how he lets it go on."

"Lets what go on?" Atalanta asked softly.

"Melina and the steward. They spent hours in the fields together. Allegedly so she can learn about the business. But I think they're having an affair. In the past my father would follow them to spy on them but after his heart attack he isn't allowed to walk for long stretches or be in the sun and …" She added scornfully, "He's becoming an old man and he knows it."

"I don't think your father would appreciate you saying such things." A handsome man had entered the room. He was tall and dark-haired with sparkling brown eyes. He had a muscular build and he moved with a careless grace. The sort of man who would turn heads wherever he went. Women would try to catch his eye, men would be instantly jealous of the power he exuded.

"My brother Giovanni," Catharina said. "Let me warn you, he is never serious."

"I was when I said Papa won't hear about growing old. He's only sixty. Not eighty, you know." Giovanni gave Catharina a playful pat on the back.

She stepped away from him as if stung, snarling, "His health is fragile and you shouldn't tell him otherwise."

Giovanni's eyes narrowed, his handsome, smiling face suddenly turning cold. "Barely across the threshold and already telling us what to do? We did well without you. You need not have come back."

"That's the most charming welcome home speech I ever heard." Catharina's eyes flashed. "Did Lorenzo push that note under my door under your orders? He never had an original idea in his life."

"What note?"

"On the Orient Express someone put a note under my door saying I shouldn't attend this party or I'd regret it. Lorenzo was on board. I saw him on the platform and I broke his nose."

Giovanni stared at her a moment and then broke into laughter. His face turned red while he bellowed, beating himself on the knees with glee, "You broke ... He said that ..." Gasping for air, he couldn't speak normally.

Catharina sighed. "It's not that amusing."

"No." Giovanni straightened up with an effort, wiping tears from his eyes. "I suppose it's not amusing at all. The poor boy is in such pain because …" He fought a new burst of laughter. "He told Papa he had been beaten by three thugs. Three! And it was actually just you?"

"Yes, it was *just* me." Catharina's voice was sharp as a knife. "And if I find out that you put Lorenzo up to that trick with the note …"

"What do you want to do? Break my nose as well? Try, sister dear. I'd break your arm first." Giovanni stared at her with ice-cold venom. Then he looked at Atalanta and his expression changed in a flash to warm and charming. "A little bickering among siblings. You know how it goes."

"Actually, Atalanta doesn't as she is an only child. An orphan, I might add. Her family left her with a large fortune and she's travelling around Europe. We met on the train and I invited her here."

Atalanta blinked; she had no idea how Catharina knew she was an orphan, or that she had a large fortune. Was she merely making this up for Giovanni's sake? Or had someone told her? Had the meeting on the train not been a coincidence after all?

"What an excellent idea." Giovanni closed in, took Atalanta's hand, and kissed it. His lips lingered on her skin a heartbeat too long. "Pleased to meet you. Allow me to get you some champagne. My sister has been neglecting you."

"On the contrary," Atalanta said. "She allowed me to play this beautiful piano. I love nothing better than a grand instrument. Do you play?"

"Like a savage, I'm afraid. But perhaps you can teach me how to get better?"

Catharina tilted her head. "You can save yourself the trouble of trying to get into her good graces. I already told her everything there is to know about our, uh … rather unusual family. I'm sure she would have no interest in becoming a part of it."

Giovanni's features relaxed into a smile. "Why don't you go and get us a few glasses of champagne, sister dear? I want to talk to your charming friend alone."

"I'm certain I can safely leave you two." Catharina nodded at Atalanta. "She's as versed in self-defence as I am." She hurried away.

Giovanni remained where he was, looking at Atalanta. "I can assure you, you won't need self-defence with me. I don't hunt the ladies. I let them come to me." He leaned back on his heels. "So you're travelling all alone and Catharina immediately turned you into a project. That is how I know her. She likes to take charge. Perhaps because she is the eldest. That's something people forget, I suppose because she's a woman. This countryside is still very traditional in its ideas. Men rule the land here. Women are … well, they have to work harder to get recognition."

"But you do believe in equality, don't you?" Atalanta asked sweetly.

"Oh very much so. I encourage ladies to deviate from the trodden path and … be a little more adventurous."

In starting an affair with him, probably, Atalanta thought, but she kept her expression friendly and mildly interested. "Your sister seems very capable. Her father would do well to leave the estate in her hands."

"Capable?" Giovanni almost spat the word. "Catharina may appear charming and innocent when you meet her at first, but everyone who knows her longer is convinced she is absolutely mad. It all went wrong when her mother died. A tragic robbery and … I guess it unsettled her. Made her feel like she was never safe. You see …" He moved closer to her and spoke in a low confidential voice, "Catharina always feels like people are being hostile towards her. She's always on the defensive. But it's all in her head really. No one is after her."

"She showed me the note she received on the train."

"The one telling her not to come to the party?" Giovanni held Atalanta's gaze and smiled slowly. "Tell me this. Before the note, were you interested in coming here? Had you already accepted the invitation?"

"Um, actually no."

"But after the note, you accepted it?"

"I did."

"I knew it. Little Catharina at work. Up to her usual tricks. You see, she knows exactly how to manipulate people. By making them feel sorry for her. Wanting to protect her. You came here to keep an eye on her."

"I saw the altercation between her and your brother Lorenzo."

"What exactly did you see? That Catharina punched him? And then later said it was in self-defence?" Giovanni shook his head with a sad expression. "Catharina should really be pitied. She has this need for attention. This urge inside to get sympathy and be seen as the victim." He took a deep breath. "She can't help it, I suppose."

"You feel sorry for her?" Atalanta asked, intrigued at the turn the conversation was taking. She couldn't deny that she and Raoul hadn't been eager to accept the invitation, that they had even wondered whether the note was fabricated by Catharina herself. But the argument with Lorenzo had convinced them to come anyway. Had they been deceived and lured here?

But what for?

Giovanni said, "I don't want to influence your judgement, for you look very well able to make up your own mind about things. But I do feel that you should be aware that Catharina is a very manipulative person. We all are in our core, I suppose. We like to have things our way and we … try to ensure that we get what we want. With a little lie or by being friendly to someone we don't actually like. It's quite harmless. It's part of the social dance. But with some people it goes further than those almost unconsciously applied ways we have that make life easier for ourselves. With them it's deliberate. They're always aware of what they should say or do to make the other person change their mind in their favour. They're even deluded into thinking they actually need this support and should contrive to win it any way they see fit. I would urge you not to get involved with whatever Catharina wants now. She has had so many plans already, each one even more outrageous than the one before. And she always needs money for it. If you're an heiress travelling through Europe alone, she must have thought you were easy prey for her scheme."

"Prey? That sounds rather serious," Atalanta said, forcing a smile.

Giovanni shrugged. "Perhaps you have so much money you won't miss a few thousand spent on Catharina's next whim. But I'd advise extreme caution in dealing with her. You wouldn't be the first who is used and then dumped by the side of the road. You should talk to some 'friends' of hers."

"I think you've told me quite enough." Atalanta gestured to the door. "Shall we return to the company?"

"But we've only talked about Catharina so far. Not about you." Giovanni stood in her path holding her gaze. "And there's so much I want to know about you. Your full name, where you came from before Catharina intercepted you and dragged you here. What your travel plans entail. Who knows, I might be able to free myself for a day and show you around?"

"That won't be necessary." Raoul came sauntering up to them. "The lady is already engaged."

Giovanni raised an eyebrow. "I'm sorry. I wasn't aware of that." With a fake bow he retreated.

"Engaged?" Atalanta echoed as soon as the irritating Lanetti was out of earshot.

"Engaged in other activities. Engaged to do things with me, whatever. I never said engaged to be married and if he understood it that way, it's probably because his English isn't so good."

Atalanta rolled her eyes. "I didn't need to be saved."

"I thought you wanted to talk to Catharina." Raoul eyed her suspiciously. "Or was this a change of tactics? A plan to charm the elder of the brothers?"

"He intruded into my conversation with Catharina. It was a shame because she was being rather talkative."

"I distrust people who freely share personal information. Why would they? It's not exactly pleasant to reveal how odd your family can be."

"Perhaps they're used to smearing each other? They see me come in, a new person in their circle, and they all jump at the chance to win me over to their side."

Raoul sighed. "Could be." He looked about him. "This is the only room in the house where there is a bit of quiet. This party is rather extensive and, presumably, costly."

"I thought you were used to such affairs."

"Cosimo Lanetti has a bigger house than most I've ever been to, and he obviously wants to impress his guests."

"Turning sixty is a momentous occasion, of course," Atalanta mused. "Especially as he might have thought he wouldn't make it."

"Why is that?" Raoul asked.

She told him about the heart attack in spring. "Perhaps Cosimo was confronted with his own mortality and it made him think."

"Also about accepting his wayward daughter back into the family fold?" Raoul hitched a brow. "I don't think her gift helped to mend relations."

"She told me it's just the thing her father would want to own." Atalanta shrugged. "Perhaps she's right. She must know him much better than we do. And their strife could even have been a little act to entertain the guests, give them something to talk and speculate about."

"A little scandal to liven the party mood?" Raoul didn't seem convinced.

Atalanta said, "They all have big personalities and aren't afraid to voice their feelings. Perhaps it's normal for them to deal with one another in this way."

Raoul thought a moment and then said, "We should try and enjoy the party. After all, we sacrificed a night we could have spent together to be here."

Atalanta felt a little stab of regret that she had let herself be dragged into the Lanetti family affairs. Then again, it was fascinating to be here, see the palazzo, and try to unravel the complicated family relations.

Raoul offered her his arm. "May I?"

"Yes, certainly."

Chapter Nine

I t was close to one o'clock in the morning and there was still no sign that the party was winding towards a conclusion. Most of the guests had had so much to drink that they were talking much louder. Jokes became more daring and couples were seen vanishing into the night to have a few moments to themselves in the gardens surrounding the house. It was warm and stuffy in the palazzo, and Atalanta was tempted by the cool breeze outside. Stepping closer to an open door she could see the moon high in the velvety sky.

"Shall we go get some fresh air?" she asked Raoul, who had just finished regaling an elderly gentleman dressed like Galileo, complete with a telescope under his arm, with stories of his races.

Raoul set his empty glass on a tray and ushered her

through the open door. They walked across the terrace, past olive trees in pots, to steps leading down into the garden. The smell of rosemary and thyme was sharp on the air, along with mint and lemon, and a sweet floral scent … rose perhaps or another bloom? It was hard to make out much in the darkness. There were lamps here and there but they only served to ensure no guest stumbled. The atmosphere was intimate, and they had to make a sharp turn to avoid colliding with a couple who were kissing.

Atalanta felt a bit awkward about her proposal, which had been made with the honest intention of breathing fresh air but now seemed to suggest an ulterior purpose.

Raoul however sauntered beside her, hands folded behind his back, while he inhaled the night air with an appreciative sigh. "Much better than it is inside." He looked at her. "Have you seen our host in the last hour?"

"I can't say I have but this house has too many rooms to be certain. I suppose it would be rude to go to bed before the guests have left."

Raoul hemmed. "I wondered because you told me about his heart attack. Wouldn't a night like this be too much exertion for him? The excitement, rich food, alcohol."

"Don't suggest he might have a heart attack while we

are here. I can do without the fuss." Atalanta stripped off her gloves and put them in her clutch. "Do you think we should also have worn costumes?"

"I saw several people who had kept their attire low-key, more like evening wear than a costume. They don't all seem to share Lanetti's enthusiasm for dressing up."

"Still, it's a gesture of respect to the host to arrive in the clothes he requested. Catharina hadn't specifically mentioned it."

"Her dress wasn't exactly a costume either," Raoul said.

Atalanta looked to their left, where a grassy patch stretched towards something that could be water. Two people walked there, arms around each other's waist. The woman leaned her head against the man's shoulder and laughed.

"Is that Catharina?" Atalanta tilted her head. "I didn't know she was romantically involved with anyone here."

"Perhaps she invited a friend to attend the party with her?" Raoul loosened his tie. "I think we should consider turning in after this stroll. It's …" He checked his watch. "Close to one thirty. That is enough party for me for one night."

"I agree. But do we even have rooms allotted to us? We arrived here when the party had already begun and …"

"I talked to Cosimo while you went after Catharina and mentioned she had invited us for a stay. He immediately ordered a servant, an elderly woman who seems to have done his housekeeping all her life, to prepare rooms. He showed me where they were, so I should be able to find them."

Atalanta laughed softly at his tone. "Thank you. You took care of everything. I really appreciate this trip. It takes me away from all the things that kept me busy in Paris."

"I want you to enjoy yourself."

"I am."

"Really? I wager you're thinking about Catharina and her father, her brothers, the man she is now kissing …"

Atalanta looked in the direction of the pair who had halted by the water. Their silhouettes had melted into each other. She felt a slight flush come to her face.

Raoul said, "Whoever he is, it's none of your business that she's kissing him. She cleverly suggested to us on the train that she needed support or even protection, but I haven't seen any evidence of it here."

"Family relations are tense," Atalanta retorted.

"They usually are."

"Yes, but how many brothers would describe their sister as mad?"

"Did Giovanni say that about Catharina?"

"Yes. To warn me against her." Atalanta frowned. "And to promote himself, I suppose."

"There you have it. He was exaggerating to make his point."

Atalanta looked doubtful and Raoul hastened to add, "I mean, he probably does think Catharina is a bit dramatic all the time and it gets bothersome for the family to deal with it."

"But he mentioned her mother's death, a violent death too, mind you, so he does seem to have an insight into the psychological background of her behaviour."

"Perhaps he merely meant to warn you against getting involved with her ... ideas." Raoul leaned over to Atalanta. "That's very good advice. I second it."

"We've had a wonderful night here, it hasn't cost us anything, and tomorrow we can continue our tour. I suppose we didn't lose out by deciding to stop by here."

As Atalanta said it, a piercing scream came from the house, as if someone had just seen a horrifying sight. It continued, one high-pitched cry after another, and Raoul broke into a run towards the house. Atalanta followed him as best she could in her heels.

When they arrived inside, everyone was talking over each other – asking confused questions as to what had happened. The screaming had stopped. Raoul pushed past a group of people towards a thronging mass. It seemed people had poured into the hallway of the palazzo and were pushing into a small corridor that led to the back of the house.

"What's wrong?" Raoul asked in Italian. Several people started to speak. Something about screaming and the name Cosimo.

Lorenzo Lanetti appeared, his nose swollen like a ripe tomato in the centre of his haughty face. He pushed through the crowd, and Raoul pulled in behind him, bringing Atalanta along in his wake.

They came to a large decorated door. It stood open and they could see inside. An elderly woman dressed in black stood in a corner, her hands clasped to her face, her eyes staring, wide with fear, between her fingers. Beside a gold-decorated desk, a body lay sprawled on the floor.

A man was kneeling over it. Raoul ran to him and grabbed him by the shoulder. "What are you doing?" he demanded.

The man looked up. He was young and blond. "I'm a doctor trying to save this man's life. He's had a heart attack."

Raoul and Atalanta stared down at the body of Cosimo Lanetti, almost grotesque now in his Renaissance finery. His features were contorted and his eyes stared up at the ceiling. The glassy look in them told Atalanta it was too late to save him.

The doctor seemed to have come to the same conclusion. "There's nothing I can do …" he muttered and rose, backing away from the body.

Atalanta saw how he put his right hand in his pocket. She had the impression there was something in that hand. She wanted to tell Raoul, but he had leaned forward closer to the body. It lay beside the desk, one arm outstretched underneath it.

Raoul pointed into the shadows under the desk. "Look." His voice trembled with tension in that one word.

Atalanta could see a large golden object lying there. It took her a few moments to make out what it was. Then her heart started to beat vehemently. It was the golden goblet Catharina had given to her father as a birthday gift. It lay almost touching Cosimo's lifeless fingers. Inside the goblet something red glittered. Wine?

"The blind fool actually drank from it," Raoul muttered in disbelief. "He poisoned himself."

"Or rather someone else poisoned him," Lorenzo's voice said. His eyes were ice cold over that ridiculous swollen nose. "Catharina knew he wouldn't be able to resist. She knew he'd drink from it and die. She wanted to make it look like a heart attack such as he had this spring. She probably intended to get the goblet away from him before he was discovered."

"Nothing should be touched in here," said a deep voice. A man in his sixties with grey hair and deep lines in his fleshy face moved in, waving along a tall, thinner man with a small beard. "I'm the chief of police. I'll take charge of this situation."

"You are the *retired* chief of police," Lorenzo said narrowing his eyes. "You have no jurisdiction."

"I was a close friend of your father. I want to find his killer. Everyone step back." He pointed to the telephone on the desk. "I'll call for a police doctor to come and see the body. He can also perform an autopsy. That" – he redirected his finger from the phone to the goblet under the desk – "will have to be analysed to see if there are traces of poison on it."

"And the contents of that carafe will also need to be tested," Raoul said, pointing at a crystal carafe on the desk containing deep red wine. "The poison may have been in there and not in the goblet he drank from."

"And you are?" the retired chief of police asked irritably.

"Raoul Lemont. I know it's easy to jump to conclusions as this goblet was used for poisonings in the past but—"

"She really had some nerve to do it under our noses." Lorenzo's eyes shot fire. "She came here, pretending to want to reconcile with Papa, and then she killed him."

"What would be her reason for doing so? She hasn't received anything from him yet. What would be the point?" Atalanta asked.

The chief of police reddened even more. "And you are?"

"Atalanta Ashford. I'm a friend of Signorina Catharina Lanetti. We travelled here together from Paris. She was threatened on the train. Someone wrote her a note that if she came here to the party, she'd regret it."

"I regret," Lorenzo cried out, "that we invited her. That we let her murder Papa in his very own house."

"Cosimo! Cosimo!" Melina came into the room. She clapped her hands together in front of her chest and stared at the body with wide open eyes. Then she screamed and collapsed.

The retired chief of police knelt beside her, ordering his assistant to bring a pillow and a glass of water, and Raoul took the opportunity to pull Atalanta aside.

"This isn't looking good for Catharina."

"Do you think she is innocent?" Atalanta asked in a whisper.

"Well, she didn't strike me as foolish and it would be very foolish indeed to poison your father with a goblet you gave him in front of dozens of witnesses."

"Perhaps she thinks it's so unbelievable that everyone will think she must have been framed."

VIVIAN CONROY

"I think she must have been. You?"

Atalanta sighed. "It was a good idea of yours to point to the carafe. The poison could have been put in there. He merely drank it via the goblet but the goblet itself has nothing to do with his death."

"My thoughts exactly. I hope that retired police chief knows what he is doing."

The man in question had risen from beside the collapsed wife, now widow, of the victim and stood at the desk to place his telephone call. "I want this room cleared," he barked at his assistant, who was still trying to shove under the woman's head a pillow he had picked from a chair by the window.

Raoul said, "Let me do that." He took over from the assistant, who started to send everyone away. Atalanta accepted a glass of water that a servant brought and stayed with Raoul to care for Mrs Lanetti. The retired chief of police was talking over the telephone. She couldn't understand all of it but Raoul would no doubt be hanging on to every word.

Atalanta looked over her shoulder. A dead body, on her vacation.

Coincidence?

There was still a chance, she presumed, that Lanetti had truly had a heart attack. The strain of playing host to

136

so many people, the heat in the overfull rooms, the wine … it was possible.

But deep inside of her she didn't believe it. It had been murder. And she was again right at the heart of it. Inside the room where it had happened. It was now of the utmost importance to imprint every little detail on her mind. The paleness in Cosimo Lanetti's features. The way his fingers had been bent, as if grasping at something. Merely the pain when he had collapsed? Or had he tried to defend himself against someone?

But if it had been poison, it wasn't likely the killer would have been in the room with him when he died. He or she could have introduced the poison into the carafe and simply waited, as a guest at the party, until it took effect.

Her gaze fell upon the elderly woman in black, who was still hovering in the corner. Her eyes were now red rimmed as she silently cried for her master. Atalanta went over and asked, "Have you served Mr Lanetti very long?"

"I came with his first wife, Anna. She made me housekeeper here. She was a good mistress. She decorated these rooms and … her heart was in this house. It was her palace, the place where she felt happy. She made that painting." The woman nodded towards a large oil painting hanging against the far wall. It depicted a beautiful woodland with tall trees and a stream of clear water. "It was her favourite place to go to. She often painted there. The afternoon she died she was headed there." The woman lowered her head and new tears ran down her cheeks.

"I'm sorry you lost your mistress through violence – and now your master as well."

"It must have been his heart. He had not been well lately. He shouldn't exert himself, the doctor had said. But he never listened. I often told him to be quiet and sit down and drink herbal tea but … he didn't listen." The woman raised her hands in despair.

Atalanta said, "I'm sure you did all you could. Now you mustn't worry. He is …" At peace now? Could she really say that? Cosimo Lanetti had been a hard man in his lifetime. He had manipulated people, had been unkind to his children. Was there peace for such people even after death?

The woman said, "He said to me that he had something very important to say tonight. Something that would come as a shock to some." Her eyes were wide. "I wonder what it is. He never said it."

Atalanta looked over her shoulder at Raoul, who had managed to bring Mrs Lanetti to, and was now encouraging her to sip a little water. Before she drank, Mrs Lanetti asked, "It isn't from this room, is it?"

"No, it was brought in fresh from the kitchens."

Mrs Lanetti seemed reassured and took a sip.

Atalanta narrowed her eyes. Had the woman known that the liquid in this room – wine, water, perhaps everything present – was poisoned? Had *she* poisoned it so her husband would die on a night with so many guests around? So many suspects? To confuse the police, to divert suspicion? Did she gain from his death? Was there a will leaving it all to her?

What had his shock announcement been? Something about who his successor would be?

Catharina, against all odds? Enraging her brothers?

Or something altogether different?

Cosimo could no longer tell them. He was dead.

Chapter Ten

"**D**on't you think it is odd?" Atalanta asked Raoul. They were seated on a sofa with gilded feet formed like lion's claws. There were several other people in the room, sitting in small groups, speaking in low voices. One man stood alone by the window, smoking a cigarette while he stared morosely into the darkness outside.

"What is odd?" Raoul asked. "That someone gets murdered while we are here? I'm beginning to think that in your company murders are quite common."

"Don't make jokes about it. It's a very serious matter. Our host was poisoned."

"I'm sorry." Raoul briefly touched her hand. "But you don't have to worry about it. If I heard that retired police chief right, he wants to take charge in this case. Now, I assume that the new police chief will also want the same, so the two of them will be bickering over who gets to do it. And with people actually fighting for a chance to solve this case, you needn't involve yourself with it."

"It's odd," Atalanta said, ignoring his reasoning, "that Cosimo drank from that goblet. I mean, why would he? It was given to him with an explicit warning about its gruesome past. Why risk it? Isn't it far more likely he imbibed the poison in another way?"

"And he just happened to collapse while he was holding the goblet in his hand?"

"He could have been admiring it when he started to feel unwell." Atalanta shrugged. "We don't know yet what poison it was. How fast it acted. Perhaps he didn't have a chance to put the goblet aside?"

Raoul studied her with a frown. "You want to argue the case away from Catharina. You don't want her to be suspected."

"All I'm saying is that her goblet may have nothing to do with it."

The door opened and the retired police chief came in. He cleared his throat ostentatiously. "I'm in charge of the murder investigation. For those of you who don't know me, my name is Foselli. I have a long and distinguished career in the police force behind me and have seen many cases. However, I've never seen one as wicked as the murder that took place here tonight. A patricide."

Atalanta rose from the sofa. Foselli turned his gaze towards her.

She smiled winningly. "May I congratulate you on solving the case so quickly?"

Foselli raised a brow. "*Scusi?*"

"You've solved it already. You call it a patricide. So you must know that the killer is a child of the victim. Tell me, which child is it?"

Foselli seemed annoyed by her sweet tone. "I can't go into details in front of witnesses we still have yet to hear. But it's clear to me, from a good look at the room where the deceased was found, that it was a patricide."

"You know then how he died and what the murder method was?" Atalanta pressed. She felt Raoul's foot touch hers in a subtle sign telling her not to do this. To back down and accept that this man was in charge. But Foselli was so full of himself. He should look at facts, not jump to conclusions.

"Since you seem so eager to speak to me," Foselli said, "I'll hear you next. Come with me."

Raoul also rose, but Foselli snapped, "One at a time."

Raoul said, "If you want to conduct the interrogation in Italian, I can translate for Signorina Ashford. She's English and her Italian is non-existent."

Atalanta felt piqued at his dismissal of her quite adequate command of the language, but she understood what he was doing. He wanted to be present when Foselli asked her questions. Most of all, he wanted to be present to hear her answers. Even if he was to translate, would he water down her answers so they'd be more acceptable to this self-conscious man?

Foselli said, "I speak English very well. Your services aren't required. You'll sit right there until you're asked to come in."

The man who had been smoking by the window turned around at this. He had deep black hair, a handsome face with a firm jaw, full lips, and deep-set brown eyes. He said, "Instead of questioning random guests, who come from abroad and know nothing about the complicated family relations that caused this tragedy, you would be better speaking to me. I know exactly what happened here tonight."

"Did you see the murder?" Foselli asked.

"No. If I had, I would have killed the murderer with my bare hands."

Foselli ignored the latter statement and merely said, "If you aren't an eyewitness, I don't see why I should give preference to you."

"My father was murdered." The man's voice trembled with anger. "He wasn't stabbed in hand-to-hand combat where he could see his assailant in the face. No, he was poisoned by something introduced secretly into his wine. It was a cowardly deed. Typical of a woman. A woman with no backbone and no morals."

"Your father?" Foselli asked with a raised brow. "I know this family well, I've dined with both Cosimo Lanetti's sons, Lorenzo and Giovanni. I don't know who you are."

The man's expression changed a moment as if he was struck by these cold words. But he said quietly, "I'm the son he wanted to leave all his property to. He was going to tell everyone tonight."

The shock announcement the maid had mentioned? Atalanta stared at the man in fascination. But if Cosimo had wanted to make such an all-important statement in the presence of all his guests, why hadn't he? The night had almost come to an end, he had retired to his study … Or had he gone there to get something? Paperwork? His new will?

But if the will had been changed already, why murder him? That made no sense.

Foselli laughed softly. "You misjudge me, young man. I'm not an outsider. I've known this family for all my life. I knew Cosimo Lanetti better than many others. He wouldn't leave his property to a stranger."

"I'm not a stranger. I'm his son. Thomasso."

A shocked ripple went through the crowd at the mention of the name.

Foselli said, "You are Thomasso? No, that cannot be." He seemed to need a moment to regain his calm. "Anyone can say he is Thomasso."

"But I can prove it. I proved it to Cosimo and he believed me. Tonight he was going to tell everyone of my return."

"But he didn't," Foselli said. He cleared his throat. "He said nothing and now he is dead."

How convenient for those who didn't like Thomasso's return, Atalanta thought.

Raoul asked, "Can you perhaps enlighten us, Signor Foselli, as to who Thomasso is? I never heard of him."

Atalanta knew this was a lie as Catharina had told them on the train about her half-brother's disappearance. But apparently Raoul wanted to know more about that and hoped Foselli would share some enlightening detail.

"He was Cosimo's eldest son by his current wife, Melina. But when he was fourteen months old, he was abducted. The family waited for a ransom request, but it never came. Everyone assumed he was dead."

"Well, I'm not," Thomasso said, eyes flashing. "You talk about me as if I'm gone. He *was* the eldest son, you say. No, I *am* the eldest son. And I intend to take what's mine."

"How did Melina feel about your reappearance?" Foselli asked.

Thomasso smiled. "She didn't know about it yet. Cosimo wanted to surprise her."

Atalanta frowned. Would a man really spring the truth on his wife like that, at a party with guests around? Oh, by the way, our son whom we believed to be dead is alive and well, and here he is? That seemed very odd. Was Thomasso lying?

Foselli said, "I'll speak to Melina later when she's recovered from the shock of her husband's murder. Now, Signorina Ashford, please come with me."

"It's me you have to talk to," Thomasso protested.

But Foselli waved Atalanta along. Raoul had to stay behind. She could sense his frustration, but she hoped he would use the opportunity to talk to Thomasso and learn something important.

Foselli took her into another room with a platform had been erected for musicians to perform. There were rows of seats in front. He himself sat down on the platform with his assistant and gestured for her to sit in a chair in the front row. She had to look up at him as if she was a defendant in court.

Foselli asked, "What is your name and why are you here tonight?"

"My name is Atalanta Ashford. I was on a trip from

Paris to Milan on the Orient Express when I met Catharina Lanetti in the dining car. We exchanged pleasantries over dinner and the topic of her father's birthday and this party came up. She invited us to come to the party."

"Us being?"

"Myself and Raoul Lemont. He is a close friend of mine and was going to show me around Tuscany."

"Are you ... in a relationship?"

"I just said he is a close friend." Atalanta sat upright.

Foselli nodded weightily. "So you came here at the invitation of Catharina Lanetti. And how did her father take this?"

"He welcomed us and seemed in good spirits." Atalanta hesitated. She had thought about this before the interrogation began and hadn't quite decided what she should do. Mention the threatening note Catharina had received – or not ...

"I should mention that, on the train, Catharina shared with us that she had received a note warning her not to come to this party or she'd regret it."

"You're aware she can be quite fanciful?"

"She showed us the note."

"She could have written it herself."

"Her half-brother Lorenzo was on the train. Catharina

believed he had pushed the note under her door. They argued about it after arrival."

"Yes, and she punched him in the face, breaking his nose." Foselli tried unsuccessfully to suppress a smile. "All night he told everyone he had been beaten by three thugs. And it turned out to be merely one upset woman." His smile vanished and he continued grimly. "An upset woman who was worried her father wouldn't listen to her pleas for money, so she murdered him for his inheritance."

"Do you know if she will inherit anything?" Atalanta asked, tilting her head. "You're drawing conclusions before you've gathered the facts."

"Don't tell me how to do my work. Did she mention to you on the train that she needed money?"

"Not in so many words."

"But you assumed that she did?" Foselli pressed.

"She mentioned she had big plans. She wanted to convince her father to allow her to make chocolate and combine that with the vineyard business."

"Chocolate and wine?" Foselli laughed. "Only a woman could think of something like that. But it doesn't matter how we may judge her plan. She wanted it. She believed in it. She asked her father to support it and he said that he wouldn't."

"Has there been such a conversation? Have you ascertained that?"

"Melina told me that Catharina was here again to beg for money. That that was the only reason she ever came here. She never loved her father. In fact she hated him."

"Mrs Lanetti was so unwell you could not question her, yet she managed to tell you all that?" It looked like the second wife had wasted no time in incriminating her stepdaughter.

"As I've explained before, I'm an old family friend. I know everything about their relations with each other. All the tensions and struggles." Foselli sighed. "It isn't easy raising children into respectable adults. Cosimo was a successful businessman, but he couldn't control his own household." Some satisfaction lined the statement. "He was too busy perhaps to keep an eye on his children."

"They're all grownups. Have been for years. How could he keep an eye on them?"

"My sons do what I tell them to do. No matter how old they become, they are my sons. And they know that. They wouldn't do anything to shame me. But Cosimo's children ..." Foselli grimaced. "Giovanni is a womanizer. Lorenzo can't run a hundred yards without collapsing for lack of breath."

"And Thomasso?" Atalanta asked.

"Thomasso is dead. I handled the abduction at the time. I have no doubt the criminals who took him weren't used to dealing with a young child. They treated him roughly and he died. That's why they didn't ask for ransom money."

"You don't know that. His body was never found."

"That doesn't mean anything. They could have buried him in the woods. He could have been left to die and was eaten by wild animals. We have wolves here in the region." Foselli looked at her with a hard glint in his eyes. "But you mustn't raise these possibilities with Melina. She never stopped grieving for her missing child. She mustn't be upset by gruesome thoughts about how he died, or what he may have suffered before he did. She must be left in peace so she can mourn her murdered husband." He sighed. "She had so much to bear already and now this ..."

"So who is the man claiming to be Thomasso?"

"I don't know. Some opportunist who heard the story and thought he could get rich? There have been others through the years. That's why I know for certain Cosimo didn't believe him. This impostor didn't speak up until Cosimo was dead. Now he can tell us whatever story he wants. About promises made to him and so on. But it won't get him a lire. I'll make sure of that."

Foselli leaned back with a smug expression. Then

suddenly he snapped, "But you're distracting me from speaking about you, Signorina Ashford. Is there a reason for that? Do you have something to hide?"

Yes, my annoyance at how you are handling this, Atalanta thought, but she said, "Not at all, Signor. I'm just naturally curious about the family dynamics. Catharina told me a few things about it and—"

"You shouldn't believe her. She's always making up stories. To put herself in a more favourable light. But she let her family down. And now she has even killed her own father. Poisoned him when he wouldn't give her the money she wanted. She must have believed she could get it after his death."

"You already said that. But unless there is a will favouring her, we have no proof that she actually stood to gain from his death."

"It doesn't matter what the will says. She believed she would get something. That motivated her." Foselli leaned across the table. "She gave him that poison cup. A beaker used to kill one's opponents."

"Yes, but it was empty then. I saw her give it to Cosimo and he looked at it from all sides."

"Did he turn it upside down?"

"No, he didn't."

"Thank you for affirming what I already heard from other witnesses. He didn't tilt the cup. That's important."

"Because the poison from the hidden compartment is only released into the contents when the beaker is tilted into a certain angle by the drinker."

"Exactly. You're familiar with the mechanism?"

"I've read about it."

"Then you understand what it means. Catharina Lanetti handed her father a goblet in which poison was hidden. He poured some wine into it in the privacy of his study and drank from the goblet. When he tilted it at the right angle, the poison was released and he ingested it. It killed him instantly."

"You know what poison it is then?"

"We're having the contents of the cup analysed."

"Poisons can be fast-acting or slow-acting. Perhaps he ingested poison earlier in the evening and it killed him later when he was alone."

"While he was coincidentally holding the poisoned beaker? Come, come, Signorina, that is too much of a stretch."

"But do you think Catharina would be so stupid as to kill her father in such an obvious manner? To have the finger of suspicion point straight at her?"

"Cosimo's body looked like he had had a heart attack. He had one in spring. I assume she wanted people to believe he had died of natural causes."

"With that beaker beside his body?"

VIVIAN CONROY

"I think she wanted to come in and remove it. But the maid found the body quicker than Catharina had anticipated."

Or she had been distracted, Atalanta thought, recalling the kiss in the garden. Had she not counted on the man who wanted to be alone with her? Had she thought she could get the goblet a little later? Had she gambled with her life, for a flirtation?

No. She was now reasoning as if Catharina had plotted to murder her father with poison in the beaker. But she didn't actually believe that.

"Have you seen or heard anything during the party that can contribute to the case?"

Atalanta thought and shook her head. "I can't say I have."

"Then you may go and send in that 'friend' of yours."

Foselli's emphasis on *friend* made Atalanta's cheeks warm. She turned away hastily. It shouldn't concern her what people thought of her or of her relationship with Raoul, but still ... it would have been good to be on better terms with the investigating police officer. Or, in this case, retired police officer. The case intrigued her and she wanted to know much more.

In the room with the lion-foot sofa, Raoul was talking to Thomasso. Atalanta told him Foselli wanted him and he grimaced at her before leaving the room.

154

Thomasso said, "Signor Lemont just told me about your time on Santorini. That he was there to explore the possibilities for a race. It's my dream to sail around the Greek islands some time."

"Oh, you love sailing?"

"I was raised on a boat. My father was a river captain." Thomasso grimaced. "The man I assumed was my father. He told me much later in life that he had found me by the side of the road and that he had taken me in because he and his wife had no children of their own."

"And how did you feel then?"

"I had never known anything but that they were my parents." Thomasso stared at the floor. "Discovering that they weren't made me feel ... lost. I didn't know who I was or what I should do in life. I had always thought I would follow in my father's footsteps: that in time my father's boat would be mine. But after he told me I ... wondered if I was destined for something else. You see, I had always been different. I devoured books and I wanted to travel. My parents were simple people with no more dreams than to have food on the table and a roof over their heads. I wondered who my real parents had been and what my chances in life would have been had I stayed with them." He gestured around him at the stuccoed cupids and the gilded frames of the paintings.

"I should have had private tutors and spent summers in Rome. I should have learned foreign languages and danced till daybreak at sumptuous parties. I'm Cosimo Lanetti's firstborn son." His voice shook with emotion. "Instead I slept in a small wooden cot in the dark underbelly of a ship. I swam in the river to wash myself, caught fish with a spear so we had something extra to eat. I never got birthday presents." His eyes flashed with anger. "I never had what I should have had."

"Do you remember anything about your abduction?"

"No. I was too small. And I don't blame the abductors. I blame these people." He gestured around him. "They lived their lives and had their wealth while they let me suffer."

"They didn't know where you were. I'm sure that if they had had an idea, they would have come to get you."

"Yes. You're probably right." Thomasso took a deep breath. "Cosimo told me he would do right by me. That he would make up for the lost years. He wanted to give me a sailboat and an income from the vineyard."

"Did he want you to become his successor?" Atalanta asked. That could have caused strife as Lorenzo and Giovanni were after that position as well. Catharina too, perhaps.

"He told me he had two sons who were both not capable. One physically weak, the other not hardworking but wasting his days with wine and women. He wanted someone able who could continue to build the property. He ... thought perhaps he had found that person in me."

Atalanta nodded. Thomasso looked proud and strong-willed like Cosimo. That would have pleased the man. And if he was, as he said, hardworking and had brains, Cosimo might have thought that his eldest son embodied the best of the two others he had never fully trusted to follow in his footsteps. The return of the missing son must have been like a lifeline to him, a solution to his problems.

"How did you find out Cosimo was your father?" she asked curiously.

Thomasso started to reply but the door opened and Catharina stormed in. Her dress was wrinkled and her hair undone. She looked like she had wandered in the woods alone. She ran to Atalanta and asked, "Is my father dead? Everyone says so."

"I'm afraid so. Where have you been? It's been an hour since his body was discovered."

Catharina didn't answer the question. She looked up at Thomasso. "What are you doing here?"

"I came because Papa wanted me to."

"He's not your papa. You're an impostor."

"I'm not and I'll prove it." Thomasso leaned closer to

Catharina. "Everything here will be mine. I'm entitled to it."

Catharina shook her head. "I know you aren't who you claim to be. I'll find out what you're truly after."

The door that was still open held the bulky frame of Foselli. He said to Catharina, "There you are. You must come with us."

"Why?" Catharina asked, backing away from him.

"Because we want to prevent you from running away and escaping justice."

Foselli reached out to catch her arm but Catharina hid behind Atalanta.

"Help me," she said in a childlike voice. "Don't let him take me."

"You can't simply arrest her without proof," Atalanta said to Foselli.

He laughed. "Her father is dead and the goblet she gave him is by his side. That is proof enough for me. I'm taking her with me to ensure she can't escape. Merely a precaution. I'll formally charge her after the doctor confirms that Cosimo was poisoned and that the cup contains traces of that poison." He smiled at Atalanta. "He *will* confirm that. It's only a matter of time."

"No!" Catharina darted away and ran to the window. She threw it open and clambered outside.

"After her," Foselli barked to the room in general.

No one moved but Thomasso. He sprinted to the window, jumped out as if he did this regularly and quickly overtook the fleeing woman. He tackled her and pushed her to the ground. Atalanta had the impression he was saying something to her and then he dragged her to her feet and brought her to the window.

Foselli stood there looking out. "Good," he said without thanking Thomasso. "Take her to the front door. I'll be there shortly."

"You're allowing him to handle her so roughly?" Atalanta asked.

"She's a murderer. We needn't have sympathy."

"You're accusing her without solid proof. I don't think your successor will like this."

Foselli bared his teeth at her. "He has nothing to say about this matter. It is *my* case."

"How convenient then that you were already at the party," Atalanta called after him. She was shaking with anger at his treatment of the case in general and Catharina in particular. But she meant her parting statement in more than one way. Was it a coincidence he had been here? Or could he actually be involved in the murder and was now hastily accusing another? Stacking the evidence against her?

She spotted Raoul at the door and went over to him. "Catharina has been arrested. Foselli claims he is taking her along to ensure she doesn't flee while he awaits the doctor's conclusions but—"

"I saw her attempting to flee with my own eyes just now. Perhaps his precaution makes sense?" Raoul touched Atalanta's arm. "You mustn't be prejudiced."

"I mustn't …" Atalanta shook off his hand in disbelief. "I'm sorry but this is too much. I'm going to bed."

She walked to the stairs leading up to the bedrooms, then realized she had no idea where she was sleeping. She caught sight of the maid who had found Cosimo and went over. "I'm sorry to disturb you as you must be very upset by what happened but is there a room ready for me? I was a late arrival to the party. Miss Ashford."

"Oh, yes, the master asked me specifically. I'll show you." The woman walked ahead of her.

"You must have been in this household for a long time." Atalanta hated to upset the woman further with these questions but she itched to know more. "You must have been here when Thomasso was abducted."

"I was." The woman walked slower, her head down. "It was a terrible blow to the master. He had always longed for a son. Even in his first marriage. But the mistress only bore him a daughter. Then after she died, he remarried and …" She stopped and looked up at Atalanta. "I've always thought the baby was born quite soon after the marriage. They said it was born too early but ..."

"You suspect Melina was with child before they married?"

"Yes. And I've always doubted whether it was from the master." The woman looked Atalanta in the eye without blinking. "When he was abducted, I assumed his father, his real father, had taken him."

Atalanta was completely taken aback by this suggestion. "You thought that Melina was with child by another man and ... but why then marry Cosimo Lanetti?"

"Because he was an incredibly powerful man. Her family made her do it. But she never loved him. She still doesn't love him."

"But it makes no sense for the real father to abduct Thomasso and then leave him by the side of the road." Atalanta frowned. "Why would he do that? What purpose would it serve?"

"To take away what the master had no right to?" The woman shrugged. "I can only tell you what I thought at the time."

"And do you believe the man who calls himself Thomasso is truly the child of old?"

"I'm certain of it."

Again, Atalanta was overtaken. "How can you know that?"

"I was with the family when Thomasso was born. I cared for him before he was abducted. I bathed him many times. He had a distinctive birthmark on his back between his shoulder blades. The man who 'calls himself Thomasso', as you phrase it, showed me this same birthmark."

"And did you tell this to Cosimo Lanetti? Did you confirm that it might indeed be his long-lost son?"

"He put little stock on the opinions of an old woman." She shrugged and shuffled further down the corridor. "In here, Signorina."

It was a beautiful room with a four-poster bed with burgundy drapes, a dressing table with a dramatic wooden rim carved into flames, a silver washing basin, and a silver dresser set – a brush, comb, and hand mirror. The silver had been recently polished and it shone. Atalanta spied her luggage in the corner.

"If you don't need anything else ..." The woman bowed and left the room.

Atalanta sank on to the edge of the bed. "What a holiday," she muttered to herself. "I land in the middle of some family drama I can't quite unravel. Is Thomasso the lost son? Did his return cause all the commotion? Even lead to the murder? Did Cosimo have to die before he could give his property to his son?"

She pressed her fingertips together. "But if the old woman is right, Thomasso might not have been his actual son. Melina's child, yes, but not Cosimo's. Did Cosimo know? At least suspect? Was he not intending to give Thomasso anything? Did he tell the man tonight?"

She stood up and paced the room, deep in thought. Suddenly there was a knock on her door. She went over and asked, "Who is it?"

"Raoul." Even in those two syllables she could sense his suppressed anger.

"I'm getting ready for bed," she called, not wanting to open the door and see his expression.

"That can wait. It's two thirty in the morning anyway. I want to talk to you, now."

Atalanta sighed and opened the door. Raoul marched in.

She said, "Last time when we were staying with the Bucardis on Santorini, your nightly visits to my room to talk caused nothing but trouble. I don't want the same here. Foselli already seemed to doubt we were just friends."

"He is old-fashioned and doesn't think men and women should travel together unless they are married, or engaged to be married. He explained to me in much detail how the mores were in his days. But it's 1930 now and I can do whatever I want." Raoul stood in the middle of the room, his hands clenched into fists. "Such as telling you my opinion about this situation we've landed in. Catharina Lanetti is a volatile woman who tells one story today, another tomorrow. She can't be trusted and you mustn't involve yourself with her. Let Foselli solve this case."

"But he thinks he's solved it already. He wants to accuse Catharina and be done with it."

"That's none of our business. We should go to sleep now and leave first thing after breakfast."

"No, we should not." Atalanta put her foot down. "I find this whole situation so odd. How can a retired police chief simply take charge? Where is the new one? Why is he not doing anything to stop his predecessor from usurping his work?"

"Because this is a case he'd rather not touch. The Lanettis are a powerful force in this region. Nobody wants to upset them."

"Apparently Foselli wants to upset them."

"No." Raoul shook his head slowly. "He is not upsetting them by arresting Catharina. That is the best option."

"Really? Why not Thomasso? He's an intruder. Either he isn't the real eldest son, in which case he's an impostor whom they must despise. Or he is the missing child nobody is waiting for any more. The brothers can't want his return."

"Catharina gave her father the poison cup. Dozens of people saw that. Foselli has his case ready made for him. He only needs to fill out a few forms and …"

"An innocent woman goes to prison."

"You don't know that she's innocent." Raoul sighed. "Atalanta, Renard agreed with me that you're working too hard. You're demanding too much of yourself. You should relax and see Tuscany. That's why I organized all of this. And then this woman comes along, who happens to be on the same train as us …"

Atalanta felt a little sorry for Raoul, who had gone to so much trouble to make this trip special and memorable for her. "I apologize for being so rude to you before I rushed off." She shuffled her feet. "I guess I should also apologize for thinking that you knew Catharina and that the encounter on the train wasn't a coincidence at all. I got it into my mind somehow that you bumped into her on purpose to start the conversation and … I guess I'm getting overly suspicious."

Raoul stared at her. "You honestly thought that … I don't want this woman to ruin our holiday. I didn't want her to be a part of it in any way. And yet you think I engineered … while you are …" He threw his arms up in frustration. "It must be lack of sleep but I'm just not feeling reasonable any more. I had better leave before I say something I'm going to regret. Good night." And he left the room, banging the door shut.

Atalanta cringed. If anyone peeked out to see who was banging doors in the middle of the night, they would see Raoul coming away from her room. The talk that could create!

But she realized at the same moment that she was fussing about the possibility of gossip about them to distract herself from Raoul's anger at her. Justified anger. He had gone out of his way to arrange a holiday for her and treat her to the best possible experience of his beloved Tuscany, and here she was forcing them into a murder investigation.

But it was all so odd. Cosimo dying during the party but in a room on his own with that cup by his side. Fallen from his hand? Or put there on purpose?

And how about the missing son, the abducted child of old, suddenly returning? That mere fact was worthy of investigation. Was Thomasso a Lanetti or not?

If not, then Melina had betrayed Cosimo into believing it was his child. Had he ever known? Suspected? If he had …

Atalanta opened her suitcase, took out a few sheets of paper and started to make coded notes – a habit she had started when she was still a teacher at an exclusive Swiss boarding school. She had deemed it essential to make notes about her pupils' quirks and progress but one of them had read them and made use of the information. Since then she had coded them, using Cyrillic letters and a simple transposition cypher to ensure that she and she only had access to them. This system came in handy during investigations when she couldn't be sure if someone went through her things.

She wrote:

Cosimo Lanetti, *paterfamilias*, domineering man who liked to dangle his children's inheritance in front of them; to get them to jump through hoops in order to please him and get their share.

Melina, his second wife. A banker's daughter from Florence. Was the marriage merely an alliance for money? Did she love her husband? And why was she out with the steward so often? Did she want to take over the vineyards? Or was there an affair with the steward?

She stared at the words realizing that Catharina had told her that Melina had spent much time with the steward. But if she had been away from home for years, how could she have known this? Had it merely been a spiteful suggestion, to put Melina in a bad light?

She continued her list.

Anna, first wife, deceased in robbery gone wrong. But robbers denied having killed her. Was the robbery really murder? Cosimo acquired his most successful vineyard through marriage to Anna. Was he somehow involved in the 'robbery'? Did Catharina suspect this?

Those brief notes already held enough drama to lead to murder, but there was more to come, much more.

Atalanta grimaced as she continued to write.

Thomasso, the eldest son of Melina and Cosimo, abducted, come back? Maid claims she recognized distinctive birthmark. But also confided Thomasso may not have been Cosimo's son as she suspects Melina was already pregnant when the two wed.

Would it be possible after so many years to find out what had truly happened? And if she couldn't find out, would it matter when it came to the murder?

Catharina, the only daughter of Cosimo and Anna. Adventuress, aspiring chocolate maker. Threatened? Framed?

Lorenzo, the one threatening her? Or was he on the same train by coincidence?

Giovanni, rumoured to drink and womanize.

Atalanta stared at the last line of her notes. She didn't know much about Giovanni and wanted to get a fuller picture of who he was and what he had wanted from his father. What might have upset him enough that he might have tried to kill him.

There was also a cousin, Danielo, and his beautiful wife, whom she had met briefly at the piano. Catharina had claimed this wife had shown an interest in Cosimo, even though she was married to the cousin. Had rejection goaded the woman to reach for poison on a night where plenty of other potential suspects were around?

But to make sense of everything she also needed to know more about the cause of death. Had it been poison? If so, what poison? Fast-acting? Slow? How had it been administered? Had the cup contained traces of poison?

A knock on her door made her jerk to attention. Who could it be? It was now after three o'clock in the morning.

She tiptoed over and called out softly, "Who's there?"

"Raoul." It sounded resigned this time.

She opened the door a crack. "I thought you needed sleep."

"I do. But I won't get any as long as you're out here involving yourself in this murder case. And as I know you are dead set on getting involved and I can't stop you anyway, I might as well help you. Let's go to Cosimo's study and see what we can discover there."

"Can we do that? Won't we be disturbing the scene? Angering the police?"

"Only if they find out. They took away the body and the cup. Not to mention their suspect. You're right about that. Catharina is about to be convicted. They won't be looking any further. If we want to help her, we have to do some investigating of our own. Starting with the crime scene."

"Fine with me. One moment." Atalanta returned to the bed and put the coded notes away inside her makeup bag. Then she cast a quick look at herself in the flame mirror. The evening dress seemed out of place for a murder investigation but she could hardly keep Raoul waiting by taking time to change. She swept back a loose lock of hair and went to the door. Raoul gave her a cynical look. "Trying to look your best while you sleuth, Mrs Holmes?"

Atalanta resisted the urge to slap him on the arm. "I was only thinking it's odd to look so festive while we're going to investigate a sudden death. What are the chances it was a heart attack anyway? Perhaps the excitement of drinking from the one and only Medici poison cup got the better of him? The cup could have fallen before he actually drank from it and the wine soaked into the carpet and the floorboards."

"That is one of the things we're going to look at." Raoul smiled at her. His features were relaxed again. "We need to handle this with order and precision. So what are our questions?"

Atalanta enumerated as they went along the corridor. "What killed him? When did he die? Was anyone with him? Did he fight back? Is there evidence in the room of an argument? Things knocked over? Perhaps something is missing?"

"A robbery?" Raoul asked with a doubtful look. "Just like how his wife died? But wouldn't a robber or thief have taken that precious golden goblet?"

"I guess so." Atalanta sighed as she followed Raoul to the study door. It wasn't locked and they could easily step inside. The door didn't even creak. Atalanta held her breath as she looked around. A man had died in here. Still everything looked peaceful in the light of the desk lamp Raoul lit. He knelt and crawled half under the desk.

"I don't see a spillage of wine here. Not a large amount in any case. Just a drop or two. We can rule out the theory that the cup was emptied on the floor and he never actually drank from it."

"Well, I was thinking." Atalanta leaned back on her heels. "He was drinking wine all evening. So, even if the doctor finds traces of poison in his stomach contents, how can he tell from which cup of wine it came? If it wasn't fast-acting, it could have been administered earlier in the evening."

"By almost anyone at the party," Raoul supplied. "Waiters were walking around with trays. It would have been easy to get access to a glass and lace it with poison. But how to get Cosimo to drink it?" He thought for a moment and then said, "Hey …" He jerked upright as he spoke and hit his head on the desk. "Ouch. I forgot I was still tucked under here." He crawled out and rubbed his head ruefully. "A good quality, heavy oak," he said with a cynical smirk.

Atalanta didn't smile. She was staring at the spot where Cosimo's body had lain. "What intrigues me," she said slowly, "is why he went here during the party. He was supposed to be with his guests."

"He wanted to try the cup."

"Right then? He could have waited an hour. Or until the next morning."

Atalanta walked over to the desk and let her gaze wander over the surface. There were some letters there, neatly in envelopes, a stack of white paper, a pen and blotting paper. "Should we try and see what he wrote before he died?" she suggested. She reached for the blotting paper and a pencil to make the indentations visible. A few crumbs of something fell away.

Raoul leaned over from the other side of the desk while she worked on the indentations. They were all Italian words and she let Raoul decipher them.

"Seems to be from business correspondence. It's about casks of wine, shipments, payments. I can't see anything potentially harmful in it. No words that suggest anything criminal."

"Hmmm." Atalanta ran her hands across the desk but didn't find more crumbs. What had those been? Was it important? She felt guilt niggle at the back of her brain that they were disturbing the scene. But the retired police chief had been so certain Catharina was the culprit. She couldn't see him combing the place for indications that it had not been her.

"Shhh." Raoul suddenly lifted a finger to his lips.

Atalanta heard it too. A sound at the window. Very soft, as if someone was there trying to … get inside?

Raoul gestured for her to come to his side of the desk. They crouched to be out of sight of anyone entering through the window. They heard the window open. Rustling as someone climbed inside. Atalanta's heart beat like a drum. What was this? Why would anyone break in? To take away some incriminating clue? Should they expose the intruder or just wait and see what he did?

There was a brief silence, then footsteps. They went to the other side of the room. Something was moved. Atalanta dared peek and saw a tall man in black lifting a painting off the wall. Behind it was a safe. He extracted a stethoscope and put it around his neck. He carefully placed the endpiece on the safe, close to the dial, which he then began turning.

Minutes passed. The man seemed to be totally engrossed in the exercise.

Raoul grimaced at Atalanta and mouthed, "Will never work."

Atalanta had the same sinking feeling. But they could hardly get up and leave the room while the intruder was busy at the safe. They had to stay hidden and wait.

After what seemed like hours, a loud click resounded, and the man opened the door of the safe. He rummaged through the contents, pulling out documents to look at them. He hissed in frustration, apparently not finding what he was looking for.

Minutes passed. Atalanta couldn't feel her legs any

more. They had gone completely numb from sitting in a hunched position.

The man cursed and stood back, lowering his arms in a gesture of dejection.

"Can't find what you're looking for?" Raoul asked.

Atalanta jumped at him speaking out, and the effect on the intruder was even greater. He turned around in a jerk, his fists up, ready to strike out. His face was familiar.

"Take it easy," Raoul said. "I don't want a fight." He stood awkwardly, leaning on the desk to keep his weight off his legs, which were no doubt faring little better than Atalanta's. He looked the man over. "Come back to see if you can still do something for the poor soul who died? You merely posed as a doctor, right? You aren't one. That stethoscope is never used on patients, just on safes you want to steal from."

The man shook his head. "I really am a doctor. And this is the first time I've ever done anything like this."

"You expect me to believe that?"

"Well, of course I practiced on the safe in the doctor's office. My partner guards it with his life. I've worked nights in order to get to the point where I could open it. Not that it matters any more." He shrugged. "What are you going to do now? Call the police? I … I have a gun. I'll shoot you if you even try to reach the phone."

"Let's not play games," Raoul said coldly. "You're not going to shoot me. You don't even carry a gun. I make a deal with you. You tell me why you are here and what your relationship is to Cosimo Lanetti and I won't call the police."

The man tilted his head. "Why would you make that deal?"

Raoul shrugged. "Because information is worth a lot to me."

The man gave a surprised intake of breath. "You're also one of his debtors. You want the IOUs as much as I do." He laughed bitterly. "Good luck finding them. They aren't in here."

"You really thought a clever man like Lanetti would hide them in such an obvious place?" Raoul asked.

Atalanta had no idea what these IOUs were that the man referred to and she wagered Raoul didn't either, but he had to play along and keep the man talking.

The intruder said, "I had to try. I guess it goes to show how desperate I am. But I am a respected doctor. It can't get out that I have incurred debts. If my IOU was found among the deceased's possessions ... I even searched his dead body for it. Thinking he might carry them on his person."

"You did take something off the body," Raoul said. "I saw you put it in your pocket."

"I felt a piece of paper closely folded together and took it on a whim. But it was merely a letter from his daughter telling him she was coming to the party. Nothing special."

"Can I see it?" Raoul asked.

The man took it from his pocket and gave it to Raoul. "Have you got anything for me? Any clue as to where that wretched proof of my debt can be? I can hardly go through every nook and cranny of this study." He looked about him with an expression of despair.

Raoul glanced over the paper the man had given him and now pocketed it. "You don't need this."

"No, I need a clue as to where my IOU is." The man closed in on him. Atalanta crouched lower to stay out of sight. "Tell me something, anything. Please."

"I can't. I don't know where it could be, But I'm staying here as a guest so I can look for it without drawing attention. Perhaps, now that Cosimo is dead, it will turn up? If you leave me your contact details, I'll be in touch when I find out more."

The man took a piece of paper off the desk and scribbled down a few words. "Don't tell anyone about my being here. The Lanettis easily carry a grudge. My entire career would be ruined." He climbed out of the window and disappeared into the night.

"So Cosimo Lanetti lent people money and then held

the IOU over their heads. How intriguing." Raoul paced the room. "If we found proof of the debts, it could reveal any number of murder suspects."

"*If* we found it. You just said it to the doctor: Cosimo must have known better than to leave it in such an obvious place as his safe."

"Cosimo didn't need to put pressure on people to reclaim money. He was incredibly rich. He did it for power. So they would all dance to his tunes. Now we must ask ourselves: who was most anxious to break free?"

"Someone with something to lose if Cosimo kept his hold on them." Atalanta reached out a hand. "Can I read that letter of Catharina's to her father?"

"Of course." Raoul gave it to her. "It doesn't say much."

Atalanta cast a quick eye across it. "It does say that she intends to take the Orient Express from Paris, mentioning both date and departure time. Anyone in the household who had access to this letter would have known she'd be on that train."

"And have put the note under her door," Raoul supplied.

"Exactly."

"We know for certain Lorenzo was on the train."

"Perhaps he acted on another's instruction. We should ask him."

Raoul nodded and bent down again to examine the floor. Atalanta looked at the bookshelves and even moved books around, looking for a hiding place for the IOUs. But they were nowhere to be found.

A clock struck the hour. Five in the morning. "We should get some sleep," she said. "This is getting us nowhere."

"I agree." Raoul straightened up and yawned. "We must speak to some people in the morning and get a better idea of the tensions in the family. I feel like there is a real goldmine to unearth there."

Chapter Eleven

The next morning Atalanta awoke to discover it was almost ten o'clock. Ashamed that she had slept so long, she hurried to freshen up, dress herself and go downstairs to see if there was any breakfast left. In the dining room she found Lorenzo standing at a buffet that had fresh bread, fruit, preserves, and cheeses.

Atalanta went over and said to him, "*Scusi*, I don't think we've been properly introduced. Atalanta Ashford. How is your nose?"

Lorenzo scowled at her. "Not good, thanks to your friend Catharina."

"I only met her on the train. I barely know her." It might help to distance herself a bit from Catharina, inspire confidence in Lorenzo, and learn something about last night.

"But that friend of yours does know her. I saw him coming from her compartment."

Atalanta felt as if she had been struck. "Excuse me?" she said coldly, hoping he wouldn't see her shock.

"I was watching Catharina's compartment in the night and saw Raoul Lemont came out from it. She has always been a man-eater." Lorenzo started to pile breakfast on his plate. For someone with weak health he had a large appetite. "I shouldn't trust her if I were you."

Atalanta tried to hide her confusion at the sudden revelation about Raoul. It revived all her earlier suspicions that he had known in advance that Catharina would be on the train and had only acted surprised at their "accidental" meeting in the dining car. She didn't want to think about that now. She had to focus on gathering relevant information about the case. "Did you send that threatening note?"

"Of course not. She made it up to get your friend to come here and protect her. Too bad she's now in jail. Or is he going to get her out again?" Lorenzo sat down and began to eat.

Atalanta said, "Isn't it strange for a half-brother to watch a compartment?"

Lorenzo shrugged. "I was looking for something to blacken her name with, something I could tell Papa to use against her. Just a tactic. They say all's fair in love and war. Well, I say, all is fair when you want a part of your legacy. I am as much his son as the others. I should get something."

"You say others. Do you mean Giovanni and Thomasso?"

Lorenzo shrugged. "Papa thought he was going to spring a major surprise on us with Thomasso's return. But I already knew about it. I had listened at the door when Thomasso was here weeks ago. Melina was out that day, as well as Giovanni. They had no idea, and I didn't tell them either. I thought it would be good to see how they responded."

Lorenzo had apparently inherited his father's trait of collecting information that could be advantageous.

Atalanta said, "Why do you call your mother Melina?"

"She doesn't like men our age calling her mother. It makes her look old." Lorenzo grimaced. "She is old to me. But she thinks she can still vie with younger women. She will probably remarry now that Papa is dead."

The steward maybe?

"Do you already know to whom? An observant man like you …"

Lorenzo shrugged. "There are several candidates. The one with the most money, or the most power …"

That didn't make it likely the steward would stand a

chance. Had Catharina been wrong about them spending time together? It had seemed unlikely she'd know what went on at home while she was away. Lorenzo's suggestions about Melina's choices in life made more sense. Did her alleged appetite for money and power constitute a motive for murder?

Lorenzo said, "She wants it all, but she'll have to make a choice. We all do at some point."

"Did you see your father before he died?"

"You mean, in his study? Oh, yes, he asked me to step in. He asked all of us, I think. He had something to say later that night. He teased me with it but as I already knew what it was, I didn't take the bait."

All of us. If everyone in the family had been in the study with Cosimo at some point during the party, any one of them could have poisoned the carafe with wine. Or even the goblet? If it was left unattended for a brief spell …

This was very important information. She couldn't wait to share it with Raoul.

Or had Lorenzo's insistence that Raoul had been in Catharina's compartment during the night made her wary about freely trusting Raoul with information? She'd already had a gut feeling the two knew each other and the encounter had been contrived. But after Raoul had responded with such irritation to her suggestion, she had believed it was foolish of her to think it, let alone say it to him and that she had to be more careful with her easily active imagination.

Now, however, she was uncertain again. Did Lorenzo lie? Why? To turn her against Catharina so she wouldn't help her?

Had Lorenzo poisoned his father and was happy that suspicion had readily settled on another? Was he anxious to keep it there and would he lie, say anything, to ensure Catharina got no assistance in pleading her innocence?

———————

Raoul didn't show up at breakfast, and after she had eaten, Atalanta went outside expecting to see him there. He was a sportive man who enjoyed horse riding and she was certain that a beautiful house like this would have gorgeous stables.

She was right – about the stables at least. They were located to the left of the house, and two stable boys were busy outside, one grooming a chestnut mare, the other walking a black stallion. They greeted her in passing and when she asked if one of the guests had taken a horse out riding, they said that several had.

"Was one of them Raoul Lemont, the race car driver?" she asked eagerly.

The boys exchanged bewildered glances, making it clear they had never heard of him. It amused Atalanta a little that there were people who didn't know and admire him, but the feeling faded again as she wondered where he could be. He had been irritated last night. What if he had decided to pack his bags and leave? Simply take his car and disappear, leaving her stranded with this odd, murderous family?

She walked away from the stables, past immaculate box hedges to a walled garden. A small wooden door stood ajar and she pushed it open and looked inside. The area had been divided into neat square beds, each holding plants. As it was late summer there were flowers scattered here and there, but most plants had blossomed earlier and had now gone to seed. A figure in a wide dark blue cape was busy watering the plants in the far bed.

Atalanta got a little closer. "Excuse me?"

The figure turned and now Atalanta recognized the woman who had played the piano last night. Her dark hair was drawn back in a simple braid and she looked completely different from the glamorous figure at the party. She gave Atalanta a weary, almost suspicious look. "What do you want?"

"I'm sorry for just barging in here but I passed the door and wanted to have a look inside. My name is Atalanta Ashford and I was a guest at the party last night."

"Quinta Lanetti," the woman said. Her guarded look didn't fade.

Atalanta enthused, gesturing around her, "You have a very beautiful garden here. Do you know a lot about plants? My mother created a wonderful conservatory in our home and as a child I often played there."

This fond childhood memory seemed to mollify Quinta. Her tired looks softened in a smile and she said, "As a child I always helped my mother with her garden. She taught me everything about plants and their medicinal properties. She showed me how you can make drops against the common cold or something to rub on grazes so they heal better. I really enjoyed exploring the natural world with her and being busy in our little pantry where we made all the lotions and tinctures."

"You still make medicines?" Atalanta asked, looking around her. "I see you have several plants here that are suitable for it."

"Yes, partly these are kitchen herbs and the cook comes here to cut them for the dishes. But there are also plants here that can be used in drops and pills. It's a

187

time-consuming process. Things have to be prepared just right."

"I see. But it must be very relaxing and fulfilling. Do you actually have takers for your homemade medicines? I know some people laugh at the idea that a plant can cure."

"Medicines you get from the doctor are often also prepared with natural ingredients. Morphine, for instance, which became widely used after the war, is derived from opium, which comes, as you probably know, from a poppy."

"Indeed," Atalanta said. She was still trying to reconcile the glamorous socialite who delighted people with her delicate piano music with this woman in the coarse cape who got her hands dirty in a garden and brewed her own medicines.

"I get quiet when I'm in this garden," Quinta said. "I listen to the birdsong and I watch how the seasons change the plants. Everything has rhyme and reason here, while life outside rarely does."

"Yes. I must convey my condolences on the death of Cosimo Lanetti. It was so sudden and how awful that it was during his birthday party."

"To me it wasn't sudden," Quinta said.

Atalanta looked at her. "No?"

"No. I knew he was suffering from heart trouble. The

doctor gave him drops for it that contained foxglove. It's a powerful plant that can cure heart problems but when taken in too high doses, it can kill. I warned Cosimo about it, but he was rather careless. He took the drops as the doctor prescribed but when he felt tired or had pain, he took an extra dose because he believed it gave immediate relief. He wanted to look strong and able, not like an old man. It was his way of keeping control over everyone. But it was dangerous."

"So it's possible," Atalanta said, "that in order to feel good during the strain of hours of partying he took an extra dose of his heart medication? Perhaps he poisoned himself."

"That's possible." Quinta nodded seriously. "But many people knew he took medication with foxglove in it. It would have been easy for them to introduce a bit extra in his wine and ..." She made an eloquent hand gesture across her throat.

Atalanta kept her gaze on the woman. "Was he very much hated then?"

"Hated? No. Why do you ask?"

"Because you suggest that several people would have felt the inclination to poison his wine."

"To speed his departure from this world," Quinta corrected. "It wasn't a matter of hating him but of looking for personal advantage. Cosimo wanted to appoint a successor and everyone wanted to be that man."

"Including your husband, Danielo?"

"I suppose so." Quinta leaned down to pick a dead leaf off a plant. "Danielo worked hard for Cosimo for many years. He feels he does deserve something."

"I've heard several people say that. That they all deserve something. No one said they deserve it all. Couldn't Cosimo have given them shares?"

"That wasn't in his nature. He wanted to play people against each other. He enjoyed struggle and arguments. He enjoyed watching people jump at each other's throats. He found it amusing and laughed about it even when others said he was causing harm." Her features contorted for a moment.

Atalanta said, "Didn't you like him?"

Quinta looked up. For just a second her eyes lit in a fiery gleam. "I saw little of him. He was always busy."

She seemed to consider the conversation over and started to walk away.

Atalanta asked quickly, "What would Thomasso's position have been?" Lorenzo had said he had known about Thomasso's return. Had Quinta also known?

"You should never mention that name. He's gone. Dead and gone. Melina is in tears when you mention his name so don't."

"But he isn't dead and gone. He was here. He made a scene last night that Cosimo had wanted to make him his successor." Atalanta gestured about her dramatically. "I saw him. 'I am Thomasso,' he said. It was quite a shock."

Quinta stared at her, now pale. "You're lying."

"No. Haven't you heard about it? He said he was abducted and left somewhere and a river boat captain found him and took him in. He learned recently that he was Cosimo's son and came here to demand his share."

"His share? He gets nothing. Nothing!" Quinta turned away brusquely, carrying off the watering can she had used for the plants.

Atalanta turned away as well, then called over her shoulder, "Oh, by the way, is there foxglove in this garden?"

Quinta froze a moment, then she said, "No. Not to my knowledge." And she hurried off.

Atalanta left the garden, mulling over what she knew. Catharina had suggested Quinta was in love with Cosimo. But she hadn't spoken about him with much feeling.

It was of course possible that she had indeed tried to flirt with him and he had rejected her. The pain and humiliation of that scene had seared deep into her being and her attraction to him had changed into … hatred? Enough hate to kill? She had knowledge of plants. She need not have created the medicine with the foxglove herself. She could have purchased it somewhere. Or even used Cosimo's own medication if she knew where he kept it.

But Atalanta assumed all family members knew about Cosimo's heart trouble and the medication he took for it. If they were also aware that in high doses those medicines could be dangerous, they had the ideal murder weapon at hand.

She was so deep in thought that she didn't notice the other person coming down the path until she almost collided with him. It was Raoul. He looked crisp in a light suit with his Panama hat throwing shadows over his face.

He said, "Finally out of bed? I spent the morning usefully in pursuit of information."

"I did as well. I have a lot to tell you. But you go first."

Raoul nodded as he fell into step beside her. His expression was serious. "I talked to a police officer. He is a fan of racing and I gave him my autograph and promised to get some signed photographs of other drivers and their cars. In exchange he gave me a lot of information about Cosimo's autopsy."

"That is bribery. You do know that, don't you?"

"As he accepted the bribes, he won't tell a soul. And

neither will I." Raoul gave her a lopsided grin. "Now do you want to hear what he had to say or not?"

"Yes please. But I'm surprised there was news about it already."

"Our friend Foselli dragged the police doctor out of bed and forced him to examine the body straight away. The poor man had to type up his report in the dead of night and deliver it to the police first thing. He handed it in before dawn. It said that" – Raoul waited a few moments for dramatic effect – "Cosimo died of an overdose of heart medication. There were traces of it in the wine in the goblet. The assumption is now that Catharina put the medication in the goblet's secret compartment so it would mix with the wine when her father drank from the goblet. She then intended to take the goblet away from beside his dead body while the party was still in full swing so that, by the time he was discovered, it would look like a simple heart attack and nobody would even think of murder."

"And why didn't she do that?"

"Because the body was discovered sooner than she had expected?" Raoul shrugged. "Or because of the distractions of the man she was kissing in the garden?"

"But when you're committing a murder and it has to proceed in a certain way to ensure you're not implicated, you don't let yourself get distracted. Your very life is at stake."

"I guess she didn't think it through very well." Raoul spread his hands. "Catharina seems like a person who loves to take risks. She must have thought she would get away with it."

"Hmmm. Did they also check the contents of the carafe on the desk?"

"Yes, they did. Nothing in it. They also checked an empty glass that was in the room. Nothing in there either. So it seems rather conclusive that the medication that killed him was in the goblet that Catharina gave him."

"In front of witnesses. If Cosimo had died and had been found, without the goblet by his side, wouldn't there have been questions about it anyway? Wouldn't people have wondered where it was?"

"Yes, but perhaps she wanted to take it away from the scene, wash it clean and then put it in the room on a shelf or something, so it would be present but not associated with his death."

Atalanta nodded slowly. "I guess she might have thought along those lines."

"What matters," Raoul said with emphasis, "is that these findings support Foselli arresting Catharina last night. He can now formally charge her. The policeman said that the case is just about closed."

"How convenient for the real killer."

"You're certain it wasn't Catharina?"

"I can never be certain as I wasn't there when it happened but … my instincts tell me it was someone using Catharina's presence at the party to commit the crime and have her accused of it."

"But whoever prepared for this party didn't know Catharina would bring the goblet," Raoul pointed out.

"They could have planned to leave some other clue on the scene pointing to her. A glove, a lost button, whatever."

Raoul looked incredulous. "Why? If you plan to put medication that someone already takes into his wine and you think his death will look like a regular heart attack, since he'd already had one months before, you have nothing to worry about. It would be deemed a natural death and you'd get away with it, without even accusing anyone else."

"I agree. But perhaps the person also wanted to implicate Catharina. Out of spite, hatred, or to remove her from the scene. What does Cosimo's will say?"

"That is the next item on my list."

"You actually know the contents? How did you bribe the notary?"

Raoul laughed. "You overestimate my powers. I only know that the family lawyer is coming here later this morning and he will read the will to the family members. Then we'll know who gets it all."

"But we don't know if that was the motive for the murder. Because Cosimo had an important announcement to make last night and he never made it."

"Agreed. But we will know who gets it all now that he didn't get to make his announcement. Assuming that he was going to say that he was changing the will ..."

"Yes, but it might have been something else altogether. 'Thomasso is back.' Or 'Catharina will get money to start a chocolate business.' Perhaps even 'I'm divorcing Melina and marrying Quinta.'"

"Who is married to Danielo," Raoul supplied. "I feel we're now getting into guessing without foundation."

"Just exercising the mind, letting it see all possibilities. We must avoid taking a limited view of the situation." Atalanta kicked away a small pebble. "Foselli is already taking that approach." She cast a look at Raoul. "I wonder how close he is to the Lanettis. Does he have an interest in influencing the outcome of this murder investigation?"

"You mean, is he manipulating it at the request of a family member?"

"For instance. Is he close to Melina? What if she was tired of her demanding husband?"

"Why not divorce him?"

"Would a man like Cosimo Lanetti have given his wife a divorce? He would sooner have ..." Atalanta fell silent. A chill went down her spine. "Killed her. What if Melina feared Cosimo would murder her and she killed him first?"

"Why would she fear he would kill her? Just because they argued? Every couple I know argues at times and they don't kill each other. They may say they want to, but they don't."

Atalanta ignored the attempt at humour and said, "I mean that Melina might have reason to think Cosimo would try it. His first wife died in a robbery that was ... well, the robbers always denied having killed her."

"So you assume that someone else killed her and made it look like a robbery?"

"If you know that there have been highway robberies in the area you live and your wife goes out regularly in a carriage, alone, you have a good way of getting rid of her leaving you free to marry someone else. He did remarry soon after."

"Lots of men do. You'd have to prove he was involved in his first wife's death. And that is over thirty years ago. There's no proof of it. Not after all that time."

"I guess not. But it's an element of the case we have to keep in mind. Also if we're looking for motive."

"You mean to say that someone may have assumed

Cosimo was involved in his first wife's death and that was a reason to hate him and murder him? But that leads us straight back to Catharina. Anna was her mother."

"Perhaps the murderer reasoned along those lines. That Catharina would seem a likely suspect because of that."

Raoul walked slowly, a look of utter concentration on his face. Atalanta realized how much she liked watching him. The liveliness in his features as his thought process unfolded. How he defended his opinions and challenged her. She was so glad he hadn't sneaked away in the night and left her alone.

And what about Lorenzo's claim that Raoul was in Catharina's train compartment during the night? a small voice nagged in the back of her head. *Can you simply forget that? Dismiss it as a spiteful lie to blacken Catharina?*

Raoul said, "We first have to know what's in the will. It will provide some solid clues."

"That we'll still have to interpret." Atalanta forced her attention back to the moment "If the will leaves all to, say, Giovanni, does that give him a motive for murder? To get it all, to prevent Cosimo from changing the will and leaving it to another?"

"Sounds plausible to me."

"But what if the will divides things between several

parties? Then we know nothing new. Besides, Thomasso's arrival threw everything into disarray."

"If he is indeed the abducted child of old." Raoul stopped and looked up at a large cypress. "At the time the police were certain the child had been killed. Why else would the abductors refrain from asking for money?"

"But perhaps ransom was never the intention."

"Then what?"

"I don't know. I have a feeling that the abduction is a crucial factor in the murder, but I can't quite see how."

Raoul touched her arm. His eyes reflected his worry. "I wanted you to have a carefree vacation. Now you're sleuthing again and diving into the dark thoughts of all these unpleasant people."

"I'm sorry. They are indeed unpleasant people. I had breakfast with Lorenzo and he suggested to me ..." She fell silent a moment, wondering how she could ask without making Raoul feel she was accusing him of something.

"What? Did he make advances?"

"Oh no. But he said some nasty things about Catharina. That he watched her sleeping compartment that night on the train and saw a man come out of her door." She watched Raoul sharply for any trace of shock at the realization that he had been seen. But there was nothing in his features.

"Can it have been the same man she was with last night?" he asked. "The one she was passionately kissing?"

"I don't think so." Atalanta steeled herself to say the words. "Lorenzo told me it was you."

"Me?" Raoul stared at her and then burst out laughing. "It was probably so dim in the corridor he didn't see much. Why would I come from Catharina's compartment in the night? I hardly know her."

"I guess he suggested it to play us against each other. He must feel unnerved for some reason."

"Can he be the murderer?" Raoul wondered out loud. "He did threaten Catharina not to come to the party. But that makes no sense. If he wanted her to take the blame, he needed her here. Why take the risk of scaring her away?"

"He's her half-brother and knows her well. He could probably guess that the note would only make her angry and more determined to attend the party. And the fight on the platform serves to prove she's violent when she doesn't like someone. That is useful in the murder case. She first attacked her half-brother and later that same day, killed her father because he wouldn't lend her money for her business. If you read that it in the paper, you'd think it was sad but you would think it likely. You wouldn't conclude she was being wrongly accused."

"I see your point. And Lorenzo has the brains to hatch a devious plan. But what does he gain from his father's death? Or did he just want to get rid of Catharina?"

They were close to the house again. A delivery truck was there. A man in a dark blue jacket with gold-coloured buttons was carrying three large cardboard boxes inside. But at the door Melina halted him. They could hear her strident voice from afar. "Take it back to the bakery. We don't need it any more. Those horrible anise-flavoured biscotti ... nobody liked them but Cosimo. Now that he's dead I don't want them in the house. Take them away."

The man spluttered something about them having been ordered and he wanted to get paid, but Melina kept shouting at him and he finally hung his head and returned the boxes to the back of his truck. Melina stood on the steps with her hands on her hips, staring after him as he drove away.

Raoul called out to her, "Good morning. A lot to take care of in the wake of the sudden death in the family?"

She turned to them and immediately pasted a smile to her features. Her hand came up to check if her hair was in place. "So much to do. But we'll get it done." She gestured for them to follow her inside. "Have you slept well? I guess it is hard after such a tragedy, but ... Cosimo would have wanted his guests to feel at home here."

"Did I hear something about anise-flavoured biscotti?" Raoul asked. "I remember having to eat them at my grandmother's and absolutely dreading to go there just because of those horrible things."

Melina's smile widened. "I always said they were revolting. But Cosimo really liked them. He had a whole ritual made out of it. Three biscotti before bed. I couldn't stand the smell of them." She shuddered. "I don't want anyone eating them now that he died. It would just remind me and ..." Tears formed in her eyes.

Raoul said, "Now, now, calm down. You're handling all of this admirably. Thrust into turmoil so suddenly. You did know, of course, that he was ill, heart trouble ... I guess after his heart attack in spring another one was only a matter of time."

Melina looked at him, tears on her lashes. "Was it a heart attack then? Not murder?" She seemed confused. Uncertain rather than relieved.

Fascinated, Atalanta watched it all play out.

Raoul said, "He took heart medication, didn't he?"

"Yes. He sometimes forgot and I had to remind him."

"Well, he must have mixed it up, taken a second dose

because he didn't recall taking the first one. It was an overdose of medication that killed him. Unfortunate, but no crime."

Melina's eyes narrowed. "How do you know that?"

Raoul ignored the question. "It must be reassuring to know he wasn't murdered at all."

"How can you be sure? That second dose could have been put in his wine by someone else. To kill him."

Raoul continued as if he hadn't heard, "I doubt that it's advisable to drink alcohol when you take heart medication. So perhaps it was a combination of the wine and the drops? Well, anyway, Catharina will soon be released then."

Atalanta was stunned that he said this because the discovery of traces of medicine in the goblet would of course keep her firmly behind bars.

Melina said, "That can't be right. She must have had something to do with it. She left us, driving Cosimo to tantrums. He had his first heart attack because of her, you know. And then she comes back and he dies the same night? It must be connected. She drove him to distraction with her questions about her mother."

"About her mother?" Atalanta echoed curiously.

"Yes: where she went in her carriage, how often and how long she stayed away. I think she was really obsessed with that robbery. As if Cosimo was to blame for it." Melina straightened up and pulled back her shoulders. "If you will excuse me. I have a lot to do."

"Such as looking into selling this house?" Lorenzo was there, only a few feet away, eyeing his mother angrily. "You hate it here, I've always known that. You can't wait to live somewhere else. And with Papa gone, that is possible. As long as he was alive, you'd never have been able to move away."

Melina flushed scarlet. "I don't want to leave here," she muttered weakly and fled up the stairs.

Lorenzo laughed disbelievingly. "I know the truth!" he shouted after her. He looked at Raoul and Atalanta and said, "Women. You can't trust them. Ever." Then he stalked away.

"He is very good at it," Raoul observed.

"What?"

"Dropping a few hints and getting everyone worked up. He lied about seeing me coming out of Catharina's compartment in the train so why not lie now? I wonder why he is so eager to throw up smokescreens."

"You think he has something to hide?"

"Well, I'll tell you what I noticed last night. He was wearing a mask. Like the waiters. Allegedly because of his busted nose. But it was of course an excellent disguise. He could have gone into his father's study to poison the goblet. Anybody seeing him walk about would have taken him for a waiter and not paid any attention."

"That's very interesting." Atalanta furrowed her forehead. "I wonder if he felt threatened by Thomasso's return. He told me over breakfast that he knew about it before the party. He said that he didn't care, but if he did, he had a chance to plot an untimely demise for his father at a moment with many people around."

"This is outrageous!" The voice resounded in the large space of the hallway, echoing back to them. A man came storming out of a room holding a newspaper in his hand. "Who did this?" He saw them and halted, looking taken aback.

Raoul said, "Raoul Lemont and Atalanta Ashford, we're guests here. You are ...?"

"Danielo Lanetti. I was Cosimo's right-hand man." Danielo held the newspaper behind his back. "Were you going out to enjoy the pleasant morning?"

"No, we just came in. Is there something upsetting in the newspaper?"

Danielo seemed to want to deny it but realized that he couldn't hide it for ever. He sighed as he produced the paper and held it out for them to read. "See for yourself."

Raoul took the paper from his hand and held it up so the front page was in full view. It said in bold letters "Poisonous Family Relations" and went on to report the murder of Cosimo Lanetti at his sixtieth birthday party. Atalanta could understand a few words here and there, but Raoul with his command of Italian whizzed through the piece and handed the newspaper back to Danielo with a whistle. "It reads like the reporter was on the scene when it happened."

"Exactly. I wonder how that is possible. Cosimo hated the press and would never have invited one of those bloodsuckers."

"But there were so many people around that someone could easily have mingled," Atalanta suggested.

"The audacity," Danielo snarled. "I'll call the editor to ask who wrote this." He turned away.

Atalanta looked at Raoul. "What did it say exactly?"

"That Cosimo Lanetti celebrated his sixtieth birthday with a party for all of his family, friends and workers but that he was killed by an enemy among them. That he was a hard man who had turned people against him by his choices and that his family relationships were complicated because of his two marriages and countless affairs."

"Affairs?" Atalanta raised an eyebrow. "Does that mean we could also be dealing with a murder out of jealousy? A betrayed husband mixing medication into the wine? Or a woman scorned, exchanged for another?"

Raoul huffed. "Won't make it easier for us."

Atalanta looked in the direction Danielo had vanished. "It's rumoured his wife fancied Cosimo too. What if he is the jealous husband who used the party to deal with his unwanted rival?"

Raoul touched her arm. "Let's first wait to hear what the will says. Then we can draw new conclusions."

Chapter Twelve

The family lawyer arrived during lunch and asked everyone to gather in the library afterwards. While they finished eating, he said, "I learned from the newspaper that Catharina Lanetti was arrested last night for possible involvement in her father's death. I went to see her at the police station and she requested that two people attend the will reading on her behalf and to see to her interests. A certain Miss Atalanta Ashford and a Signor Raoul Lemont?"

There was a shocked gasp from Melina, and Giovanni said, "I don't want them there. There is no point. Catharina killed Papa and as his murderer she can't inherit from him anyway."

"She has not yet been convicted," the lawyer said calmly. "I must ask you to allow the mentioned persons to be present or I'll reveal the contents of the will to them later."

Giovanni rolled his eyes but remained silent.

Melina said, "I consider this all very odd. If Catharina had a husband or something, we would have to allow him to attend, I suppose. But two strangers?"

Lorenzo said, "Perhaps Mr Lemont is Catharina's husband-to-be? I know for a fact that they spent nights together."

Raoul reddened. "We did not, so don't say that."

"I think he's right," Quinta said. "I saw Catharina at the party with another man. They kissed in the garden."

"One doesn't preclude the other," Lorenzo said with aplomb.

Raoul rose from his chair. "I understand now why Catharina broke your nose. You're insufferable."

Lorenzo cringed as if he feared his nose would take another beating. But Raoul simply left the room.

"I don't see," Melina said, "why the idea that he slept with Catharina should upset him so. It's well known that those race car drivers use every opportunity to get willing women into their beds. It's part of their lifestyle."

The lawyer cleared his throat to get their attention once more. "I'm charging my normal hourly rate for my presence here. The sooner you end lunch and join me the less money it will cost."

This led to a quick emptying of wine glasses and the scrape of chair legs on the floorboards as everyone scampered to leave the room and reconvene in the library. There was a long table there and they all sat down around it, the lawyer at the head. To his left sat Melina, Giovanni, Quinta and Danielo, with Lorenzo, Atalanta and Raoul sitting opposite. The door opened again to allow a man to enter.

Atalanta recognized him at once, but the others seemed to have no idea who he was and Melina even asked in annoyance, "What do you want? We have a will to discuss."

"I know. That's why I am here. My name is Thomasso Lanetti."

Melina stared at him. "Take back that joke."

"It's not a joke. I am Thomasso. Cosimo knew that I had come back. He was going to tell everyone yesterday at the party. But he died before he could do so."

Melina blinked. "Thomasso? My son Thomasso?"

"Yes. I was left by the roadside to die. But a river boat captain found me and took me in. I learned only a short while ago whose son I truly was."

"And you couldn't wait to run out here and get part of the property," Giovanni said with a snarl. "You can't prove you are related to us. Anyone can say he's Thomasso. The story of the abduction was widely known. But we'd need more than your word to accept you as one of our own. Proof of your blood tie to us, which you can never deliver. Leave. Don't show your face here again."

The lawyer said, "I'm afraid I have to agree with him. You may say you are a Lanetti and you even may be, but we can never be sure of it. And I may add that this will was made before you returned, so there is no mention of you in it. You have no business being here."

Thomasso laughed, a short harsh sound. "That is the welcome I get after all these years? Nobody is glad to see me? Happy I didn't die? No. I should never have come back."

"No!" Melina cried. She half rose. "If you are Thomasso ..."

Giovanni pulled her back into her seat. "He's a liar, Mama. An impostor out to milk your grief. But we will not let him." He shouted to Thomasso, "Leave! Or I have you thrown out."

Thomasso stepped back. "You'll regret this." There was cold rage on his face. "You will all regret this."

When the door had closed, the lawyer rearranged his papers. The rustle sounded impossibly loud in the sudden silence.

Melina said, in a shaky voice, "But if there's a chance that he really is ..."

"We won't be able to ascertain it either way," Lorenzo said. "It's too long ago." He sounded reasonable but the gleam in his eyes betrayed that he was just as pleased as Giovanni that the alleged older brother had been dismissed.

The lawyer said, "Shall we begin the reading?"

He cleared his throat and launched into the traditional formal opening. Atalanta listened with bated breath. Who was the main beneficiary of the will?

"To my wife, Melina, I allot the right to live in the house until she remarries. She can keep the jewellery I purchased for her, but the family pieces as described in the added list must be returned immediately upon my death."

"Those are all the best pieces," Melina protested.

The lawyer continued, "To my son—"

"Don't I get any money?" Melina asked. She was pale, either with shock or rage.

Atalanta felt Raoul's foot touch hers. He was probably thinking the same thing. Melina had obviously expected a lot more from her husband's will. A powerful motivation to speed his death.

"To my son Giovanni I leave the hunting lodge in the mountains, which he might like to use for his parties. He gets one third of the vineyard, on the condition that he cannot sell it to an outsider and that the profits from the vineyard are invested back into the company with the exception of ten per cent for his personal use."

"A measly ten per cent?" Giovanni fumed.

Lorenzo was suppressing laughter. He obviously expected to get more.

The lawyer continued, "To my son Lorenzo I leave my book collection as he will certainly enjoy the knowledge contained in it. He gets one third of the vineyard, on the same condition as described before."

Giovanni grimaced at Lorenzo. "Just ten per cent for you too, brother dear."

"But wait," Lorenzo said, half rising, "who gets the other third?" He was visibly shocked that it wasn't his.

"To my daughter, Catharina, I leave the family jewellery for her to wear as she goes to parties and tries to interest people in her outlandish ideas. She cannot sell the pieces or otherwise make money from them, and after her death they must go to her children under the same conditions. She gets the last third of the vineyard, provided she won't sell it to an outsider and that the profits are invested back into the company, except for ten per cent, which she can use to live off or invest in her own business, which she seems so keen to start."

Atalanta was sorry that Catharina wasn't here to hear this for herself. Apparently her father had known that she wanted to have a business for herself.

The lawyer continued, "My cousin Danielo will remain a worker in the vineyard. He cannot be dismissed or sent away. He will earn reasonable wages."

"That is all?" Danielo cried. "For all the work I did?"

Quinta moved restlessly in her seat as if she was worried she might not get anything.

"To his wife, Quinta, I leave the use of the herb garden, which she enjoys so much, and the ivory chess set from my study, in gratitude for our enjoyable games."

Quinta flushed to her hair roots. She clenched her hands into fists.

The lawyer continued to read out minor bequests to staff members but none of these were worth substantial money, so Atalanta assumed they didn't provide a motive for murder. She was unpleasantly struck by how mean Cosimo had been in his will, using the wording to belittle his closest relatives. He had to have been a difficult man to deal with.

A man one could easily grow to hate.

Melina said in a strangled voice, "He knew how I hated this house; this shrine to his first wife. *Her* rooms, *her* decor, *her* choices. Nothing of mine. He knew it and now he leaves me the 'right' to live here … I don't want to live here! I want to leave!" She jumped to her feet and ran from the room. The door banged shut.

Giovanni said, "He got us good. Nasty old bastard."

"That is no way to speak about your father," the lawyer said. "He worked hard all of his life to build his business empire and he made the choices he thought were best for it."

"I do wonder though," Raoul said, leaning on the table, "what he wanted to announce last night before he died. Was it a big change to the way in which his property would be divided after death? If he believed Thomasso wasn't an impostor and he wanted to deal him in, the shares of the others would have been diminished. Or perhaps he would even have cut out one heir in favour of the returned son?"

They were all eyeing each other as if to calculate who it might have been.

Giovanni said, "We don't need you to make accusations, Lemont. We all know with whom you side and why. You hoped Catharina would come into money and that's why you courted her."

"Yes," Lorenzo said eagerly, "you came here knowing she would kill Papa and you two would have one third of the vineyard."

Raoul scoffed. "I barely know your half-sister. I have no intention of being with her, for whatever reason, let alone money. Were you listening to the reading at all? One third of the vineyard that she can't sell and ten per cent of the profits to live off? That's not exactly a king's ransom. If I wanted to find myself a wealthy wife, I would look elsewhere."

"You know that *now*. But Catharina may have lied to you. Told you she would sell her share and you'd be rich. Or that she'd inherit the lot. She's always been a little liar." Lorenzo rose and turned away. "A liar and a killer now."

One by one the family members left the room. Atalanta and Raoul remained seated with the lawyer. Raoul said, "Thank you for allowing us to be present on Catharina's behalf."

The lawyer made a dismissive gesture. "I've always felt she suffered unduly when her mother died so suddenly. Her father didn't have much time for her and her stepmother, well, they weren't close. Then the tragedy of her half-brother's abduction ..." He shook his head and adjusted the glasses perched on his nose. "She has had her share of tragedy in life and now she is being accused of murder."

"But you don't think she did it."

The lawyer smiled bleakly. "That's not for me to decide but for the police." He gathered the papers he had brought and put them back in his briefcase. "It's inevitable when someone wealthy dies that their relatives argue about the division of his riches. I've never been to any will reading where the family members fell into each other's arms cheering for what they each got. I ..." He hesitated a moment and then continued, "I've always felt there was injustice in their angry or hurt responses. The money and assets to be divided are not theirs. The testator has often worked long and hard to gain property and he or she is the sole person entitled to the benefits. The assets are divided only because that someone has died – the beneficiaries haven't worked for it."

"Many think they have a right to it because they were nice to the testator," Raoul said. "I have several friends who will visit an old aunt or uncle regularly and complain about how boring they are and how tedious it is to see them, but they are only after a share of the inheritance. If they were to find out later that they didn't get a thing, they would feel cheated. You might say that would be unjustified for them to feel this way because they had never been promised anything, but a person acts on their expectations."

"I agree," the lawyer said. "I just wanted to point out that their behaviour is in no way unusual for a family after the death of a patriarch."

He bid them farewell and left the room.

"If he was trying to convince us that these are normal people," Raoul said with a grimace, "he hasn't succeeded. I think they are all odd – and potential murderers."

"All of them?" Atalanta asked with raised brows.

Raoul sighed. "I don't mean that they all conspired together to kill Cosimo. I mean that they all had powerful motives to want him dead. It's obvious they expected a lot from him. And if they felt like he wasn't about to give it to them they might have acted in anger."

"When I think of someone acting in anger, I imagine them lashing out and pushing another person. Or grabbing an object and bashing them on the head, in the heat of an argument. But this was a murder by poison. With an ingenious way to divert suspicion, if we assume that the goblet wasn't actually drunk from but used to suggest the poisoned wine had been imbibed from it."

Raoul nodded. "I see your point. Still it's possible. If we assume that someone harboured hatred for Cosimo or wanted the inheritance early and thought the party was a good time to act and incriminate another. These feelings of resentment could have been long in the making."

"With a family history that includes a murdered first wife and an abducted son, you're probably right. Such wounds can start to fester." Atalanta took a deep breath. The atmosphere in the room still seemed heavy with tension and unease. "At least we can tell Catharina she is getting a third of the vineyard and some sort of income. If the wines are so successful, ten per cent of what she earns should be something."

Raoul said, "How much can it actually be? I can understand that they feel it's a pittance. But at least Cosimo didn't make a choice between them. He could have given it all to one child and disinherited the others."

"Perhaps they would have liked that better. Now they're stuck with each other."

They walked out and heard voices from a room on the other side of the corridor. Raoul snuck to the door and listened. Atalanta joined him reluctantly.

Lorenzo was saying, "You never enjoyed working in the vineyard. You want to do something else with your life. If you sell your share to me, you're free to go into the world and become whatever you want to."

"The will said not to sell."

"To an outsider. You can sell to me. Papa wanted the property to stay with a Lanetti."

"And you can work in the vineyard? After half an hour you're panting for breath."

"I have medication now that makes it better."

"Those herbal concoctions Quinta provides you with? You only take them because you're in love with her."

"Shut up. Shut your filthy mouth!" There was the sound of a scuffle. Raoul threw the door open and stormed inside. He grabbed Giovanni by the shoulder and pulled him away from Lorenzo. "He already has a broken nose. Don't make it worse."

Lorenzo used his brother's distraction to throw a punch, but his hand merely brushed Giovanni's cheek. Even then, Lorenzo cried out and held his hand as if he feared he had broken his knuckles.

"You're a weakling," Giovanni snarled. "A mother's baby. Quinta only gives you the medicines because she pities you."

Lorenzo hissed in anger, but Giovanni pulled free from Raoul's grasp and left the room.

Raoul said to Lorenzo, "Wouldn't it be wise to try and heal rifts now that you're the heirs of the vineyard? I mean, you have a company to run together."

"Together?" Lorenzo scoffed. "We'd sooner kill each other."

"Or buy each other out," Atalanta said. "Did you really think he would accept your offer?"

"It makes sense." Lorenzo still rubbed his injured hand. "Giovanni never liked the seclusion of this place. He wants to live in Florence or Rome and go to parties, spend time with friends, chase the ladies. As he doesn't want to hide away here, I thought he'd agree to sell his share to me. Once I control the entire vineyard, I can make it into an even bigger success than it was under Papa's lead."

"But Catharina also owns a third," Atalanta pointed out gently.

Lorenzo made a derisive sound. "She can't inherit. Murderers can't inherit from their victims. Her share will come back to the other heirs. Giovanni and I have halves then and he will sell his half to me." It sounded determined, almost grim.

Raoul said, "Was this your plan all along? To kill your father, blame your sister, and then in the confusion after his death take control of all of the property?"

Lorenzo blinked. "I didn't kill my father. Why would I? I had a good relationship with him."

"But under his control it's unlikely you would have been able to make a single decision. He determined everything and you were just his puppet."

Lorenzo's eyes flashed. "Don't talk to me like that. This is my house now. You're not welcome here."

"This house belongs to *all* of the heirs," Raoul said, gesturing around him. "Catharina asked Atalanta and me to act on her behalf and so we are staying." He leaned closer to Lorenzo. "To prove her innocence."

Lorenzo held his gaze. He seemed undecided as to what to do. Try and evict them or accept the situation as it was?

After an awkward silence that seemed to stretch endlessly, Lorenzo said, "Good luck with that. The evidence against her is strong. I can't see how you will persuade Foselli to look in another direction. If even *he* thinks Catharina is guilty, she must be."

"Even *he*?" Atalanta latched on to his word choice. "Why would Foselli not think her guilty?"

"He's been a close friend of the family from the days when her mother was still alive. He always liked Catharina and even gave her money to support her travels. Why would he suddenly think she's a killer? He's been forced to believe it due to the overwhelming evidence. The goblet beside the body, the poison in it ..." Lorenzo shook his head. "Not even the great Inspettore Foselli can save her." He smiled softly and walked away.

"What an unpleasant character," Raoul said with disgust. "He actually enjoys Catharina's predicament."

"What he shared is interesting though," Atalanta said. "I had the impression Foselli was against Catharina and was looking for reasons to arrest her. But if it's the other way around ... if he likes her and doesn't want her to be guilty, but feels he must act on the evidence because he can't afford to show partiality ..."

"Then," Raoul completed her sentence, "we may be able to persuade him that another did it, if we build a strong enough case for their guilt."

"Exactly. We need motives. We need proof that other people could have accessed the heart medication and put it in Cosimo's wine."

"Motives we have in abundance. Greed, jealousy, hatred, anger. Even Thomasso is a suspect in my book. He told us that Cosimo intended to reveal to everyone that he was back and would be joining the family business. But what if Cosimo didn't want that at all? His will proves he had a nasty habit of hurting people where they're vulnerable. Thomasso felt he had been denied his birthright and wanted to be reinstated in the family. What if Cosimo told him he didn't believe him, or that he was happy with things as they were? How hurtful that would have been to Thomasso."

"Yes. You're right. We're acting on the assumption that Cosimo wanted to change his will in favour of Thomasso and that someone acted to prevent him, but it could have been the other way around. Cosimo didn't want to change anything and Thomasso murdered him to let another take the blame."

"Why Catharina though?" Raoul mused. "Was it coincidental? Had Thomasso already decided to poison his father during the evening, and when he saw the gift Catharina had brought, he saw a chance to do it in such a manner that another would be thought guilty?"

"Or was she his intended victim all along?" Atalanta looked at Raoul pensively. "Thomasso was born when Catharina was a little girl. She didn't like her father remarrying. She missed her mother and didn't love her stepmother. She might also have felt resentment against the baby that was born."

Raoul nodded. He took a deep breath before he said, "A terrible thought crossed my mind."

"What is that?"

Raoul looked about him, as if he was worried they would be overheard. "Let's go outside and walk in the gardens," he suggested.

Atalanta followed him out of the room's French doors. They walked in silence for a few minutes until they were well away from the house. It was hot in the bright sunshine and not even a gardener was around. They had probably watered the plants in the morning or did that at night.

The silence around them made Raoul lower his voice. "I've been thinking about Thomasso's abduction. I talked to that old maid who has worked here all her life. She recalled it vividly. The boy was taken from the crib that stood in these gardens. It was thought to have been an intruder. But what if ... what if it was a family member? What if it was Catharina?"

Atalanta stared at Raoul. "You think she took her baby brother, half-brother, and carried him off and left him somewhere to die? That would be extremely cruel. How old would she have been at the time? Seven perhaps? Could a child that age think up such a wicked plan?"

"And execute it." Raoul nodded slowly. "I agree that it is unlikely. But once I had thought it, I couldn't unsee it any more: this little girl, carrying off her baby brother, smiling to herself that she was removing the one who had taken her place in her father's affection. Cosimo must have been so happy it was a boy, a son, an heir. Catharina had lost her mother and now she had lost her father as well to this newcomer."

"It does sound plausible from a psychological point of view, but do young children reason with such accuracy?"

"The old maid told me Catharina knew the layout of the land around the house like the back of her hand. She would always play outside and no one really looked after her. She could stay away for hours."

"And do you know how Catharina behaved after the abduction?" Atalanta asked.

Raoul nodded. "I asked about that too. The maid said that while Catharina had kept her distance after the baby had been born, she spent more time with her father after the abduction. She tried to comfort Cosimo and distract him from his grief. They were closer than they had ever been." Raoul sighed. "It makes me think that Thomasso's disappearance gave Catharina everything she wanted."

"I'll keep it in the back of my mind," Atalanta said. "But it seems far more likely an adult took the boy, intending to ask the family for money. What do you think of Giovanni's remark that Lorenzo is in love with Quinta?"

"She's an attractive woman. But I was more interested in the revelation that she makes medication for him. To help with his shortness of breath apparently. But if she can make that, she could also ..."

"Make something out of foxglove and use it to poison her husband's uncle?" Atalanta nodded thoughtfully. "I saw the garden where she grows herbs and medicinal plants. There was no foxglove there and she denied having it. But she could be lying."

"She need not have got the foxglove from her own garden. It also grows along the roads in summer."

"I know." Atalanta began to pace, her hands folded behind her back, contemplating all the angles of the case. "But why would Quinta murder Cosimo? Danielo didn't get much in the will."

"Perhaps it wasn't about money. You said yourself that Cosimo had a mean streak. If he insulted her somehow ... she and Danielo don't have children. Perhaps Cosimo made vicious remarks about that? Or he humiliated Danielo in another way. Quinta seemed upset he was treated as nothing more than a cheap labourer."

"Yes, I agree, but murdering him would be an enormous risk to take, for likely only a small return. Or do you think Danielo can negotiate a better position now that he's dealing with the siblings rather than their father?"

"I have no idea," Raoul said. "But what if Quinta reasoned like Lorenzo does now? Catharina is accused and so can't inherit. The brothers share the loot. Giovanni wants to leave and sells his share to Lorenzo. Then Lorenzo would be left to run the vineyard alone – it's a physically demanding job, so he would need help. Danielo would be the man to step up. In that scenario, Quinta's murder of Cosimo would promote her husband to a very important place in the company. The right-hand man of the new owner."

"I think that is very well thought out. I have to make new notes now that we know what was in the will. But we have to keep in mind that we can't be certain that the siblings, or indeed anyone else, knew what the will contained. To murder someone on a gamble of the outcome is rather—"

"But Cosimo was an unlikeable person. It would always have been better to have him dead. And it might bring financial gain too. What's not to like?"

Atalanta cringed under Raoul's cynical tone.

He continued, "Besides, Thomasso had shown up.

That was a danger to all of them. He might upset the power balance and take things away from them. But as soon as Cosimo was dead, Thomasso would no longer be a threat. Melina might want him in the family fold again, but she has no influence here in the house or at the vineyard. The siblings decide everything now and they won't let Thomasso anywhere near the property."

"Agreed. So Thomasso's appearance might have triggered the murder. But who knew about it? Lorenzo admitted to me that he knew. He said that the others didn't, but what if he was wrong? They could have been prompted by fear to act."

"How would Melina feel, I wonder?" Raoul stopped at a pond and stared into it with a frown. "She's Thomasso's mother. Would she not have been pleased he was still alive? Why murder her husband? She has three sons. Any of them could become heir and she'd hold the position of mother of the heir."

"Yes, but did she believe Thomasso was Thomasso? Or did she think it was an impostor after money? Was she worried Cosimo would fall for it and did she kill him for that reason?"

Atalanta followed the shadow of a fish moving under the surface. "There's another thing. The old maid told me that when Melina married Cosimo she was already with child. What if it wasn't his? What if she agreed to marry him quickly because she knew she was with child from another man, from an affair her parents would never agree with?"

"Thomasso not being a Lanetti at all?" Raoul asked. "That would be explosive."

"Melina came into the marriage with a secret. She hoped Cosimo would never find out. When the child disappeared, she was sad, of course, but it removed the threat of discovery. However, when Thomasso re-entered their lives ... We have to consider what Melina's feelings would be if Thomasso came back and she knew he was not Cosimo's child."

"Would fear have prompted her to kill Cosimo?" Raoul nodded slowly. "I see your point. Melina never liked Catharina so she'd certainly think her the best person to take the blame."

Atalanta said, "We also have to find out who leaked information to the press. There was a large article in the paper this morning with details about the party. A guest must have revealed all. Now why would they?"

"How do you intend to find out?"

"You can call the newspaper. You're a celebrity. They will certainly want to talk to you."

"And want an interview." Raoul grimaced. "But you're right, it could reveal something useful. I'll make the call right away. Shall we return to the house via that path?"

The path had a low hedge separating it from the road. They could see across the land on the other side. Danielo stood by a tree talking to another man. The man shook his head several times, but Danielo seemed persuasive as he pushed something into his hand. It was an object that gleamed in the sunlight.

"What is he doing?" Raoul asked Atalanta. "That looks like an artefact of some sort."

"Is he pawning items for money?" Atalanta wondered aloud. "Cosimo didn't seem to pay him much."

"Well, if he is, I wonder if he is entitled to whatever he is handing over." Raoul swung his leg over the hedge. "I'm going to find out."

Atalanta wanted to protest that with her dress she couldn't follow but Raoul had already jumped the stream that lay on the other side of the hedge, crossed the road, and then agilely ran down a dirt path to the tree where the two men were standing. They saw him coming and the unknown man took off. Danielo was left looking sheepish as Raoul closed in on him.

Atalanta hated that she couldn't hear what was being said. But Raoul came back to her soon enough. He looked grim. "Danielo said it was none of my business what he was doing. But he was sweating profusely."

"It is a hot day." Atalanta gestured around them. "He doesn't have to tell you anything."

"I know, but I find it telling he might be selling off items from the family estate."

"We didn't get a proper look at what it was," she warned him. "We mustn't cause trouble, for ourselves or for Catharina."

Raoul dabbed his forehead. "I'm going inside to call the newspaper. Why don't you go and find Quinta and ask her about her husband's actions? Pretend you saw him accept money for the item. Pressure her to tell you what is happening."

"I can't do that. I know too little to go around making accusations. It could cause an argument between them." She waited a moment and said, "Like Lorenzo's lie that he saw you come from Catharina's compartment on the train."

Raoul looked at her. "Is it really a lie in your mind or are you beginning to think he might have told the truth? Why else bring it up again?"

"To demonstrate how harmful lies can be. Raoul ..." She touched his arm. "I want to trust you. And you must trust me. We have to handle this with the utmost care. We're merely guests here. I haven't been hired to look into anything."

"Yes, you were. By Catharina. On the train she asked us to come with her to this party."

"She didn't know I am a detective. Or did she? Did you tell her?"

Raoul looked down. Atalanta's heart beat fast. What was he going to say? Did he have something to confess?

"I told her, but only last night during the party. Not on the train."

"You told her last night? When? Why?"

"You were chatting to that couple from Pisa and I had gone to get us another drink. Catharina passed me. She looked upset and I asked her if she was all right. She said that she had talked to her father and he had said things were about to change drastically. She didn't understand what he meant and was worried about what he might be planning. I told her you knew a little about the law and justice and things and that if she got into trouble with her family, you might be able to assist her with advice. That cheered her up again. I didn't say anything about you being an actual detective, because why would I? There hadn't been a murder yet."

Atalanta sighed. "Again we hear of Cosimo's reference to a dramatic change in the situation but we still have no idea what he meant. Thomasso's return? His entry into the family business? Turning it all over to him?

Or something far different? I can't piece it together. I wish I understood more of Cosimo's personality. Was he truly the man to embrace a long-lost son?"

"Not if he had doubts he was a Lanetti. Any grown man could come here and claim to be Thomasso. The case was all over the papers at the time. I'm off to make the call then. You do whatever you think best."

Atalanta stood there and sighed. It felt like the weight of the world was on her shoulders. She had to act fast to protect Catharina's interests but how could she, knowing so little?

Chapter Thirteen

Atalanta had hoped to find Quinta in the piano room. She didn't intend to approach her with outright lies as Raoul had suggested, but it couldn't hurt to have a little chat and find out if she knew about her husband's transactions. Atalanta could always suggest she only had the best interests of the couple at heart.

However, the piano sat empty, the wood gleaming in the light coming through the high windows. Atalanta cast her eyes across all the art on the walls and pedestals. This house was a treasure trove. A rich inheritance. Melina had to be angry she could only live here until she remarried. The jewellery wasn't even hers to keep. Just the pieces Cosimo had purchased especially for her.

That meant he had given her family heirlooms to wear. The same that Catharina's mother had worn? Had that created more bad blood between Catharina and her stepmother? Had Melina hated her enough to pin a murder on her?

"There you are." Raoul stepped into the room. He looked about him, came closer, then whispered, "I have terrible news."

"What do you mean?"

"I spoke briefly to the editor of the newspaper. He said that the article had been written by one of their reporters who was at the party last night. As a guest."

"But Cosimo would never invite a reporter. Or would he? Had he wanted his explosive statement to be on the front page the next morning?"

"I don't know. But the editor said that his man was eager to hear more about any new developments and asked if we would meet him? He suggested a roadside inn in half an hour. I agreed to it thinking we might learn more. But we must be careful not to give him anything he can print. Do you want to change before we go?"

"I'd better." Atalanta rushed upstairs to find a different dress and do her hair. While going through the familiar motions, her brain worked to put everything into perspective. Who stood to gain the most by Cosimo's death? Had it even been about money or the vineyard? Had Cosimo's mysterious references to a dramatic announcement made someone panic, thinking a huge secret was about to be exposed?

How had the wine been poisoned? When it was in the goblet? Or before? Why had Cosimo drunk from the goblet at all? Or hadn't he? Had it merely been placed by his side for show? No, there had been poisoned wine in it. Introduced later? A completely staged crime scene? By whom? Who would have the intelligence for it, the nerve? Lorenzo had said all the children had been alone with their father at some point during the party. Who was the most likely to have executed the murder?

When she met Raoul outside, he had the car ready. They got in just as a police car approached the house.

"It's Foselli," Raoul said, as they passed the car. "What can he want?"

"We'll hear when we get back. We must now first meet our reporter. What do you think he wants to know? The editor mentioned developments, but surely we're not going to tell him anything about the autopsy or the will? We can't. We learned about that through, um … protected channels."

"Let me do the talking. I'm used to dealing with the press. I'll say you're a friend of Catharina's and I came along as your driver for this Tuscany trip. I want to avoid any speculation that I am her boyfriend."

"Of course." Atalanta held her purse in her lap, brushing the leather absentmindedly.

They arrived at the inn on time. Raoul parked the car in the shade of some trees. Two boys came up to admire it. He told them not to touch it and not to let anyone else touch it either. "Then you'll get a hundred lire each."

They nodded enthusiastically. Raoul led the way around the inn to a terrace at the back where simple tables and chairs stood. A girl of no more than sixteen came to take their order. The reporter was nowhere in sight. Raoul leaned back and looked around him. "This is how I imagined our vacation. Leisurely touring the countryside, sitting down for coffee and cake every now and then. Letting you soak up the beauty of this land. Now I feel like we've been thrust into some play. But it's not a *commedia dell'arte*. It's more like a Greek tragedy. And we already had one of those on Santorini."

"I feel sorry for the people it happened to. Imagine, Cosimo loses a wife in a robbery. He remarries someone who might have lied to him when she said that the baby was his. Then the child is abducted and never found. Now Cosimo himself is murdered. That murder pits the siblings against each other. How can they ever find peace?"

"I'm glad I'm an only child. You?"

"I did want a sister when I was younger. To play with, tell stories to. It was lonely growing up alone."

"I had lots of friends who came to the house. I don't think I ever felt alone." Raoul frowned. "I liked all the attention." He grinned at her. "I guess I chose the right profession to continue that."

Atalanta had to smile as well. "You certainly did."

A man approached them in long strides. *"Buona sera."* He had a very handsome face made all the more charming by his appreciative look at Atalanta. "Antonio Gati. My friends call me Tony." He turned to Raoul. "Mr Lemont, I've been a long-time admirer of your racing. Daring, never accepting less than first place."

Raoul shook his hand. "Do sit down, we've already ordered."

Atalanta studied the reporter. She had indeed seen him at the party last night. But not innocently mingling with guests or looking around the beautiful home of the great Cosimo Lanetti. No. Outside, in the dark, kissing Catharina.

Her throat tightened. Had Catharina known that the man she was flirting with was a reporter? Or had he deceived her to learn more about her family? Had he used her to get into the party and …

"You wrote that well-informed article about the murder," she said to Tony. "I was surprised it was in the paper this morning. You must have worked all night to finish it."

"People forget that the paper also needs to be printed. I had to hand in my report before two o'clock. It lacked finesse in my opinion, but I'm pleased you liked it." Again he flashed her his winning smile.

"This must be great for your career," Atalanta continued, "to be present, however coincidentally, when an important man was murdered."

"The most important man in this region." Tony nodded. "You're right. My editor called it serendipity."

"So you didn't tell him you used Catharina to get into the party?" Atalanta kept her tone friendly but her eyes were on the reporter with a steadfast intensity. "That you lied to her, giving her a false name, so she would trust you and bring you into the house you wanted to see?"

"I didn't give her a false name." Tony's eyes flashed. "She didn't know me. She had spent a lot of time in Turin, she told me. She never read the local newspaper here. And if she had, I doubt she'd have looked closely at the byline."

"The point is," Atalanta continued, still in a conversational tone, "that you didn't mention being a reporter. And she would never have asked you to come if you had."

"I wonder if that's true." Tony leaned back, crossing

his legs. "She couldn't stand her father. She would have liked to see him rolled in the mud."

"So you actually convinced yourself it was fine to kiss her because your piece about the Lanetti family wouldn't shock her as she didn't like them anyway? But you forgot that she came here to ask her father for an investment in her chocolate business and she'd never get it if he found out she had leaked to the press."

"How would he find out? He would see a name in the paper and not know it was me." Tony flashed a smile again. Instead of charming, Atalanta now found it predatory. She said, "Let me get this straight. You came to the party to …"

"Know more about the Lanettis. They're influential. Important. Rich. The sort of people readers love to learn more about. I was assigned to the social column …" Tony rolled his eyes. "Which is really not where I belong. But I thought if I gave them an amazing piece about the Lanettis, I could move up the ladder."

"And it worked out." Atalanta leaned towards him. "You didn't get the column on page seventeen but the front page. With a murder story."

"Yes, well, it's not like I killed anyone for it." Tony uttered a forced laugh. "Lanetti died while I was there. I wrote about it. That's all."

"And it didn't bother you at all that you had to cast

Catharina as the killer?" Raoul asked. His voice was chilly.

"I only wrote about the facts of the case. I can't help it that she never liked her father. She told me that her mother died when she was young and she blamed her father for it." He shrugged. "I guess that gives her motive."

The girl brought their coffee and cakes and Tony ordered a glass of limoncello. "You should try it too," he enthused. "It's homebrewed here and delicious."

"So we can toast to your success as a crime reporter?" Raoul asked. "I wonder how far you would go to further your career. You were at the house. You could have gone into Lanetti's study to—"

"Wait a moment. Are you now trying to hang the murder on me? What is this? Why did you invite me in the first place?"

"To have a little chat about your relationship with Catharina," Raoul said. "I'm a close friend of hers and I wouldn't like to see her hurt. If you don't have honourable intentions, you'd better—"

"Honourable intentions? Man, we shared a drunken kiss at a party." Tony sounded indignant. "It didn't mean anything. Catharina feels the same way. She flirts with men wherever she goes. I even saw her standing in a corner whispering with that cousin of hers, Danielo. The one who's addicted to pigeon racing."

"Pigeon racing?" Atalanta echoed, recalling what Raoul had told her about the popular pastime.

"Yes, he bets on pigeons and gambles away bucketloads of money. He keeps telling his creditors he will strike it rich soon but they're beginning to lose their patience. If he doesn't pay those debts, they'll likely come one day and break his arm. As an example to others as well."

Atalanta again saw the scene by the road, the item exchanged. The man had initially shaken his head because he wanted money, of course, not whatever Danielo had to sell. Eventually he had accepted it, but if Tony was right about the number of debts, one item wouldn't cover them. There had to be a lot of pressure on Danielo to find a way into more money, soon. Was that his motive for murdering Cosimo?

She looked at Raoul to see if he had also caught on but he was just staring at Tony with a dark look. He had told her before their arrival here that she was supposed to be Catharina's friend and he the driver on the Tuscan trip, but now he had said he and Catharina were close friends …

Was that merely to put fear into Tony and get him to

confess what he had been up to with Catharina and at the Lanetti home?

"They all have skeletons in the closet," Tony said. "Giovanni has a few jealous husbands on his back and one pregnant woman who is divorcing her husband to be with him. Not that he will marry her. He's waiting for a prize catch. Someone who can take him away from dependence on Papa." Tony recrossed his legs. "Cosimo Lanetti made sure he controlled everything. I even heard from people I interviewed that, after his son Thomasso was abducted, he never let his wife, Melina, go out alone. He had her watched day and night. She couldn't do anything. Only after the other two boys were born and growing up did he relax a little. Imagine how they must have been raised. To be their father's puppets. They want to break free. I can easily see one of them murdering him. Perhaps the lot of them were in agreement on it."

"But it is Catharina who is in jail now."

Tony shook his head. "Catharina was mad to give him that goblet. I told her not to."

"You knew she was going to do it?"

"Yes. I pointed the goblet out to her in an antique shop in Turin. I had to woo her a little to get the birthday party invitation, you understand. I told her by way of a joke it was a perfect birthday present for her father. I had no idea she'd actually buy it and bring it and give it to him with dozens of people seeing it. Any of them could have seen the chance to slip in poison and be done with the old bastard."

"Why did you really befriend Catharina?" Atalanta asked. "Do you have a grudge against Cosimo Lanetti?"

"Ha, the next question will be: did you kill him?" Tony accepted the limoncello from the serving girl and raised his glass. "To a fine afternoon in Tuscany."

Raoul said, "We'll look into you. We can dig just as well as any second-rate reporter."

Tony laughed. "You're welcome to. But you will find nothing on me. I'm not guilty of anything but having a bit of healthy ambition. I want to move up in life and the Lanettis provide perfect fodder for stories the readers eat up." He sipped his limoncello and cast Raoul a pitying look. "You're also feeling sorry for Catharina. It's the sad story of her murdered mother and how she was always the outcast when her father remarried and the boys were born ... She plays it well. But she's really a very smart woman who doesn't like her family at all and wouldn't hesitate to stick a knife in their backs."

"If she is so smart, then why not kill her father in a way that wouldn't immediately lead back to her?"

"She wanted it to look like a natural death. If she had removed the goblet, it would have worked."

"But she didn't have the opportunity because you

had lured her away to kiss her." Atalanta's mind raced to understand what it meant. Had Tony planned the murder and kissed Catharina to make it look later as if she had been distracted from retrieving the goblet? But why would he kill Cosimo Lanetti? Merely to have something to write about?

Raoul was right. They did have to dig into this man's past. Look for any connection that would provide a motive for murder.

Tony emptied his glass. "I would have loved to hear more about your racing. But I guess you won't tell me a thing, huh? This whole trip out here was a waste of time. I should send you a bill for my time."

"You have a lot of nerve for someone who wormed his way into a woman's confidence with lies." Raoul's eyes flashed.

"Catharina wasn't exactly honest with me either. Oh, she told me the sob story of her troubled past, but she forgot to tell me that she has an inheritance from her deceased mother. Money that was set aside for her when her mother died. I looked into the provisions via a lawyer friend of mine who owed me a favour. Catharina is a rich woman. She doesn't have to beg her father for a start into the chocolate business." Tony put his glass on the table and rose. "That makes you wonder, doesn't it?

Why she came to his birthday party at all." He touched an invisible hat in mock farewell and walked off.

Atalanta said, "He's an insufferable man, but his last point does deserve consideration. Catharina made it very clear to us on the train that she needed her father's financial support. Why would she lie about that?"

"Perhaps Tony is lying?" Raoul gestured at her. "He could be telling all kinds of lies to blacken Catharina's name and have her convicted for the murder he committed."

"If we want to prove that, we'll need a good motive." Atalanta tilted her head. "Do you have any connections that can dig into him? I'll call Renard to see how far his long arm reaches."

"Do that. There's a phone in the inn. And order another coffee for me. I could barely taste the first one because I was so angry at that cad."

"I know how you feel. But we mustn't let ourselves be distracted by the idea that he could have done it, not while we still have so many other things to look into. I'll go and place the call."

Chapter Fourteen

Renard was happy to hear from her. He took notes of everything she wanted to know and promised to find the information as quickly as he could. "Can I call you at the Lanetti residence?"

"Certainly. I'm there under my own name. You can safely say you're my butler and you need to speak to me about my social calendar or something. I hope you can help us because we are swimming in suspects."

"This was not how your holiday was supposed to turn out." Renard sounded indignant. "But then again, it is like your grandfather used to say: 'Trouble has a way of finding me.'"

"He said that? So he also had these cases sprung upon him?"

"Frequently. I thought that perhaps the letter I put in

your suitcase would tell you more about that. As it was meant to be read on holiday."

"Oh yes, the letter about his experience on the Orient Express. I never did finish reading it. I was so busy. I'll do so soon. I promise. *Merci* and *au revoir*." She disconnected.

The girl who had served them stood looking at her. Atalanta was glad that the use of rapid French ensured that the girl hadn't understood much. But of course she had heard the mention of certain names.

The girl said, "Is it true that Cosimo Lanetti is dead?"

"It's true," Atalanta confirmed quietly.

The girl nodded. There was a brief look of relief on her face.

"Did you know him?" Atalanta asked.

"Not well. He came here every now and then for a drink." The girl took a step back, her back growing rigid.

"Was he unkind to you?" Atalanta asked.

"No." The one word conveyed enough to make Atalanta understand. Cosimo had been friendly. Too friendly. A man close to sixty flirting with a girl no older than sixteen. She was young enough to be his granddaughter.

"He'll come here no more. You needn't worry. And we would like two more coffees. They're excellent."

The girl nodded with a hint of a smile and

disappeared into the kitchen area. Atalanta went back outside. She told Raoul about the conversation.

Raoul said, "Cosimo grew up in a time where it was common for wealthy men to cast their eye on pretty servant girls. They were in a position where they couldn't complain."

"I wonder ..." Atalanta sat down and stretched out her legs. "Catharina's friend died during a stay at the house, remember? Fell out of her bedroom window. People wondered why she had tried to climb out of it."

"You think it's because Cosimo made advances on her?" Raoul's eyes darkened. "That is a very nasty thought."

"But one we can't disregard. Catharina blamed him for her mother's death. Perhaps also for the death of her friend. That gives her motive for the murder."

"We've been over that. We need information to exonerate her."

"But we're not getting much. If Renard confirms she had money of her own, her reason for visiting her father also falls through." Atalanta sighed. "What have we got ourselves into? Perhaps she is guilty."

The girl brought two more coffees and they enjoyed the rich aroma and taste in silence. Atalanta was aware of the beautiful surroundings with the golden late afternoon light kissing the land. But her heart wasn't in it. Couldn't be in it as she pondered the strange events that had unfolded ever since they had met Catharina Lanetti on the train.

Raoul put down his cup. "I'll make a few calls to find out more about Danielo's alleged addiction to pigeon racing. Friends of mine place a bet now and then so they should have inside information. I'll also ring the police station to ask how Catharina is doing and to inform her that her father did make her heir."

"No, don't tell them that. I want to tell her myself. Ask if we can visit her."

"Why would you want to tell her yourself?" Raoul eyed her. "To see a guilty look on her face? Or do you want to reveal that the man she kissed so passionately was only a reporter after a story? That will crush her spirit. And she needs to keep her chin up to get through this ordeal."

"I know that. But we need to put her on her guard. Tony may contact her and if she doesn't know who he really is, she might let things slip that will end up in the papers."

"I'll tell the police not to let that man or any other reporter near her. I'll tell them not to say to her that someone from the press is preying on her. Then we can tell her more when we go and see her." Raoul walked away two paces and then said, "But we should be careful what we share."

Atalanta watched his back as he walked off. Why was he so adamant in protecting Catharina? Was there something between them? But no, she shouldn't let suspicion get the better of her. She needed Raoul's help to sort all of this out. Tony had made an interesting observation about Catharina whispering with Danielo. What about? Who sided with whom in the family?

When they came back to the house, the butler was in the hallway talking excitedly to the housekeeper. They didn't even look up when Atalanta and Raoul passed. Raoul halted and asked, "Excuse me, I hear you're talking about Signor Foselli. Is he still here?"

"No, signor." The butler's left eye twitched nervously. "He went away with what he found in the safe."

"In the safe?" Atalanta echoed. The IOUs came to mind. Had the blond doctor not checked thoroughly, under the strain of his clandestine entry? Did Foselli now hold some explosive information that would point at other possible suspects for the murder? Could it clear Catharina?

"It was shocking," the butler said. "It was the ring."

"What ring?" Raoul asked.

"The ring Signora Lanetti wore when she was murdered by the robbers. It was taken off her body and never found again. The robbers were hanged but the ring wasn't recovered among their loot. Now it has been found in the safe. The master's safe."

Atalanta's heart skipped a beat. If Cosimo had kept his dead wife's ring in the safe, it could mean but one thing. He had killed her and made it look like a robbery.

Raoul said, "Is it the exact same ring?"

"Yes, Signor Foselli knew it well. He came here often when she was still alive. He took it along and now he intends to determine whether there are fingerprints on it."

Raoul looked at Atalanta. "Did Foselli say anything about the murder case? His evidence against Signorina Catharina?"

"No, signor."

"*Grazie.*" Raoul ushered Atalanta up the stairs and into her bedroom, closing the door behind them. "Did you hear what he said? The ring worn by the first wife on the day she was murdered was actually here in the safe all these years. That will be devastating news for Catharina. It proves that her father murdered her mother."

"And if she suspected it, she had a huge motive to kill him."

Raoul paced the room. "Foselli took it to look for fingerprints. If he finds Cosimo's prints on it, the case is shut. Cosimo killed his first wife in order to marry someone else who could bring him new financial gain. That Melina was pregnant with another man's baby didn't matter to him as he hadn't married her for love anyway. He wanted her assets. How cold-hearted can one man be?"

Atalanta took her coded notes from her luggage and started to add information about the parties. The picture they were uncovering of Cosimo Lanetti was that of a ruthless man who had not hesitated to harm even the people closest to him. He must have been utterly hated. The obvious murder victim.

Who had decided they had had enough?

Melina. The second wife who had been forced to live in the house decorated by the first wife. Who was always reminded she was second choice, in spite of her money. Her eldest son abducted. Or removed by the half-sister who hated him?

Giovanni. The son who wanted to get away but couldn't. Who'd had to endure his father's remarks about his womanizing, knowing his father was the same. Or worse?

Lorenzo, who was eaten by frustration that he was the more intelligent but despised by his father for his physical weakness. Was he in love with Quinta. but she had flirted with Cosimo? Had Lorenzo killed his father to do away with a rival?

Danielo, the underestimated and underpaid worker. Pushed by his wife to be more ambitious. Had he learned from her how to make medication? Had he been forced to act by his debts from the pigeon racing?

"How much did your friend say Danielo owes?" she asked Raoul, who stood at the window.

"A hundred thousand lire, at the least."

"How can he ever repay that?"

Shaking her head, Atalanta added more notes about Quinta and also wrote about the ring that had been found in the safe.

Suddenly she looked up. "The intruder, the doctor from last night, he searched the safe. He must know if there was a ring in there."

"Why would you want to verify that? Do you doubt Foselli found it there?"

"Well, he could have wanted to strengthen the case against Catharina. He may have brought in a ring similar to the one Mrs Lanetti wore and put it in the safe, then pretended to find it. The ring was lost thirty years ago. Who could recall in detail what it looked like?"

"Hmmm. Does he *need* to strengthen the case?"

"I don't know. But we can always ask our intruder. He didn't leave us contact details for nothing."

Raoul stepped away from the window. "You're right. I'll look into it. I feel too restless to sit around here. I'll report back later." He left the room.

Atalanta studied her notes with a sigh. There was so much to go on and still nothing materialized into a stable theory. She could speculate but that wouldn't convince Foselli. Why had he wanted to test the ring for fingerprints? He had Cosimo's dead body at the station. Could he put the dead man's prints on the ring? To make sure he got Catharina convicted. But why would he want to do that?

He had been a close friend of the family during the time the first wife had been murdered and also when Thomasso had been abducted. Had he later suspected that Catharina had taken her brother away? Had it stung him that a little girl had committed a crime he had been unable to solve? Had he been on a quest to implicate her for something? Had the murder given him the ideal opportunity?

Could the wily retired police chief even be Cosimo's killer? Framing Catharina by placing the goblet by the dead man's side? With his experience, he would know everything about crime scenes and evidence. And now that he was in charge of the investigation, he could steer everything in the desired direction.

Atalanta folded her notes and hid them again. Her palms were clammy and she swallowed with difficulty. If she was about to take on a retired chief of police, accusing him of murder and of letting an innocent woman take the blame for the crime he had committed, she had to make sure she had real evidence against him. Else she'd get into deep trouble and destroy her reputation and Raoul's.

Chapter Fifteen

The next morning they set out for the police station to speak with Catharina. Raoul said, "I can't fit all of it together. The intruder told me that he touched everything in the safe in his search for the IOU. He was thorough because he thought Cosimo might have folded the paper and put it in some container or other. He is certain that there was no ring. So it seems you were right in assuming Foselli planted it there to strengthen his case against Catharina. But why would he?"

"I'm still working on that," Atalanta said. It seemed better not to reveal she suspected Foselli of Cosimo's murder. Raoul would immediately see the potential dangers of such a line of reasoning and might try to persuade her not to pursue it. She would be a little disappointed in him if he did. Because a good detective followed up on every clue, even the ones that were inconvenient or downright risky.

Raoul parked the car in the village square. The police station was housed in the same building as the community hall. Having entered through a large wrought-iron gate they came into a small courtyard with several doors opening out on to it.

Raoul pointed to their left. "That is it, I suppose. I see a barred window there."

Atalanta gasped at the idea that Catharina was kept prisoner behind that window. They entered a hallway that had a tapestry of a battle scene hung on the right wall. There were wooden chairs with red pillows for visitors to sit and wait until they were seen. Very quickly a policeman appeared and spoke to Raoul. Atalanta could follow little of the very fast conversation, which was accompanied by many hand gestures.

Raoul said to her, "Catharina isn't here. It seems that Foselli is holding her at his house."

Atalanta's stomach clenched. Why had he decided to do that? Did he hate Catharina so much that he contemplated harming her? Could he make up a tale about an escape attempt in which she would be killed?

"That seems very unusual. He's no longer the chief. Why would he have so much power?"

"That's the way things are in these small

communities." Raoul shrugged. "We can do nothing but drive out to his house hoping he will let us see Catharina."

Atalanta nodded, even though she hardly wanted to go to Foselli's house. Now that she suspected the retired chief of involvement in the murder, she had the eerie feeling he would be able to read her suspicions in her expression. She shouldn't make him aware of any doubts about his integrity. Not until she had a much stronger case against him.

"Are you certain we need to speak to her?" she asked when they returned to the car. "I mean, we could also pursue other angles."

"We need to know how much Tony told her about his background as a reporter. What exactly he said to her about the poison cup. I have a theory that he pointed it out to her on purpose, hoping she'd buy it for her father and he could use it to poison him and let Catharina take the blame."

"Why?"

"I'm still working on that. Did Cosimo ever hurt his interests or did their paths cross in the past? There must be a reason why our friend Tony is so eager to throw dirt at the Lanetti family. What he told us proves he has dug deep into their past and business transactions. It must be more than just a story to him."

Atalanta had to agree that the journalist had struck her as a clever man with a forced careless attitude. What was he really up to?

Raoul backed the car up, waiting a moment while a cart passed with large wooden barrels on it. "Could be *novello*, the new wine," he said. "I wish we weren't knee deep in this murder case and could enjoy more of the land."

"I'm sure we'll have time for that after we have completed the case."

"You make it sound like it will be completed soon." Raoul glanced at her. "Have you got a crucial lead?"

"I'm working on a few theories. But I need more information to put everything together." Her heart skipped a beat again at the idea of taking on Foselli. It was a recipe for disaster. If only she hadn't accepted Catharina's invitation … But it was too late for such regrets now.

They drove down a winding road with a cypress here and there while the vineyards rolled away left and right. A man with a large hat pulled over his eyes was checking the grapes. "They regularly see if they are sweet enough for harvesting," Raoul explained. "The wine will have a certain taste depending on the sugars in the grape. I'm no expert on it but I find it a fascinating process. You?"

"Certainly." Atalanta let her gaze wander past the vineyard to the fields beside it. "Oh, I see a deer."

"Yes, there are a lot in the countryside. You can see them especially at dawn or dusk. We should take an evening stroll tonight and try to find some wildlife."

"That would be lovely. My head is too full of thoughts."

"And worries?" he asked. "I can sense something is weighing on your mind. More than the case itself. You enjoy the intellectual exercise of that."

He was right. It surprised her that he knew her so well. But perhaps it was logical as they had worked together on two intense cases. Santorini had been especially challenging, even stretching their tentative friendship to the breaking point. She wanted to avoid the same complications here.

"Can't you tell me?" he asked, and added after a moment's silence, "You're not still thinking about that louse Lorenzo's lies that I went into Catharina's compartment at night? I assure you there is nothing whatsoever between us. Besides, you saw her kissing that reporter."

"I don't know. I mean, I do believe you when you say there's nothing between the two of you. But I don't know what to make of Catharina's relationship with Tony. He said he wooed her in Turin to get her to take him to her father's birthday party. That suggests they spent time together before they came here. Yet he dismissed their kiss as something insignificant, claiming they were both drunk. But how does Catharina feel about it? Does she have feelings for him? Or did she only want a little distraction from the difficult choices she faces now that she has come back home?"

"Well, Tony will certainly not be on her mind much at the moment. She's in deep water and must worry every waking minute how she can get out of this mess. Look, that is Foselli's house in the distance."

He pointed out a beautiful apricot-coloured house on a hill with vineyards on the slopes. "Is he also a winemaker?" Atalanta asked.

"I don't know. Perhaps the vineyards are just for show?" Raoul grimaced. "Foselli struck me as a man who likes to impress others."

They drove down a road with trimmed hedges on each side and passed a fountain spraying water high in the air. "See?" Raoul asked. "Such a thing is not authentic to this land. He put it here to give the place a touch of Rome."

"It must have cost a lot too." Atalanta frowned. "Would a chief of police make that much money?"

"I have no idea, but he's probably from an influential

family. That house and everything with it must be his estate, a legacy passed down from father to son."

"Still the upkeep of such a property costs a lot of money. He must have income," Atalanta speculated.

Raoul parked the car beside the house. As they got out, the sound of hoofbeats resounded and a woman of about thirty rode a majestic white horse in their direction. A stable boy ran to catch the bridle and she dismounted looking at them with a welcoming smile. "*Buongiorno.* Can I help you?"

"I'm Raoul Lemont. This is Miss Atalanta Ashford. We're staying with the Lanettis. We would like to see Catharina Lanetti. We heard she was here?"

"Oh, yes. My father brought her yesterday. He didn't tell me what it was all about. 'Police business,' he said."

"But you must know that Cosimo Lanetti was murdered." Raoul looked at her sharply. "It was all over the newspapers."

"I never read newspapers. It doesn't interest me." The woman brushed the horse across the neck. "You can take him away now, Gianni. Cool him down properly before you water and feed him. I pushed him rather hard."

With a fond smile she watched the horse walk away, then turned to her guests again. "I'll show you in and to Catharina's room. We had such fun together last night."

"Fun?" Raoul echoed. He threw Atalanta a bewildered look.

"Yes. We talked about all the places she has been and things she has done. I made *rustici* for the occasion."

Atalanta asked, "What are *rustici*?"

"Uh, I don't know what you would call them in English."

"Sausage rolls," Raoul said. He sounded half amused, half cynical. Atalanta could understand that he didn't quite follow how someone accused of murdering her own father could be sitting down with the daughter of the retired police chief prosecuting her and eating sausage rolls while discussing her adventures abroad.

"I still have two left if you'd like to try? Do follow me." She strode ahead of them into the house. In the hallway, which was decorated with lots of marble and stuccoed flower vases, she clapped her hands together and halted so abruptly that Atalanta, walking behind her, collided with her. "I'm so rude. I haven't even told you my name. Felicia." She broke into stride again, waving her arm. "This way. Up the stairs."

They climbed what seemed like endless steps until they came to the door of a room in what had to be the highest point of the house. Atalanta had to admit it was a good place to put a prisoner as Catharina wouldn't risk climbing out of the window and breaking her neck.

Felicia knocked on the door and then opened it. Catharina sat in a chair at a low table. There was a board on it with chess pieces. She was staring hard at it but looked up at their arrival. Her expression lit when she saw Atalanta. Or was it the sight of Raoul behind her?

She rose and approached them, wringing her hands in a dramatic gesture. "Good that you're here. I heard my case looks quite desperate. That everything points to my guilt. But how could it? I haven't done anything."

Felicia said, "I'll go and get refreshments." She left the room, humming.

"Isn't it a bit odd," Atalanta said, "that Foselli put you up here?"

"Better here than in a damp cell. He offered it and I agreed right away. I hoped it meant he wasn't fully convinced I did it." Catharina sank back in the chair. An embroidered pillow slipped through the open armrest and fell to the floor. She didn't notice, gesturing wildly with her hands. "I haven't killed my father. I didn't put poison in the goblet. There must have been some inside it when I bought it. I never checked. I thought it was a copy, not the real deal. I only wanted to give Papa a gift he would enjoy."

"Tell me about how you found the gift." Raoul sat down opposite her. "Did you see an advertisement in the paper or …"

"No, it was mentioned to me by a friend. He had seen the goblet in an antique shop's window."

"A friend? Could it be he pointed it out on purpose? Was he also at the party?"

"As a matter of fact he was, yes. But …" Catharina's tense features relaxed in a smile. "He would do nothing to hurt me. You can be certain of that."

"Can we?" Raoul leaned back and crossed his arms over his chest. "We're talking about Antonio Gati, aren't we?"

"Yes. He's madly in love with me." Catharina played with a thread on the hem of her skirt.

"And how do you feel about him?" Atalanta asked.

"I like him. I can't say more yet. I haven't known him that long and besides, I'm far too independent to fall head over heels into a man's arms."

"That's not the impression I got when I saw you kissing him at the party," Raoul said. "That looked pretty much head-over-heels to me."

"Are you jealous?" Catharina batted her lashes at him. "I can tell you I'm not engaged to him or anything. We're just having fun together."

"I see." Raoul waited a few moments.

Atalanta's mouth was dry; she suspected that he was going to tell Catharina the terrible truth now.

Raoul said, "Do you have any idea what he does for a living?"

"No, he didn't really tell me and I wasn't about to ask. It might look as if I was after his money and I'm not. I have plenty of my own."

"Really? I thought your father had cut you off."

"I make my own money with my travelling. People sponsor me."

"People like Foselli," Atalanta said. "Is that why he was kind enough to put you up here?"

"I don't know. He only paid for a trip once, years ago. It's not like he funds my every move." Catharina sounded defensive. "And stop interrogating me."

"We're only wondering how well you know Signor Gati." Raoul pursed his lips. "He might be taking advantage of you."

"Because I am Cosimo Lanetti's daughter? I'll have you know it has nothing to do with it. Tony told me that I could be a garbage collector's daughter for all he cared. He loves me."

"Oh, and that's why he wrote a piece in the newspaper about the party, the murder and your part in it?" Raoul held her gaze. "He is a reporter, Catharina. He's digging up all kinds of dirt about your family. Your half-brothers, Danielo. He plans to burn you all down publicly. I don't know exactly why yet, but it's not merely for a story. I fear he has a vendetta against your family and he used you to get to them. To get inside the house. Perhaps even murder your father."

"No. You're lying." Catharina was deadly pale. "You're lying. Lying!" Her voice rose into a high-pitched scream.

Felicia entered with a tray in her hands. She cried, "What's wrong?" She put the tray on a table close to the door and rushed to Catharina, throwing an arm around her shoulders. "Calm down." Staring at Raoul and Atalanta with flashing eyes, she demanded, "What have you said to her? Why are you making her all upset?"

Catharina said, "It's not true."

"Yes, it is," Raoul said. "I can show you the newspaper article." He reached into his pocket.

"No, don't." Catharina backed away from him. "Don't break it. Please don't. Finally someone loved me for me and now ..." She burst into tears.

"Hush now." Felicia threw her arms around her and pulled her close. She patted her back and brushed her hair. "It's not that bad. I promise."

Raoul looked at Atalanta and hitched a brow. It was indeed odd that these two women seemed so close if they had only just met when Foselli brought Catharina here for safekeeping. Or ... had they been friends in the past?

After all, Felicia looked to be of Catharina's age and Foselli had been a family friend.

Catharina sobbed with long, ragged intakes of breath. Felicia spoke in soft soothing tones, meanwhile glowering at Raoul. He remained seated with his arms crossed, like an immovable force.

After a while he spoke. "I'm not here to ruin Catharina's dream of being loved. I'm here to warn her against this person who has inserted himself into her life with the express purpose of ruining her family. It could be because of him that Catharina is accused of murder. She must never see him or speak to him again."

"You bet I will see him." Catharina tore herself free from Felicia's grasp and stood. Her face was blotchy and her hair was wild. She stared at Raoul. "I *will* see him and demand he tell me what he did and why. Why, why, why." Her voice screeched.

Felicia touched her arm. "There's no point, Catharina. He won't tell you. You can't make people tell you the truth. They keep it close to them like a precious treasure you're not allowed to ever see." She sounded a bit sad. "You can't claim any right to hear it."

Catharina stamped her foot. "I do have a right. I let him close to me, I let him love me. I ... was vulnerable and he abused me." Tears streamed down her face. "I hate him. I hate him. I could just ..." Her hands clenched into fists.

"You will not see him ever again." Raoul's voice carried a hint of steel. "He'll only laugh at your anger and pain. He's a ruthless man without any sense of regret. You'll only hurt yourself more if you seek confrontation."

"I must hear from him why he did it, or else I'll never be able to go on."

"Catharina." Atalanta walked over and leaned over the devastated woman. "You lost your mother and you were able to go on. Your half-brother was abducted and you were able to go on. You were cast out of the family and had to find your own path in life and you did it. You're a strong woman. You can conquer this too. Believe me."

Catharina looked her in the eye. Her lips wobbled. "A strong woman? Ha!" Her eyes filled with new tears. "I keep dreaming about my mother. About the afternoon she took off her wedding ring and showed it to me. She said it was proof of her bond to my father and that I too was part of that bond. That she would prove it to me by etching a little C into the ring. She did it in front of my eyes. She said she'd always wear that ring, with the first letter of my name in it, as a token of her love for me."

This bittersweet memory could be hugely important

for the case, Atalanta realized with a shock. They had assumed there was no way to prove that the wedding ring Foselli had allegedly found in Cosimo's safe belonged to Catharina's mother, but if a letter C was found to be scratched into it ... and if there was *no* C on it, it was the wrong ring. If Foselli hadn't known that the real wedding ring bore such an identifying mark, he might have made a crucial mistake when building his supposed evidence against Catharina. By pulling at such a tiny thread they might make his entire case unravel.

Catharina continued. "But she was killed and the ring was taken. I had nothing left. Nothing."

She gasped for breath. "When I met Tony, I ached for him to tell me that he loved me. I ached to fall into his arms and feel safe. Safe at last. I would have a place to turn to somewhere in the world when things got hard. And now, all lies." She clenched her fists again. "Lies because of the Lanetti name. That accursed name. I wish I had never got it. I wish I could get rid of it. Wash it off."

"I'm sorry" – Raoul's voice was low now and compassionate – "if I hurt you more by springing it on you like this. But we also learned of it from the paper and ... we were so angry because of you. We only want to protect you. Help you now that you're accused of murder. You must tell us how the goblet came to you, what part Gati played in this. Did he put the goblet in your hands on purpose? Can he be your father's killer?"

"I don't know." Catharina sank into the chair again and bowed her head in her hands. "I don't know."

"You must tell us everything ..." Atalanta tried.

But Catharina said, "I already told you. Tony said it was at an antique shop and would make a great gift. He sounded as if he was joking. I thought it might actually work to get me in my father's good graces again and bought it. I didn't check the poison compartment. I gave it to my father and later that night he died. That's all I know."

"Had you been in the study during the party? Lorenzo said everyone had to come there during the night."

"Not me. I didn't go in there." Catharina's voice was muffled by her hands.

"Did you have an argument with him?"

"Yes. He told me that he wouldn't fund my chocolate business. He said it quite brusquely. That's how you'd know it was final with him. I was mad and went outside. Tony came and we ..." She fell silent.

Raoul said, "Did you see anything meaningful? Who went to Cosimo? Lorenzo? Giovanni?"

"I didn't see much. I was too busy with my own affairs. I drank quite a lot." Catharina pulled her hands away and sank back with a sigh. "I won't get off, right? I'm headed for the noose."

"Not so fast," Raoul said as he leaned forward, elbows on knees. "Why were you whispering with Danielo?"

"He asked me for money. He was in trouble again because of his pigeon racing. I think it's a dumb sport. I mean, pigeons are pretty intelligent creatures – they can navigate home using the stars or something – but I wouldn't lay down ten lire on one, let alone the thousands he pumps into it. Thousands he doesn't own. I told him I had nothing either and that was it."

"Did he say anything revealing?" Atalanta asked. "Think back carefully."

Catharina stared at the ceiling for a few minutes. "Nothing I can think of. Just the usual about Quinta murdering him if she found out how much debt he had. That he needn't ask my father as he would just laugh at him. That he had already asked Giovanni, who told him no as well."

"Had he asked Lorenzo?" Raoul queried.

"He didn't say, but it's unlikely he would have tried. Lorenzo has always been terribly tight-fisted. Even as children, we knew he'd never treat us to anything. He never even bought us gifts on our birthdays. He would always come with something like flowers from the garden, or a thing he had made with his hands. Nothing that cost him a single lira."

Felicia said, "You must try the *rustici*. They are delicious. And I will pour the coffee, yes?" She busied herself by the tray.

Catharina looked at her in annoyance, then smiled as if she was reminded of the other's good intentions. "You mustn't blame Felicia," she said. "She doesn't believe I killed my father, so nothing bad will come of it. It's all a misunderstanding, and it will soon be resolved."

"Do you think so because you have so much faith in your father's abilities?" Atalanta asked. "Do you think he can find proof of Catharina's innocence?"

"I think so, yes," Felicia said as she set out the cups and saucers . "He's always been successful in his cases."

"He didn't manage to solve Thomasso's abduction," Raoul observed quietly.

Atalanta added, "Your father was also the police chief when Catharina's mother was murdered, wasn't he?"

"Yes. And he caught the gang who did it," Felicia snapped, the allusions to her father's failures had clearly made her defensive. "They terrorized the countryside and stole from everyone. They were all tried and hanged."

"But they denied having killed Signora Lanetti," Raoul pointed out.

Felicia scoffed. "Who would take the word of liars and thieves? Of course they denied it. They hoped for a reduced sentence." She tried to put a cup of coffee into Catharina's hand. "You must drink something. Please."

Catharina accepted with a sigh and sipped.

Atalanta tried one of the *rustici*. "It's very nice. The meat is spicy and the pastry nice and buttery."

"We make it with butter from our own cows. You can't see them around the house. They graze down the hill. My father owns all the land around here for acres and acres. He lets farmers work it and collects rent and payment in milk and eggs."

"Your father is a rich and powerful man," Raoul observed.

"It has always been common in these parts that someone well-to-do is chosen as chief of police," Felicia said. "It prevents criminals from being able to bribe him. He has enough money to live well so why would he be susceptible to payments? A good system."

Catharina took another sip of coffee and Raoul used the moment of relative quiet to tell Catharina about the contents of the will.

With a weary smile she looked at Raoul. "So I do get part of the vineyard. But what good is it to me as long as I am under suspicion? Can you do something to shift the blame?"

Felicia was pouring more coffee for Raoul, and Atalanta had the impression her hand was unsteady for a moment. Was the idea that Catharina might be cleared unwelcome to her? But her kindness to her implied she genuinely liked her.

Raoul said, "We're compiling information about everyone involved. There are certainly motives there."

"But" – Atalanta cut across him before he could reveal anything significant – "we can't really share much about it yet. We only came to warn you against Antonio Gati and ask if you had any more for us about the night of the murder."

Raoul looked at her with a slightly raised brow as if to question why she hadn't let him finish. Atalanta moved her head a tad in Felicia's direction. He had to understand that they couldn't possibly discuss the case with the main suspect in front of the daughter of the man handling it.

Raoul said, "Yes, can you tell us anything useful? You must have thought about the night of the murder."

"I did, I tried to go over every little detail. But the truth is that I drank so much that I don't remember everything."

Raoul let out his breath in a hiss. "That's not good, Catharina."

Catharina put her cup down with a bang and jumped

to her feet. "Then what do you want me to do? Tell lies about things I supposedly know? I was back home after years, it was tense, I was worried, Papa rubbed me the wrong way by immediately denying me any money. I drank too much and I can't remember what happened. If you don't understand then you've probably never felt lousy in your life. Lucky you." She turned her back on them and stared out of the window.

Raoul rose and went over to her. He gently put his hand on her arm. "I do know what it's like to be tense, disappointed, and down on your luck. I also know what it's like to have a demanding father for whom you can never do anything right. But you asked us to help you and for us to succeed you must be the first one to open up completely. Tell us all you know. You do know more than you let on now."

"I don't." Catharina turned and eyed him, her face pale. "Honestly I don't. The night is a haze in my mind. I keep seeing all those masked waiters, hearing the music playing in exaggerated false notes in my ears. Nothing was real about that night. And now you have told me Tony's kiss was a lie too, that he was just after a sensational story about my family. It's always my family who ruin it for me." She pressed her hands to her face. "I should never have come back home. It could only end in disaster. Now I've been arrested and ..." She looked up. "I'm going to die, right?"

Raoul caught her shoulders and shook her. "Stop being so dramatic. Of course you're not going to die. You have to fight. Show some spirit. You have travelled the world; you have conquered many dangers."

"But I can't now." Catharina broke into tears again. "I can't."

Raoul let go of her and Felicia rushed over. "You're a monster," she snarled at him. "Can't you see she is devastated? You're forcing her to relive a night she wants to forget."

Atalanta watched the exchange with a frown. What was Felicia's role in all of this? The sympathetic friend? The daughter of the man gathering evidence against Catharina, strategically placed to see if she would confide in her and incriminate herself?

Raoul walked back to Atalanta. "We had better go. There's nothing for us to do here."

He left the room.

Atalanta said to Catharina, "We'll do everything in our power to help you. Please believe me." Then she ran after Raoul. He was already halfway down the stairs. Catching up with him, gasping for breath, Atalanta said, "Why did you handle her so roughly?"

"Did I? She should help us. She knows more than she

lets on. She is part of that odd family. And what does she do? Play the weeping willow. I can't understand her." He raced down the stairs and stalked to the front door. He pulled it open and came face to face with Foselli.

His huge form filled the door frame. "What are you doing here?" he asked with a mix of surprise and immediate suspicion.

"We came to see Catharina." Atalanta gave him a forced friendly smile. "You have a charming daughter, by the way."

"Felicia?" Foselli's features softened. "She is the light of my life. My wife died five years ago. Felicia runs my household so very efficiently. I don't know what I would do without her."

"She's also a great support to Catharina." Atalanta took a deep breath and added, "I must say I misjudged you. I thought you were set against her, but you managed to keep her out of the cell by bringing her here. The company of your daughter cheers her up. Thank you for that."

Foselli seemed uncomfortable about this sudden gratitude. "You needn't thank me. It was just a practical measure." He stepped aside to allow them to leave the house. "Have a nice day."

"A nice day?" Raoul grumbled when they were in the car. "How can we have a nice day with this whole case hanging over our heads? You may be convinced of his good intentions—"

"I merely said so to mollify and confuse him. I want him to be uncertain whether we are friend or foe. And I think I succeeded." Atalanta nodded towards Foselli, who was on the steps watching them.

Raoul said, "He has too much experience to be fooled."

"But this case is different." Atalanta settled into the seat. She was glad they had made the trip out here. It had confirmed her suspicions that Foselli was somehow more than just the police chief in this matter. He had wanted Catharina to meet Felicia. He had wanted his daughter to be nice to her. To lure her into personal confessions? Was Felicia working with her father to knot a noose for Catharina?

She turned to Raoul. "What did you think of the situation?"

"Catharina is a fool to have fallen for that liar's charms. How could she not see through his ruse?"

"No, I mean the chief's daughter. Charming Felicia. Letting the main suspect cry in her arms."

"Either she is very guileless, not even reading newspapers, or she is as cunning as Lucrezia Borgia." Raoul grimaced. "Inserting herself into Catharina's confidence."

"While she is at her weakest," Atalanta added. "I'm afraid that we've warned her against Antonio Gati but a much greater danger lurks there in the house behind our backs. If Catharina tells Felicia too much ..."

"She assured us she knows nothing. If that's the truth, she can't reveal anything to her either."

"But what if she kept something from us? Perhaps because she's ashamed of it or doesn't know if she can fully trust us ... She must be so confused after discovering Gati only used her to get close to her family. How can she determine who really wants the best for her and who is lying?"

Raoul gripped the wheel. "We should never have agreed to go to that party. We've landed in so much quicksand we're bound to be sucked under." He glanced at her. "While I was sitting in that room, I realized a horrible thing."

"What is that?"

"That if Foselli is somehow involved we could never get Catharina acquitted."

Atalanta didn't know whether to feel joy that Raoul was thinking along the same lines as she was, and that she need not force her unwanted theory on him, or dread that they would indeed have to cross swords with someone so powerful.

She tried to sound positive when she replied, "I don't

agree. Foselli is retired. There is a new police chief. He won't like the old one meddling in his affairs. If we build a strong enough case, we may convince him. Let's be honest. If we can accuse Foselli of any kind of wrongdoing, present or past, it will remove him from the scene and the new chief will have his hands free to work the way he wants. Wouldn't that be tempting to him?"

"Perhaps." Raoul didn't seem convinced, looking ahead with a grim expression. "But we'd need solid evidence to persuade him to try and go after Foselli. Have you got any?"

"I need information from Renard. Hopefully he'll call me soon. And I also want to talk to Thomasso. When you spoke with him while Foselli was interrogating me, did Thomasso mention where he was staying?"

"Yes, he mentioned a hotel that I happen to know well from previous stays in the region. I can give you the phone number."

Chapter Sixteen

When Atalanta arrived back at the house, a servant informed her that her butler had called. She returned the call from Cosimo's study, but it felt awkward to sit in the dead man's chair so she remained standing while she waited for Renard to answer. When he did, she asked, "There was something urgent to discuss?"

"Yes. You need not reply in any manner that can give something away should you be overheard. I will talk. I looked into the will of Catharina's late mother. She did leave money to her daughter to be turned over to her in portions. At her twenty-first birthday, at her twenty-fifth, thirtieth, and so on. Quite substantial amounts, so she could live comfortably off it. She's also entitled to jewellery and paintings that came from her mother's family. I understand that her mother, being an only child from a wealthy family, had a lot of property. I can of course not judge another's spending and Catharina Lanetti might have already sold off a lot but …"

"I see." Atalanta frowned hard. The house was full of beautiful art. It had been mentioned several times that the first wife, Anna, had decorated it. Was this all her family's property? Did it actually belong to Catharina? Had Cosimo never told her? She had been but a child when her mother had died. Had she never learned about the provisions in the will for her? Something to look into further.

"Interestingly, the lawyer told me that a reporter had tried to flirt with his secretary, taking her out for drinks, and so on, to get access to the provisions of the will."

Atalanta sucked in a breath.

Renard said, "You need not ask who. Antonio Gati. He is a reporter with an Italian father and an American mother. He lived across the Atlantic for most of his life and has only recently returned to Italy. It seems he has set his sights on Catharina. Either to get into her money or into her family. Or both. In any case I would be highly suspicious of him."

Atalanta's mind whirled. Had Antonio realized Cosimo would stand in the way of Catharina ever getting the money from her mother? Had he killed him for that reason? But wouldn't he then have laid a trail to accuse another family member of the murder? Wouldn't it have been an ideal scenario if Giovanni or Lorenzo were accused and convicted and their share in the vineyard go to Catharina? Then Antonio, as her partner, would hit the jackpot.

Leaving a clue pointing directly at Catharina made no sense. If she was convicted, she'd never get anything out of Cosimo. And Antonio would have no access to the wealth from Catharina's mother's side of the family either.

Renard said, "Lorenzo Lanetti has had health problems since childhood. He has been away to the mountains several times for his lungs. But recently he has been spending all of his time in Tuscany."

To be near Quinta? Had Lorenzo killed his father to finally get a position of control in the estate? But what about Danielo? Wouldn't Lorenzo have killed Cosimo and implicated Danielo so as to get rid of the husband and be able to charm the devastated wife?

Quinta ... Had she killed Cosimo thinking the will would bring money and influence to Danielo? Had Lorenzo been her second bet, in case Danielo didn't get enough? There was obviously no love lost between her and Catharina so implicating the hated half-sister was logical. And knowing everything about the medicinal properties of plants, Quinta had been the perfect person to use poison as a murder method.

Renard had still been talking so Atalanta said, "Could you repeat that? I was distracted for a moment."

"Is someone there listening in? I'll be brief. Giovanni Lanetti is always getting into some scrape with a woman. He is moderate in his spending, though, never gambling and he actually knows a fair deal about wine. Some say he's keeping his philandering image alive to conceal how cunning he is."

And how ambitious? Atalanta wondered.

"I tried to find old newspaper articles about the earlier tragedies related to the family. The robbery in which Catharina's mother was killed was covered but briefly as it was considered a tragic killing following a theft. The abduction made headlines for weeks, with people taking clues to the police in order to get their hands on the reward being offered for information that would lead to the recovery of the child."

Odd then that the river boat captain hadn't known about it. Or …

Of course! Being always on the move he had probably left the area and not heard about the reward.

She had to talk to Thomasso right away and learn more about the exact circumstances in which his adoptive father had found him.

Renard said, "About Cosimo I learned the usual things: brilliant businessman, ruthless in getting what he wanted, kept a tight leash on his family members. They were all afraid of him. He had lately started to believe that someone was doctoring the books and was funnelling money away."

"Really?" Had that been his big announcement? Exposing someone as a fraud and throwing them out of the family business? But who? Lorenzo? Giovanni? Danielo? Quinta via Danielo? Melina even, if she had access to paperwork?

"I would advise you to be very cautious. If the person who killed him thinks you're closing in ... I understand that with Catharina in jail the general idea is that she is guilty but ... a paranoid killer may take no chances and come after you too."

Atalanta was glad she needn't respond. His warning was kindly meant but rather futile when poison was at play. Anyone could put something in her food or drink and ...

For a moment she thought of the *rustici* that Felicia had so kindly offered them. They had tasted wonderful, but there had been so much spice in them that it would be easy to hide a certain taste. She didn't feel sick or disorientated though.

Not yet.

Renard said, "I'll call again should anything of interest come up. Take care. Goodbye."

"*Merci et au revoir.*" Atalanta put down the receiver and looked around in the room. It had happened here. Cosimo had sat here, or stood here, and then the poison had started to act. It had caused him to collapse and die.

She stared at the desk's surface, trying to picture the scene. Had the killer remained nearby? Had he or she watched as Cosimo died? Had they then set the scene with the goblet?

But there had been poisoned wine in the goblet.

So maybe the goblet had been on the desk and someone, perhaps stopping by to discuss something with Cosimo, had put the poison in it behind his back? Had there been an argument? Had he been pacing and gesticulating, not noticing the movement behind him?

She sighed in frustration. She didn't know enough. It didn't fit.

She picked up the receiver again and called Thomasso's hotel. He wasn't there but the receptionist said that he knew where he was and would get him to call her back as soon as possible. Indeed, within a few minutes he rang.

"I always play chess with the villagers in the square," he explained. "I could come over right away. What is the matter?"

"Where exactly were you found by your adoptive father?"

"Along the road near Pisa."

"Pisa? That is so far away from here." Atalanta could now dismiss her theory that a little girl had carried off her unwanted half-brother. She felt oddly relieved that Catharina hadn't done something so wicked. "And your new family took you away on their boat?"

"Yes, they often ferried loads into Switzerland or Germany."

"I see." That would have taken them away from the region for long periods of time. The news about a reward had never reached them. They had been blissfully ignorant of the background of the child they had taken in. "How did you find out your father was Cosimo Lanetti?"

"After my assumed father told me that he had found me by the side of the road, I wanted to know more. I advertised in newspapers around Pisa to learn if anyone could remember anything from the time. Then a reporter contacted me. He said he found the timing oddly in line with the abduction of Thomasso Lanetti. He could put me in touch with a servant in the family who had cared for the young boy. She recognized the birthmark on my back."

"So you've actually met that old servant woman."

"Lucretia, yes. She was so happy to see me. She cared for me day and night after I was born. My mother, Melina, was apparently always busy with other things and she abhorred changing diapers. Lucretia said she felt like my mother. She'd never had any children herself, she told me."

"She prompted you to come here and reveal to Cosimo that you were back."

"Yes. She said she would help me regain my rightful place in the family. That her testimony about my birthmark would be very important. That it would remove any suspicion that I was an impostor after money."

"I see."

Thomasso said, "I have hopes it still can. Melina must accept me."

"But she has no influence in the family now that Cosimo has died. You'd have to convince your siblings to accept you back into the family fold. And frankly I can't see them doing that."

Thomasso sighed. "I know. Cosimo died at the worst possible time for me. Now, can I return to my chess game? Someone else will have probably already finished my biscotti and wine."

"You take your biscotti with wine?"

"Yes, they must be soaked in something or they break

your jaw. It's usually coffee but in this region they often use wine. It's a delicious combination, with the spices in the biscotti and the additional tang of the wine. You should try it some time. *Arrivederci*."

Absentmindedly muttering a farewell, Atalanta slowly lowered the receiver. Biscotti and wine.

She remembered the crumbs that had fallen away from the desk when she and Raoul had been in here looking for clues. She had wondered at the time what those crumbs had come from, but now she knew. Anise biscotti. Like the shipment the baker had tried to deliver – the one that Melina had said wasn't needed any more. Cosimo had always eaten three before he went to bed.

Three biscotti and a cup of wine to soak them in. The taste of both the anise in the biscuits and the wine would cover any addition. That was the wine that had been in the room, the wine into which the poison had been introduced. After Cosimo had finished eating the soaked biscotti and taken an additional sip, or two or three, he had felt unwell and collapsed. The murderer had then put the last of the wine in the goblet to ensure it contained traces of poison. They had removed the other glass but hadn't seen the biscotti crumbs.

She now knew how the murder had been committed and how the false trail to Catharina had been laid. The remaining questions were by whom and why?

Chapter Seventeen

Atalanta entered the kitchens and looked around. A tall wiry cook stood at the table kneading dough. The muscles in her bare arms strained as she pushed it into shape, picked up the ball, and slapped it with force onto the table.

Atalanta shrank back under the thuds. "I'm looking for Lucretia," she cried over the sounds.

The woman gestured with a dirty hand to the door leading into the back garden. Atalanta called, *"Grazie,"* and went out of the door.

Lucretia stood a few paces down a path made of crushed shells. She was scattering seeds and dozens of pigeons had landed to feast on them. Atalanta walked over and said softly, "They are beautiful birds."

Lucretia looked up at her and smiled. Her dark eyes

sat deep in her lined face. She could be seventy or eighty or even older – impossible to determine. A woman who had spent a lifetime working in this household. Seeing everything.

"Do you do this often?"

"Every day. They know exactly when I'm coming. They land even before I appear. They're intelligent creatures."

"Yes, they always find their way home." Atalanta waited a moment and then added, "Like Thomasso. He was abandoned far away but he found his way home."

Lucretia's features set in pain. "He was but a small child when he was taken away. It was a brutal thing to do."

"Criminals have no conscience," Atalanta agreed. "But sometimes injustice can be set right."

"Indeed, it can." Lucretia made cooing sounds to the pigeons.

"You helped Thomasso find his way back here. A reporter connected the dates but you recognized the birthmark on his back. How did this reporter find you?"

"He came here to the house one day when all of the family were gone to Rome for a party. He talked to several servants but they knew nothing. I'm the only one who has always been here." Lucretia smiled softly. "I told him how I'd cared for the little boy. He offered to take me to see him. I was overcome ... I thought he was lying. But when I saw Thomasso I recognized him right away. It was so good to hold him in my arms."

"You promised to help him regain his rightful place here."

"It would be hard. No one wanted another to share with." Lucretia rubbed a finger along the rim of the now empty bowl that had held the pigeon food. "But I was determined to set an old wrong right."

"You felt Thomasso deserved his place in the family?"

"Of course, he is the eldest son. The others are but second best." Lucretia sounded determined.

"And Catharina?"

"She doesn't want any of this. She went away and she lives her own life."

"But not any more now that she's been accused of murder."

"Someone must take the blame." Lucretia muttered it half to herself as she watched the pigeons. "Melina should never have left him alone as she did. It was so easy for someone to take him."

"And where were you when it happened?" Atalanta asked.

"I was ill; I was in bed with a fever. I couldn't watch him as I normally did. I always blamed myself for that. I should have been there."

"You need not blame yourself for anything. Wicked people took him away for their own gain."

"Yes." Lucretia looked up at her. "It was wicked and it deserved punishment. All of those years, that boy didn't know who he was, what he was entitled to. He was raised like a pauper while all of this was his. Those years were stolen away from him and they can never be given back. That is a burden he will always have to bear. Regardless of what happens now, I can't make that better for him." Lucretia shuffled away to a small fountain. She washed the bowl in the water.

Atalanta felt sorry for her as she watched her stooped shoulders and stiff movements. The woman probably suffered from gout or a similar affliction.

"Do you know how Cosimo reacted when he found out Thomasso was his long-lost son?"

"He wanted to make a big announcement at the party."

"Yes, and you believed it was to say that Thomasso was back and the vineyard would be divided differently? The property would partially be his?"

Lucretia swung the bowl to and fro to shake off the excess water. The drops sparkled in the sunshine as they fell. "I don't know what he would have said. He never had a chance to do so."

"Do you know about the anise biscuits he ate every night?"

"Yes. They're put ready in his study so he can eat them before bed. He always reads paperwork before bed." She corrected herself hastily. "He always did."

"I'm sorry for your loss."

"Thomasso was lost to me for many years. My heart was broken by that. Now I am old and I feel nothing." Lucretia gave her a resigned look. "I must be getting on with my duties. The pigeons are a private pleasure of mine. If I get caught, I will be punished."

"I won't tell anyone about it," Atalanta readily assured her. She watched the old woman shuffle away and enter the kitchen. It had to be difficult to spend a lifetime in service, always having to do what others asked. Being loyal, even against your own better judgement. But perhaps one got used to it?

She now had confirmation that the biscuits and wine had been set out in the study. The poison had been introduced before Cosimo came in to take his evening snack. But by whom?

She had a feeling that something the old woman had said had been very important, but she couldn't quite determine what it was.

Chapter Eighteen

Atalanta was walking down a winding road lined with cypresses. In the distance she saw the Lanetti house but it lay on a hill now, as Foselli's house did. There were cows grazing around it, but they weren't eating grass; they were eating grapes. They were destroying the beautiful vineyards. As she came closer, she saw the old woman, Lucretia, milking one of the cows. Atalanta could see the liquid streaming into the bucket placed at the old woman's feet. It wasn't milk but wine. The cows actually gave wine. Voices rang in her ears: Lorenzo saying everyone had been in the study that night; Catharina whimpering that someone had finally loved her for herself and talking about her mother's ring with the C etched into it, a token of her love for her little girl; and above it all, someone was repeating over and over, "An old wrong that must be set right".

An old wrong …

Atalanta shot upright in her bed. She stared into the darkness, her eyes wide. *Of course. That was it.* The answer she had been looking for. The motive for murder. She put her hand over her heavily beating heart. This was devastating. It would hurt so many people in the household. She would have to tell them terrible things. But it had to be done. To acquit Catharina. To … set an old wrong right? Yes, perhaps.

She couldn't sleep any more and pored over her notes to ensure she had drawn the right conclusion. The light of dawn seeped into her room and, with it, the realization she had to do this quickly, not put it off. She tried to steel herself for the task ahead, the pain associated with it. Pain that would not be hers but would still hurt her as she would be the cause. She would have to reveal family secrets that had lain dormant for many years.

She went to her suitcase and removed her grandfather's letter from the lining, the one she had started reading on the train but had never finished. He had been about to expose the nephew, the actor who had come on the train to rob his aunt and take her inheritance.

She looked for the point where she had stopped

reading. Oh yes, there it was. Seeing her grandfather's strong handwriting calmed her a little.

The cousin had abandoned his education to join the stage. I reasoned that, as an actor, he could easily have assumed a role and been on the train in disguise to conduct the robbery. I asked around whether there had been any new staff hired for the journey. The cook told me that the usual help hadn't shown up because of a family emergency and another had taken his place. He had been helping with food preparation for almost the whole trip, but for one brief moment in which he had been sent to the luggage car to get some more oysters. To reach the luggage car he had to pass all the compartments. He knew the passengers were in the dining car. It would have been easy to step into the compartment in question and steal the jewellery, putting it in the bucket with the ice that he carried to transport the oysters. By the time I had worked this out, we were pulling into another station. Of course the cook's help stood ready to step off the train.

The station official stopped him and handed him over to the police, but we didn't find the jewellery on his person. I asked where his luggage was, but he said he had carried none as he was on the train as an employee not a passenger. Still, I noticed the question flustered him. I went back on the train, which had to wait for about fifteen minutes at the station, and asked the man in charge of the luggage car whether the cook's help had been in there.

"Yes," he said, "to get oysters."

I asked him if there was any luggage in his care that was to be picked up later. There was a single suitcase. He showed it to me. The address on the label had been changed. I opened it and the jewellery was in there. Our friend, the greedy cousin, had used his oyster knife to open the suitcase and put the jewellery in, and had quickly rewritten the address on the label to ensure he could later collect the suitcase.

A clever man. But not clever enough. I guess it was his downfall that I was on the train that night.

Yes, Atalanta thought, it was also going to be the downfall of Cosimo Lanetti's killer that she had been on the Orient Express with Raoul. That she had met Catharina Lanetti and accepted her invitation, albeit reluctantly, to join her father's birthday party.

She read on:

Crime is never far away, not even when you're on holiday. But see it as an opportunity to exercise your mind and learn more about human nature. Everything you learn will help you in the future to become even better at what you do. There must be people like us, Atalanta, who protect the interests of the innocent. Who confront those who, by clever means, seek to further their own situation while they let others take the blame. The conductor who had been accused of the theft had a family. If he had been fired and ended up in prison, what would have become of them? Always remember that when you solve a crime, whether it's theft, or murder, or something else altogether, you save lives. You restore things. You put wrongs right.

But at what expense? Atalanta wondered. The truth would set people free. But it would also send other people to prison and to the noose.

She put away the letter and got dressed. Her heart was heavy but her mind made up. She had to do this. Right away.

———

They all sat around the breakfast table. Melina at the head, Giovanni to her left, Lorenzo to her right. Beside Lorenzo sat Quinta and then Danielo. Beside Giovanni, Atalanta, and Raoul. The butler had poured the coffee and left the room. At Atalanta's request, Lucretia now shuffled in. Thomasso followed her. He stood at the door, back straight, looking around the family circle.

"What is he doing here?" Lorenzo asked sharply.

Atalanta said, "I asked him to come. I have something to say to you. To all of you."

Before he could protest, she continued, "Two more people should have been present here. Catharina, because she's your sister and fellow heir."

"Our father's murderer?" Giovanni grimaced. "I think not."

Atalanta didn't look at him. She said, "And Antonio Gati, a journalist who inserted himself into the birthday party to find delicious titbits to report upon. But I thought it better he doesn't learn what I am about to reveal."

"Reveal?" Melina said. She sat up straight, looking majestic in a sky-blue dress with her hair pulled back. She gave Atalanta a cold look. "You are but a guest here. What could you possibly know about us? Our family?"

"Quite a lot." Atalanta smiled. "I'm a detective. I'm used to finding out people's secrets."

Melina blinked a moment.

Quinta moved in her seat. "Detective?" she asked in a high-pitched voice.

"Catharina asked me to come to the party. She had been threatened on the train. A note was shoved under her compartment door telling her to stay away from the party or she would regret it."

"If she had heeded that good advice," Lorenzo said,

"our father would still be alive and she wouldn't be in custody."

"Did you write that note?" Atalanta asked him. "You need not deny it. You were on the train."

"I was. I was travelling home for the party. I had no idea that Catharina was also on the train until I saw her on the platform and she attacked me like a mad woman."

"That isn't true," Atalanta said quietly. "I placed a few calls this morning and I spoke to the conductor on the train. He told me that a well-dressed man with glasses asked to see the passenger list as he wanted to check if a friend of his was on board. He wanted to surprise him, he said."

Lorenzo flushed fiery.

Giovanni said, "I wager you gave the man money to let you see the list. They're not allowed to share personal information about travellers. That's all private."

Atalanta ignored him and said to Lorenzo, "Not only did you know Catharina was on the train, but you also knew what compartment she was in."

"Very well, so I knew. And I did push a note under her door. But only as a well-meant warning. She had no idea how the atmosphere was in this house. That no one wanted her to come back."

"No," Atalanta said slowly, "you were right there. No one wanted her back. Not Melina, who wasn't her mother and had never cared for her. Not her two half-brothers, who wanted the property for themselves. Not Cosimo, who hated his daughter's independence, perhaps because she reminded him of his first wife, who had valued her freedom and often left his house to wander the countryside and be alone. Be away from him, I wonder? I'll come back to that later. But I first want to determine whether Lorenzo, while on the train with his half-sister, trying to deter her from coming to the party, hatched a plan to kill his father and blame Catharina for it."

"If I wanted to blame her for my crime," Lorenzo spluttered, "would I have tried to scare her away?"

"Perhaps you thought that a note would make her angry and determined to come anyway. Reverse psychology? You're very intelligent, Lorenzo. And not afraid to play people against each other."

Lorenzo's eyes shot sparks at her from behind his glasses.

Atalanta said, "Especially after Catharina had attacked you and broken your nose, you knew your plan had a good chance of succeeding. She'd come to the party. She'd never stay away because you had told her to. She was violent – your bloodied nose proved that to anyone who laid eyes on you. Your lame tale of being attacked by a few thugs would convince no one.

They would soon enough realize the truth and assume you hadn't admitted it was Catharina straightaway because it was embarrassing. But you plotted to have your sister be accused of murder. You wore a mask over your face for long periods during the party, you looked just like one of the waiters, so you could freely move around and no one would notice. You entered your father's study and poisoned the wine that was waiting for him with his anise biscotti. You waited until he had drunk it and collapsed, then contaminated the goblet Catharina had given him so she would be accused. You put the goblet beside the body as if it had slipped from his hand as he fell to the floor. Your father was dead, you'd inherit part of the vineyard, and with your sister accused of the murder, her share would revert to you and Giovanni. All you had to do was buy him out ..."

"You tried to negotiate that with me," Giovanni said. "You bastard."

Lorenzo glared at him across the table. "I didn't kill Papa. That woman is lying."

Atalanta kept her gaze on him. "It was easy enough for you to get your hands on some foxglove drops: Quinta prepared medicines for you. You were in love with her."

Lorenzo flushed a deep red.

Quinta said, "I never gave him any poison. What fantasy is this?"

Atalanta said, "Perhaps Lorenzo didn't put the poison in the cup, but you did. You wanted to get rid of Cosimo, who had spurned your interest in him. You also wanted to bring money to your husband Danielo, who was deep in debt because of his gambling."

Quinta scoffed. "It's no secret Danielo always needs money. But we need not kill for it." She glanced at her husband.

Atalanta said, "Each of you was uncertain, after Cosimo died, whether the other was behind it. You felt suspicious of each other. Quinta, you thought Danielo was desperate enough for money to do it. And Danielo, you knew your wife had a way with medicinal plants."

Danielo said, "I never suspected Quinta. I thought Melina had done it."

"Oh yes." Atalanta looked at the woman at the head of the table. "Melina, the dutiful wife whom Cosimo kept on such a short leash. He didn't appreciate you, he often humiliated you in front of others. Over the years you must have grown to hate him."

"He was the father of my children."

"Your sons who never got a chance to take responsibility as Cosimo kept everything to himself."

Atalanta waited a moment. "If he were dead, your sons would finally get their inheritance."

Melina said, "This is madness. You're accusing us one by one. What kind of detective are you? Merely speculating to make Catharina go free? It's pathetic."

"I want to show that all of you had good reason to want Cosimo dead. He was an unpleasant man who enjoyed playing people against each other. He would withhold favours to make people grovel for them. He laughed at pain and heartache."

Melina's eyes darkened a moment.

"Yes." Atalanta kept looking at her. "The loss of your son, Thomasso. It was Cosimo's reason to keep you here all the time, to never let you go anywhere alone. Someone told me that only after the boys were born and were growing up did he relax. Now isn't that odd? That was the time when the children might have been snatched like Thomasso had been. But then he didn't seem to care as much any more. What was Cosimo really after? To keep you, his wife, near him all the time, to ensure that the sons you bore were truly his?"

Melina turned pale. "How dare you ..." Her voice shook.

"I've heard that you were with child when you married Cosimo. He feared that it wasn't his. When Thomasso was born, he couldn't enjoy the baby. Holding him, looking at him, he kept wondering if the child was another's. A cuckoo in his nest, after his money."

Atalanta looked around the table. Everyone was staring at her in silent disbelief.

She had to swallow before she could say it. "And therefore Cosimo decided he had to get rid of the child. Thomasso was not abducted by strangers. His own father took him from his crib and brought him far away from this house. He left him by the roadside, leaving it to chance whether he lived or died. A river boat captain found him and took him in. The abduction story featured in the media for weeks, but the captain didn't see it as he was ferrying loads across the border. Cosimo used the alleged abduction to force Melina to stay at home all the time. Only when his sons and heirs had been born and were growing up did he allow her more freedom. Because then it didn't matter any more. He knew for sure that the children were his."

"Thomasso was his," Melina said. She beat her fist on the table. "How dare you accuse me of infidelity in my own home? I want you to leave, right away."

"I'm not accusing you of anything. I'm raising the question of whether Cosimo believed Thomasso to be his son. And I'm convinced that Cosimo never believed it. He hated Thomasso. So when he returned and Lucretia confirmed that the man calling himself Thomasso Lanetti was indeed the child of old, the one with the birthmark on his back, Cosimo had a huge problem. The child that he had so conveniently disposed of had found his way back home. He had to do something about it. And he intended to. At his birthday party."

"The announcement he wanted to make ..." Giovanni rasped.

"Indeed. It wasn't that Thomasso was going to be his successor. No. Far from it. He was going to announce that his wife had betrayed him and that he was divorcing her. He was casting her out along with her son, Thomasso. Cosimo rejoiced at the prospect of publicly humiliating her in front of all of his guests."

Melina said, "He wouldn't have ..." Her eyes were wide.

Atalanta said, "If you knew he was going to do that and you were angry about it ..."

"But I didn't know. This is the first I have heard about it."

Giovanni said, "Don't harass Mama."

Atalanta looked at him. "You seem upset by the suggestion your father was going to divorce your mother. Did you want to prevent a family scandal by killing him before he could do so? You went to his study as well. All of you had to go and see him."

"I didn't go. He couldn't order me like a dog."

Giovanni's eyes flashed with anger. "He wouldn't have told me anything anyway. He always loved to do that: dangle a carrot and let the donkey follow. I was tired of playing the donkey."

Melina said, "I don't feel well. I want to go and lie down. Lucretia, come with me to help me."

"No," Atalanta said. "You're not leaving with Lucretia. I need you here."

Melina sank against the back of her chair reaching for her face. "I feel light in the head. Perhaps I'm going to faint."

Quinta rose. "Can I go and get something to revive her?"

"No!" Melina cried. "Stay away from me with your herbal concoctions, you witch. You tried to enchant Cosimo but he didn't fall for it."

Quinta scoffed but sat down again.

Atalanta said, "You all had a chance to go to the study and poison the wine. You all hated Catharina enough to let her take the blame for it. After all, she was the child from the first marriage, the half-sister. She still missed her mother and grieved for the unhappiness of her childhood."

"As if I could forget Anna," Melina said. "She was present here, everywhere."

Atalanta nodded. "This house was of her making. A

living memory and testimony. That was the odd thing, the thing I couldn't reconcile. You see ..." She let her gaze wander the table. "The person who killed Cosimo didn't do it because of money, or to prevent a disastrous divorce, or because advances had been rejected. No. The murderer did it because they thought that Cosimo was a murderer himself."

Melina stared at Atalanta. "But ... Thomasso is still alive. Even if Cosimo took him away, like you claim he did, he survived."

"I'm not talking about Thomasso, but about Anna."

"Anna was killed in a robbery gone wrong," Giovanni said. "As a detective you should get your facts straight."

"The gang apprehended for the robberies in this region always denied having killed Anna Lanetti. Even before they were hanged, they protested their innocence. Why?"

"Because they were criminals who were used to lying?" Lorenzo suggested.

Atalanta shook her head. "They had indeed not killed Anna Lanetti. Someone else had. And why couldn't it have been Cosimo? His wife often left the house to take tours in her carriage. She was away for hours, alone. She might have been seeing someone else. A lover. Cosimo knew she hadn't married him for love but because her father had made her. He had wanted Cosimo in the family as a profitable alliance to keep the vineyards alive and ensure a future of prize-winning wines. Cosimo married Anna for her father's property. That was the deal. If he knew she had never had feelings for him, perhaps he suspected her of loving another? To end this unwanted situation, he followed her and killed her, taking away her jewellery to make it look like one of the robberies that had plagued the area for some time. He hid the jewellery in his own safe. Foselli found the wedding ring there."

There was a deep silence in the room. Melina swallowed hard. Giovanni put his hand over hers. Lorenzo sat with his head down as if he couldn't quite grasp it.

Thomasso spoke first. "He was an evil man. Jealousy made him kill his first wife. Then he suspected that I wasn't his son and he put me out to die. He was capable of anything. Anything!"

Atalanta said, "Your return put everything into motion. Because you were still alive and could tell what had happened, the killer understood that it was Cosimo who had taken you away, blaming it on a kidnapping. Cosimo had no intention of bringing you back into the fold and repairing the injustice, he intended to cast you out again, along with your mother. Thinking back, the killer realized that Cosimo must also have killed his first wife, again blaming it on criminals operating in the area. That was the final straw. This evil man had to die. On the night of his sixtieth birthday party. The killer put the poison in the wine and waited as Cosimo soaked his anise biscotti in it and ate them, then sipped the wine, as he did every night. He began to feel unwell and tried to stagger to the door to ask for help, but the killer had made sure the door was locked and that he couldn't leave. The killer was in the room with him when he died. The killer watched and waited and then contaminated the goblet Catharina had given her father, placing it beside the body to let another take the blame. It was justice, wasn't it?"

Atalanta slowly turned to where the guilty party stood. "It was setting an old wrong right, wasn't it, Lucretia?"

Chapter Nineteen

There was a gasp of shock around the table.

Lorenzo cried, "Did you do it? Did you kill our father?"

Lucretia stood up straight, her wrinkled features calm. "He was an evil man. I've had to watch for decades as he ruined people. He killed his first wife without remorse. He drove a young girl to her death when she jumped out of her bedroom window in panic to escape his harassment. He left a baby on the roadside to die. Then, when the child miraculously survived, and came back to claim his inheritance, he made new plans to abandon him once more and throw out the wife who had endured all of his wickedness. I could stand it no longer. I had to kill him. I wanted to make it look like a heart attack. He'd had one in spring. But while he was dying, he looked at me and he cursed me and hissed that I would never get away with it. On impulse I poured the dregs of the poisoned wine into the Medici goblet and put it by his side. I thought it was a fitting ending for a vain man – that he had died because he wanted to be like the Medici, who also destroyed each other with greed and jealousy."

Atalanta asked softly, "Didn't you care at all that Catharina would be accused and perhaps even condemned? She is Anna's daughter. If you killed Cosimo because he killed Anna …"

Lucretia shook her head. "I killed him for Thomasso. The boy must have a share in the vineyard." She looked at the people seated around the table. "You must allow him to have a share. He is the eldest son. He was cruelly denied his inheritance, his name, everything. He was forced to live in poverty far away from his birthright. You must set that right."

"I don't have to listen to you," Melina said. "You're nothing but a servant. And a killer."

"I did what I did for this family," Lucretia said. "You can be close. You can take care of the vineyards together. Without Cosimo here to drive you apart, you can make it work."

"Call Foselli and let him come and take her away."

Giovanni sat back with a disgusted expression. "I don't want to hear any more from her. Let her rot in prison."

Lucretia's eyes dimmed. Atalanta felt a stab of pain for this old woman who might have committed a heinous crime but who had done it for the sake of family. To reunite people driven apart by a tyrannical father who had cast his shadow over everything. She had hoped that once he was removed, things could be different. But how much of the Lanetti need to dominate and control was in his children? Were they doomed to repeat the same mistakes and become utterly unhappy?

Raoul said quietly, "I'll go and call the police station to send someone over to pick her up."

Lucretia stood very still. "I'll not try to escape. I take responsibility for what I did. I don't regret it. Someone had to stop him." She looked at Thomasso, tears in her eyes. "I held you in my arms when you were a little boy. I sang you songs at night when I put you to bed. My heart broke when you were abducted. I kept telling myself over and over that perhaps you had not died. That you were alive somewhere. I hoped that you were well. When you came back, stood before me …" A tear spilled down her cheek.

Thomasso went over and hugged the fragile old woman. "Thank you," he said in a hoarse voice, "for never letting go of me."

Atalanta bit her lip. She had had no choice but to expose the old woman to save Catharina.

Thomasso straightened up and looked at Melina. "I am your son," he said. "You must know me. Would a mother not recognize her own child?"

Giovanni tightened his grip on Melina's hand. "We are your sons," he said to her, nodding at Lorenzo on her other side. "We can't allow some intruder to step in and demand a share of what is rightfully ours."

"Yes," Lorenzo said, "we will help you to deny the claims of this fraud. Don't worry, Mama, we are here for you."

Ironic, Atalanta thought, how two brothers who couldn't stand each other were suddenly united in their desire to stave off Thomasso.

Giovanni said, "Luckily Papa's will doesn't give Thomasso anything. So we can continue as we always have."

"With Catharina," Atalanta reminded him. "She didn't kill her father, so she's entitled to her share."

"I think I heard something ..." Lorenzo sat up with a cunning smile. "About her wanting to start a chocolate business? If we give her enough money to do so, she might agree to sign papers that she can't claim a share in the business any more."

Giovanni grinned back at him. "What a good idea. We

must discuss this in more detail. Make her an irresistible offer."

Atalanta looked at Raoul. "We'd better go and see Catharina to tell her the good news."

"Is it good news?" Raoul asked cynically as they left the room. "She will no doubt be happy she is no longer a suspect, but her family members are already conspiring against her to buy her out."

When Atalanta didn't respond, he asked, "Or do you think it's even better for her to take the money and start her own business, far away from these conniving types? It would be hard to work with family members who couldn't wait to see you executed as a murderer."

They left the house and headed for Raoul's car.

Atalanta took a deep breath of the fresh morning air. She spoke at last. "I'm not thinking of Catharina's chocolate business or whether she must try and stay in the family vineyard or not. I'm imagining how she will feel when I tell her the truth."

Raoul's expression darkened. "Yes, it must be terrible for her to learn her father killed her mother. She must be outraged. In fact, it's probably good that Cosimo is dead already or we'd run the risk she'd rush to confront him and kill him anyway."

Atalanta looked at him as they stopped at the car. "Cosimo didn't kill Anna."

"But you said ..." Raoul looked confused. "Did I misunderstand?"

"No. I told them what Lucretia must have been thinking when she decided that Cosimo had to die." Atalanta closed her eyes a moment. Then she looked at Raoul again. "But Cosimo had nothing to do with Anna's death."

"Then how did the wedding ring end up in his safe? Did Foselli plant the ring there? We can check on that, I suppose. Anna Lanetti's ring wasn't like any other, we know that now. The tiny C scratched into it proves that."

"I know. I called the police station this morning and asked about the ring. The officer who was with Foselli when he found it had filed it for evidence and told me about the C in it. He thought it was a C for Cosimo, the beloved husband."

Raoul rubbed his forehead visibly confused. "So it really is Anna Lanetti's ring, not a replica planted to suggest a motive for murder. And still you say Cosimo didn't murder his first wife?"

"I do." Atalanta gestured for them to get into the car. "Everything will become clear soon."

Chapter Twenty

At Foselli's house they asked to be admitted to see Catharina Lanetti. Foselli wasn't there, it seemed, for no mention was made of him. Or of Felicia. Atalanta's heart beat quickly as she walked up the stairs. Was she too late?

Catharina rose from a chair at a little table holding her breakfast. She had barely touched it. Her features were pale and there were dark shadows under her eyes, suggesting she hadn't slept much either. She approached them quickly. "Is there news? Can you help me in any way?"

"There is wonderful news," Raoul said, grasping her outstretched hands. "Atalanta exposed your father's killer. She's being arrested by the police as we speak. She confessed so there is no doubt as to her guilt."

"She?" Catharina looked perplexed. "Was it Melina? Or Quinta perhaps? I knew she was in love with Cosimo."

"No, it was Lucretia," Atalanta said.

"Lucretia?" Catharina frowned. "I don't know who that is."

"The old servant woman."

"Oh, her. I tend not to"– Catharina flushed – "pay much attention to servants."

"She loved your mother very much." Atalanta held Catharina's gaze. "She killed your father because she believed he was responsible for your mother's death."

"Because he let her go out on her own, in her carriage, into the woods? While there had been other robberies on the roads?"

"No." Raoul pushed Catharina into her chair. "You'd better sit down while you listen to this."

"Lucretia thought your father had actually killed your mother." Atalanta spoke quietly. "That he had used the alleged robbery as a cover to get away with it. Because the robbers always denied having done it."

"I see." Catharina stared in the distance, her face seeming younger, more vulnerable. "The thought had crossed my mind from time to time. I never dared really embrace it because it was too horrible."

"Lucretia thought she understood it all. But she acted

foremost because of Thomasso. Because it was your father who took him away and left him to die. And then, after all those years, when Thomasso found his way back home, Cosimo didn't acknowledge him but wanted to turn him out. Him and Melina."

Catharina sat motionless. "He was an evil man. Hard to the core. Ruthless. And defensive of his property. Which wasn't even his. My mother brought everything with her into the marriage." She clenched her fists. "How could he kill her and leave her by the side of the road?" She looked up, her eyes wide. "And the ring! He stole it off her finger and kept it and ... it's too terrible for words."

"But Lucretia was wrong, Catharina." Atalanta said it softly, leaning over. "Your father may have been guilty of many things in his life, but he didn't kill your mother. The ring was put in his safe to accuse him wrongly. To provide a motive for you as a suspect in the murder."

Catharina blinked. "He didn't do it?" She grabbed at her head. "Why do you confuse me so?"

"Because I want you to learn of these things gradually." Atalanta took a deep breath. "You loved your mother so, you ached for her to come back to you while you knew she never could. Because of her killer. It's not your father, but it is someone you know."

Catharina held her gaze. She was shivering now. "Tell me."

Raoul said, "Yes, tell me too. I don't know yet, you know." He said it in a matter-of-fact tone as if to break the tense emotional moment.

Atalanta said, "It was Foselli."

The two others stared at her. Catharina echoed, "Foselli? You mean, the retired chief of police? The man in whose house I'm staying right now? He killed my mother? But why?"

"Because he was her lover. Your mother was forced to marry your father for property. Foselli was a policeman at the time, not yet having the high position he later did. His family may have had money, but he couldn't compare with Cosimo Lanetti, who was not only wealthy but also had an interest in vineyards and wine. Being both shrewd and ambitious, he was considered the best choice to marry Anna and continue the wine business. The relationship between your mother and Foselli continued after the wedding. When she went out to ride in her carriage, she saw Foselli. I believe that she didn't want to continue the affair. She tried to tell him, but he kept pressuring her to see him again and again. That day, when he killed her, she told him that it was over. That she wasn't going to come out to meet him any more. She wanted to give her marriage to Cosimo an honest chance.

Also for your sake, Catharina. But Foselli couldn't bear her choosing a man she didn't love over him. He had always been jealous of Cosimo, and Anna's decision was a rejection, and an insult, that he couldn't accept. He stabbed her and took her jewellery to make it look like robbery. But he took her wedding ring for another reason. He removed, from her dead body, the token of her bond to another man. He kept it all these years. And when Cosimo died and you were accused, he put it in the safe to be found and to strengthen the case against you."

Catharina stared at her. "He wanted me to be convicted for his crime? But ... if my mother had an affair with him, while she was married to Cosimo ..."

"You might be Foselli's daughter." Atalanta nodded. "Yes, I've considered that. Could he implicate his own child in a heinous crime and have her convicted? Of course. Remember how he killed the woman he had claimed to love. Because she had not chosen him, he had wanted to destroy her. As he now sought to destroy you."

"But ..." Catharina shook her head. "He was kind to me. He didn't lock me up in a damp cell. He allowed me to stay here, in his house. He has treated me well. He even allowed his daughter Felicia to come here and talk to me and ..."

"Of course. Can't you see?" Atalanta felt a deep

sadness as she had to express the twisted thoughts of a bitter man. "He wanted you to be here in his house, where you had never had a chance to live. He wanted you to see the luxury and comfort that might have been yours had you been acknowledged as his child. He had done well for himself, rising far above the man he had once been, who had been spurned as unworthy to marry your mother. By bringing you here and letting you see everything he had achieved, he was spiting your mother, her parents, Cosimo, everyone who had, in his mind, underestimated him and done him injustice. He also wanted you to see his daughter, Felicia. He wanted to see you two together before you were taken away to be tried and executed. That was justice, in his mind. You had to be punished for the choice your mother made all those years ago. You had to die, like she had."

"I can't believe it ..." Catharina whispered. "I've known him all my life. He pretended to be a family friend, he—"

"But I am a family friend," a voice said. Foselli entered the room. He smiled but his eyes were watchful. "Don't believe a word they're saying, Catharina. It's all made up."

"No, it's not." Catharina rose to her feet. "You killed my mother and took her ring. You kept it and placed it in my father's safe to suggest he had killed her. You wanted me to hate him for killing my mother while you yourself did it. *You* did!"

Foselli walked over in a flash and slapped Catharina in the face so hard that she fell to the floor. "I don't have to listen to you," he hissed.

Raoul said, "That's outrageous, Foselli ..." But the man spun around and pointed a gun at him. "Back away. That's better. I won't let you outwit me. You see, I can't allow you to leave here with this tale. It would harm my reputation ... even though it isn't true."

Atalanta's gaze swept the room for a weapon to disarm Foselli but there was nothing within reach. She wished she had thought about this better. But she had been contemplating how to tell Catharina and she had believed Foselli was busy with Lucretia's arrest. She should have realized that he would conclude they had gone to tell Catharina the news and rush out here to ...

"There will be a fire and you will die in it. All three of you." Foselli walked backwards to the door. "Don't try to escape via the window. There is nothing to support you and a fall would certainly kill you. You don't have to be afraid of pain when the fire reaches the room. The smoke will render you unconscious and you won't feel a thing."

Atalanta glanced at Raoul. His tense expression betrayed he was thinking up ways to attack Foselli without getting shot. But there were none. The man had a gun pointed straight at them and with his experience in the police force he had to be an excellent shot.

Suddenly someone appeared behind Foselli and struck at the arm holding the gun. Foselli cried out in pain and the gun clattered to the floor and slid away from him.

Felicia stood behind him with a poker in her hand. "How could you? Kill an innocent woman? Frame her daughter for murder? All because you felt rejected?"

Foselli looked his daughter in the eye. "Did I ever do anything to hurt you? I gave you everything you own. You have a beautiful room here, money to buy dresses, rich food on the table every night. You have nothing to complain about."

"Oh, you gave me everything. Except for freedom. I can never go where I want, see who I want. I always have to tell you what I do, how much I spent. You even have a man watching me. For a long time I called it love. But now I see it for what it is. It's an illness of your mind. You can't let go. You can't let me be myself."

Foselli hissed in anger and made a lunge for the gun. Raoul also dove for it and their shoulders made contact as they collided on the floor. Arms reached, hands grabbed. Atalanta held her breath. Who would get the gun first? If Foselli regained control of the situation, would he still execute his plan? Would he still light a fire that would kill Catharina, Raoul, and her? Felicia knew now. Would Foselli go so far as to include his own daughter among the people who had to die to keep his secrets safe?

Felicia looked at Catharina and then at her father fighting with Raoul. She stepped closer, lifted the poker high and ...

Atalanta raised both hands to her face for fear the solid iron instrument would strike the wrong man and Raoul would be seriously injured. But the poker made contact with the side of Foselli's head and he gasped. His body went limp and he sagged to the floorboards. Raoul grabbed the gun and emptied out the bullets. They clattered on the wood and rolled away, one catching the sunshine in a blinding reflection.

Felicia stood with the poker in her hand staring at her father's unconscious form. She drew breath in an audible intake. Her voice shivered as she said, "Papa ... what have I done?"

Catharina rushed to her side and put an arm around her shoulders. "It's over now. It's all over now."

Felicia broke into long sobs and Catharina held her tightly, patting her back. It mirrored the scene earlier when Felicia had comforted Catharina in her pain over her situation.

Atalanta looked at the two dark heads close together.

Two half-sisters? Daughters of a man just as ruthless as Cosimo Lanetti had been? But his power was broken now. He would be tried and convicted. His daughters would have freedom at last.

If they could ever enjoy it.

Chapter Twenty-One

R aoul had driven them to a hill from which they could see for miles across the rolling land. The sun slowly completed its course along the sky, dipping everything in orange light, then turning the horizon fiery red followed by deep purple. The first stars appeared.

Atalanta and Raoul sat on a blanket on the grass and ate crostini, olives, pecorino, and truffles. They drank wine from beautiful crystal glasses. This was Tuscany as it was supposed to be.

Atalanta tried to soak up the birdsong and chirping of insects, to impress every memory of this afternoon and evening upon her mind. Raoul was with her, and she felt at ease. The world might be far from perfect, but for these few hours it came very close.

She looked at him. "What would have happened if we hadn't come to the party?"

"With Foselli in charge of the investigation, Catharina would certainly have been accused and brought to trial. I don't know if a good lawyer would have been able to save her." Raoul smiled at her. "I doubt he would have unearthed the links to the earlier murder of Catharina's mother and Thomasso's abduction. You solved three crimes in a single, clever stroke. Four if we count the unhappy fall from that bedroom window of Catharina's schoolfriend."

"We will never know for certain if Cosimo was behind that. And I don't feel clever at all." Atalanta waved a hand. "Foselli made a terrible mistake putting the ring in the safe. It ruined everything."

"Yes, but he couldn't know that there had been an intruder who knew the exact contents of the safe and could vouch that the ring hadn't been there before. He really had bad luck with that."

Atalanta took a sip of wine. "Or Catharina had a bit of good luck, depending on your point of view. What do you think? Will she let herself be bought out by her half-brothers?"

"I don't know. The arrangement as it is laid out in the will isn't very attractive for her. She has to share control of the vineyard with her half-brothers and must invest ninety per cent of her profit back into it. If they make her a generous offer to buy her share, she would do well to take it."

"I was thinking the same thing. But Catharina seemed set on helping Thomasso get a share as well. If she is an heir, she can more easily push for his acceptance into the family."

"She only controls a third. Giovanni and Lorenzo may not like each other but I'm certain they will suddenly be as thick as thieves when it comes to keeping Thomasso out of it."

"Lorenzo seemed to want to buy out Giovanni as well."

"But Giovanni won't hear of it and Lorenzo doesn't have the money to do so."

"What about Danielo? Will they keep him on as a worker?"

"Probably. His debts make him easy to manipulate. And Lorenzo is in love with Quinta."

"Which is a recipe for a new disaster." Atalanta shook her head. "I'm glad I'm not part of that family. I would never have an easy moment."

"I guess with such family members you would have to look over your shoulder all of the time," Raoul agreed. "I can only hope Catharina cuts herself free and starts over elsewhere."

"If she does open a chocolate business, I must become a customer. I love chocolate."

"I knew that and that is why I asked her to make us some special chocolates. I have them here."

Raoul produced them from the bag in which he had kept the wine chilled. "Try some."

Atalanta bit into a dark bonbon with a little red decoration and savoured the rich taste of raspberries and a spice she couldn't identify. "Are you not trying any?" she asked Raoul.

"I don't like sweet things. You seem to enjoy them, so try them all."

Atalanta let her gaze drift to the countryside stretching away from them. "I'm glad we came here to see your second homeland. You've convinced me how beautiful it is."

"Already? We're not through yet."

"It's a land that is easy to love." Atalanta let another bonbon – white with a hint of lemon and ginger – melt on her tongue. "Perhaps I should buy a house here."

"Felicia Foselli might sell her father's house now that he is in jail."

"I don't think I'd want a house where I was kept against my will at gunpoint with the threat of death in a blaze hanging over my head." Atalanta grimaced.

"Besides, the countryside might be a bit too lonely for me. I was thinking about a house in Florence."

Raoul nodded. "A great choice. I have friends who can keep an eye out for you and let you know if something suitable comes on the market." He smiled at her. "If you were living in Florence, it would be much easier for me to pop over from Rome and spend a day or two with you, exploring the city. I mean, I love driving but Rome to Paris is a bit far even for me, and I do have the obligations of my racing." He leaned over to her. "And if you're in Italy, I might persuade you to come and see a race some time?"

Atalanta didn't know if she could stand watching Raoul risk his life in a fast car at high speeds, but she nodded. "Who knows?"

"It doesn't sound like you're very eager," Raoul said with a grin. "But I can work on convincing you."

"That would be great." Atalanta stretched her arms in front of her. "I guess my grandfather was right. Crime is never far away from me, but I have the chance to enjoy my life because of everything he left me."

She lifted her glass and toasted Raoul while the stars sparkled against the velvety blue overhead. "And I fully intend to take that chance."

Acknowledgments

As always, I'm grateful to all agents, editors and authors who share online about the writing and publishing process. Special thanks to my fabulous editor Charlotte Ledger for her thoughtful feedback; to the entire One More Chapter team for their work on the series; and to Lucy Bennett and Gary Redford for the gorgeous cover illustration which captures the Tuscan sights brilliantly.

As a huge Agatha Christie fan, when I started writing mysteries, I knew sooner or later one of my characters would have to travel on the Orient Express. So when I sat down to take Atalanta to Tuscany from her home in Paris, the Orient Express offered itself as the perfect way to do it. The history of this illustrious line is well documented, and so gorgeous photos of the train's interior and even old menu cards provided ample inspiration for Atalanta and Raoul's luxurious journey. And how could one visit Tuscany without thinking of many people born in this very region who shaped the history of Italy by their contributions to literature, art, politics? Their personal lives have enough drama, including allegations of murder, to form a fascinating backdrop for our sleuths' visit. I fictionalized it all, of course, but still I hope it gave you, reader, an escapist experience exploring the region alongside Atalanta and being enchanted by the delicious food and beautiful sights.

Do check out other instalments in the series, which always have Atalanta visiting gorgeous locations where baffling mysteries await. Happy reading!

Don't miss Atalanta Ashford's next adventure when she's asked to attend a debutante ball in snowy Austria where a blackguard moves among the white-clad girls in
LAST DANCE IN SALZBURG

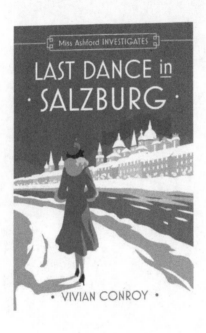

Coming November 2023

Available to pre-order in eBook and paperback now

Read on for an extract from Mystery in Provence

A beautiful French estate

A wedding

A murder

And a novice detective intent on solving her first case!

Fresh from teaching at her prestigious Swiss boarding school, Miss Atalanta Ashford suddenly finds herself the most eligible young lady in society when she inherits her grandfather's substantial fortune. But with this fortune, and an elegant new Parisian home, comes a legacy passed down from grandfather to granddaughter... sleuthing discreetly for Europe's elite.

Mystery in Provence: Chapter One

JUNE 1930

When the news that would change her life forever reached Miss Atalanta Ashford, she was climbing the rocky path to the ruins of an old Swiss burg, fantasizing those tattered grey remains were the white marble columns of the Parthenon.

Her vivid imagination filtered out the tinkling of bells attached to the sheep grazing on the grassy slopes of the surrounding mountains and replaced them with the murmur of tourists' voices, speaking all the languages of the world. Beside her she pictured eager young people whom she was telling everything about Greek mythology, and a few feet away walked a handsome man with intriguing deep brown eyes who had cast interested looks in her direction as she explained about the Hydra of Lerna.

He might invite her later to try baklava at a table under a large old tree in a shaded courtyard while a sole musician lured melancholy notes from his mandolin. 'I've rarely heard,' her male admirer would say, 'someone speak about a multi-headed monster with such passion, Miss Ashford.'

'Miss Ashford!' A voice echoed the words from her imaginings but it was not male or admiring. It was female, young, and decidedly impatient.

Atalanta halted her upwards movement and slowly turned to look over her shoulder. At the bottom of the steep path, one of her younger pupils stood waving a white item in her hand. 'Miss Ashford! A letter for you. It looks awfully important.'

Atalanta sighed as she gave up on the glittering vision of the Parthenon behind her back and made her way, precariously, down the path to her real life. She had done this many times before, always with a sharp stab of regret that the fantasies that made her so happy were just that: daydreams.

But she also renewed her determination with every step she took that she would one day see Athens or Crete or Istanbul. Now that she had at last paid off her father's debts, she was finally in a position to save money for her travel plans.

If only the letter wasn't from another debtor, who had found his way to her via the others who had been paid. It had taken her years to settle things and finally be her own woman. She wanted to enjoy that freedom. Admittedly, her vacation this year would just be a small trip to a nearby valley, but it would be the first money she could spend on herself since she had stood at her father's grave, knowing she was now all alone in the world, faced with two choices: running away from responsibility or paying the debts, no matter how long it took, and making a fresh start of it. The idea that that money might be snatched away by yet another debtor made her heart sink.

'It looks like a crest on the envelope,' the girl called, studying the item in her hand. 'Perhaps it comes from a duke or an earl.'

Atalanta smiled involuntarily. She liked it when people expected the winds of change to blow through the cobwebs of their daily treadmill existence. Still, it was extremely unlikely that a duke or earl would write to her. Her father had come from an aristocratic family but he had broken off all ties with them, forging his own path in life. He had so wanted to achieve something, make a name for himself, away from his birthright. He had longed to prove to his father that he could be more than merely an heir to a title, a man waiting in the wings to take his place in the row of ancestors who were commemorated in the family tree.

Sadness washed through her. Her father had died feeling that he had failed. Not failed himself, but failed her, his only child.

I wish he could know how well everything turned out for me.

Swallowing quickly, she forced her attention back to her pupil. A frown furrowed her brow. 'Why are you still here, Dotty? Shouldn't your father's driver have picked you up already?'

Dorothy Claybourne-Smythe was the daughter of an English diplomat who had a house in Basel. She was supposed to spend the summer vacation there, if the family didn't decide to go to their Tuscan villa. If Atalanta was lucky, Dorothy would send her a postcard that could further feed her fantasies about travel abroad. She had entire albums full of postcards and pictures cut from newspapers with an invisible promise written beside them: *one day I will see these sights for myself.* The albums were her lifeline when things got hard.

Dorothy's expression set. 'I don't want to go home.'

It didn't sound rebellious, just achingly sad.

Poor girl. Atalanta jumped down the last few feet across a large boulder and landed beside her pupil,

350

putting an arm around her narrow shoulders for a moment. 'It won't be that bad.'

'But it will. Father never has time for me and I hate my stepmother. She will comment on everything from my wardrobe to my freckles. I want my mother.'

Atalanta's gut clenched. How could she say something uplifting to his girl whose situation was similar to her own? Like Dorothy, Atalanta had never known her mother. From her untimely death onwards it had been just her father and her, rocked on the tides of his spending, with times when money was abundant and they could afford books and clothes and desserts, and months when they had absolutely nothing and Atalanta was sent to the door when the debt collectors came because they might take pity on a little girl in a tattered dress.

She had learned quickly how to read their posture, the look in their eyes, and to determine whether she could bargain with them to give her father a little more time or whether she should offer right away that they could take something from the house by way of payment.

She had kept her face composed while her mother's jewellery was taken. Only after the door closed had she sobbed like a baby. Nothing left of her mother but memories, and the photograph beside her bed.

'At least you have family, a place to call home,' Atalanta said softly to Dorothy. A stable home instead of constantly changing addresses and an existence walking a tightrope between hope that their circumstances would this time really change for the better and fear that it would never turn out the way her father projected. In his enthusiasm he often overlooked risks.

'Home?' Dorothy grimaced. 'Often I feel like my presence is too much. It's just about the boys.'

The boys were the rambunctious twins her stepmother had borne. Especially the elder, and heir to the estate, who never got corrected or punished for anything he did, Dorothy had often explained to her.

Atalanta couldn't deny that male descendants—heirs —mattered, a lot, in any well-to-do family. Still, she couldn't stand to see her pupil so dejected. Being able to adapt, constantly, to new circumstances was a great asset in life, as well as understanding that you could not always have your way. And that unpleasant situations could be made better if you changed your outlook on them.

'You'll have to devise a plan then.' Atalanta pressed Dorothy's shoulder. 'Whenever your stepmother isn't nice to you, just imagine yourself someplace else.'

'Where?' the girl asked, rather perplexed.

'Anywhere you'd like. A place you've read about, a

place you've been to. A place you made up, all to your liking,' Atalanta enthused. 'It can be your secret castle where you hide away when the world feels like a lonely place. In there you have everything you need. Friends, even. That's the beauty of imagination. It has no limits.'

Dorothy looked doubtful. 'Does that really work? My friends are here and they can't come with me. I'm not allowed to bring even one friend. My stepmother says we get too loud and it gives her headaches. But when the boys scream all day, it doesn't hurt her ears at all. It's so unfair.' She sighed and pressed her head against Atalanta. 'I wish I could stay here with you.'

The simple gesture and words raised a lump in Atalanta's throat. To have a younger sister like this, to feel an unbreakable bond... But the boarding school director was very strict. The pupils shouldn't form too close a connection with the teachers. Emotion was discouraged, empathy disapproved of. She had to keep her distance even though she didn't want to.

'But I'm not staying here.' Atalanta smiled down on her warmly to soften this blow. 'I've found a little village in a remote valley where I can climb and explore to my heart's delight.'

'So I can't write to you either,' Dorothy said, her expression setting. 'I so wanted to write to you whenever I feel sad or the boys tease me.'

'Then write it all down and pretend you send it to me.' As a girl she had written countless letters to her mother, telling her what she had learned to play on the piano or how gorgeous the park looked with the budding blossoms. She had never written about her father's business transactions, or when the jewellery had been taken. That would only have made her mama sad.

Dorothy didn't seem to have heard her. 'But I couldn't have written anything meaningful anyway,' she said, pursing her lips. 'Miss Collins would have read it. She steams open the envelopes and glues them shut again, you know.'

'It's not polite to say such things about other people.' *Even if they were true*, Atalanta added to herself. Miss Collins was their housekeeper, postmistress, and much more. She was kind to the girls and an ally when Atalanta had a more unusual educational plan, but she was also insatiably curious.

Now, Atalanta took the envelope from Dorothy's hand and studied the flap to see if it had been opened, but the sender had taken the precaution of sealing it with an old-fashioned red wax seal. He had even pressed his ring into it. It wasn't a crest, though, as Dorothy had suggested. Rather, initials: an I and an S entwined like vines on an old tree. Whose initials could they be?

She turned the envelope over and studied the front

with the neat name and address directing it to her at the International Boarding School for Young Ladies of Good Repute.

No sender address though. Mysterious.

'Dorothy Claybourne-Smythe.' The name should have been pronounced with indignation but the speaker's lack of breath made it sound rather like an engine that had run out of steam. Miss Collins stood beside them, putting her fleshy hands on her hips. 'Your father's chauffeur has arrived and is waiting for you. Why are you not packed and ready? Where is your hat? It does not do to run around bareheaded.' She cast a half-reproving, half-amused look at Atalanta. 'That goes for you too, Miss Ashford.'

Atalanta reached up with her free hand to feel across her head as she became suddenly conscious she wasn't wearing a hat. 'Yes, Miss Collins,' she murmured obediently, noting to herself that if, by some miracle, she did ever get to the Parthenon, a stylish sunhat would be an essential.

Dorothy said, 'Bye, Miss Ashford. Thank you for what you said,' and ran off down the broad paved footpath leading back to the school.

Atalanta felt the emptiness where the girl's head had rested against her. Her pupils trusted her and confided in her, but those wonderful moments reminded her sharply that she herself had no one to turn to. That she had to fend for herself.

Miss Collins stayed in position, glancing curiously at the letter in Atalanta's hand. 'I didn't know the mailman had come.'

Apparently, Dorothy, skulking about to avoid her father's chauffeur for as long as she possibly could, had managed to lay her hands on the letter before the postmistress had even noticed its arrival.

'It reached me without problems, *merci*.' Atalanta smiled. 'I will now continue what I was doing. *Au revoir*.' And she retraced her steps up to the burgh ruins. She knew Miss Collins thought it very unladylike to 'scramble up paths', as she called it and would not follow her, giving her the privacy she craved to look inside her mysterious letter. If it was bad news, she would have time to compose herself before returning to the school.

And if it was good news... But what good news could it possibly be?

After a few minutes of climbing, she stood on the top of the small hill amongst the cracked stones and mossed formations of what once had been a burg overlooking the village below.

Pink and white wildflowers bloomed between the stones, bees buzzed, and overhead the red kite let out its eerie high cry as it circled against the blue sky, its wings spread wide to catch as much rising hot air as it could to stay soaring.

She pulled a pin from her hair to use to slit open the letter and then dropped the pin carelessly in her jacket pocket to look inside as soon as she could.

Extracting a leaf of fine, high-quality paper, she unfolded it and read the opening lines, written in a strong—probably male—hand with expensive blue ink.

> *Dear Miss Ashford,*
>
> *I trust this letter finds you well and in good health. It pains me to write to you expressing my condolences at the death of your grandfather, Clarence Ashford, Esq.*

Atalanta gasped, pushing her heels hard against the cracked stones under her feet to maintain balance. She had only seen her grandfather once. She had been about ten and he had come to their house to offer her father his help in paying off his debts. Atalanta had believed the arrival of a fine coach and a well-dressed man was the answer to their prayers but her father had only fought with their visitor, throwing terrible accusations and insults at him, and sent him off with a sharp order never to call on them again.

Later, as their situation got increasingly desperate and her father's health began to suffer, she had been tempted to pick up a pen and write to her grandfather, begging him for assistance. But she never had. It would have been too painful to receive a cool reply stating that he was too mortified by the earlier treatment to look kindly upon her request, or something of that nature. Her father had treated him horribly, and such a response would be natural.

Besides, she hadn't known how the revelation that she had contacted his family would affect her father. What if he became so angry with her that he suffered a heart attack or a stroke? She couldn't risk it. The chances of a happy outcome were simply too slight.

And now it was too late.

Her grandfather had gone.

The breeze felt suddenly cold on her neck and she blinked against the burn behind her eyes. She steeled herself to read on.

Your grandfather left very specific instructions concerning his last will, which I must convey to you in person. I have taken up residence in Hotel Bären across from the station. I will await you there at your earliest convenience so you may learn something to your benefit.

Yours faithfully,

I. Stone, lawyer.

She read and reread the short message. Her heart pounded painfully in her chest. On top of the shock that her grandfather had died without her ever having properly known him, she was now informed she had something to do with his last will.

And the letter said she could learn something that would benefit her. But how was that possible? Surely, after her father's terrible behaviour, her grandfather wouldn't have been open to supporting her in any way?

What could it mean?

Pushing a hand against her hot cheek, Atalanta forced herself to think, to ignore the turmoil inside her about the death, and the memories of that one time she had seen the imposing man with his grey hair and walking cane, and the baritone voice that exuded natural authority. He had smiled at her with a sudden kindness.

Before Father had said all those hurtful things.

She bit her lip. She shouldn't judge what had happened between them before she had been born, and couldn't fathom what bitterness of past injury had driven her father to react in that manner.

She looked at the letter again. *At your earliest convenience*, it said. And she was leaving for her remote valley the next morning. So the only opportunity to do it was today.

She checked her watch. Three in the afternoon was a

perfectly suitable time, she assumed. All she had to do was dress for the occasion.

Meeting an unknown lawyer about a will was something very special. Despite her sadness over her grandfather's death, and confusion as to how she might be involved, she should try and enjoy this unique experience. It would probably never again happen to her.

Ready to find out what happens next...

Mystery in Provence **is available in eBook and paperback now**